DEATH MARCH 4
TO THE
PARALLEL WORLD RHAPSODY

KARINA
The second child of Baron Muno.

LULU
Born in the Kuvork Kingdom. She is Arisa's older sister.

ARISA
A former princess of the Kuvork Kingdom. She was Japanese in her previous life.

SATOU
A twenty-nine-year-old programmer who has been transported to a parallel universe.

Lulu pressed her hands to her cheeks and mumbled to herself.

"Hee-hee... A bride, huh?"

DEATH MARCH
TO THE PARALLEL WORLD RHAPSODY

④

★ ★ ★

HIRO AINANA
ILLUSTRATION BY SHRI

YEN
ON

NEW YORK

Death March to the Parallel World Rhapsody, Vol. 4
Hiro Ainana

Translation by Jenny McKeon
Cover art by shri

© Hiro Ainana, shri 2015
First published in Japan in 2015 by KADOKAWA CORPORATION, Tokyo.
English translation rights arranged with KADOKAWA CORPORATION, Tokyo through Tuttle-Mori Agency, Inc., Tokyo.

English translation © 2018 by Yen Press, LLC

Yen On
1290 Avenue of the Americas
New York, NY 10104

Visit us at yenpress.com
facebook.com/yenpress
twitter.com/yenpress
yenpress.tumblr.com
instagram.com/yenpress

First Yen On Edition: January 2018

Yen On is an imprint of Yen Press, LLC.
The Yen On name and logo are trademarks of Yen Press, LLC.

Library of Congress Cataloging-in-Publication Data
Names: Ainana, Hiro, author. | Shri, illustrator. | McKeon, Jenny, translator.
Title: Death march to the parallel world rhapsody / Hiro Ainana ; illustrations by shri ; translation by Jenny McKeon.
Other titles: Desu machi kara hajimaru isekai kyosokyoku. English
Description: First Yen On edition. | New York, NY : Yen ON, 2017–
Identifiers: LCCN 2016050512 | ISBN 9780316504638 (v. 1 : pbk.) |
ISBN 9780316507974 (v. 2 : pbk.) | ISBN 9780316556088 (v. 3 : pbk.) |
ISBN 9780316556095 (v. 4 : pbk.)
Subjects: | GSAFD: Fantasy fiction.
Classification: LCC PL867.5.I56 D413 2017 | DDC 895.6/36d—dc23
LC record available at https://lccn.loc.gov/2016050512

ISBNs: 978-0-316-55609-5 (paperback)
978-0-316-55616-3 (ebook)

1 3 5 7 9 10 8 6 4 2

LSC-C

Printed in the United States of America

CONTENTS

Disturbance at Dawn

Satou here. They say necessity is the mother of invention, but you still need to understand the basics of what you're trying to do in order to turn an idea into reality. I think the father of invention is consistent day-to-day effort.

After the potion debacle with the witch of the Forest of Illusions and the viceroy's aide, our new friends saw us off as we departed Sedum City.

The younger four girls sat in the back of the horse-drawn carriage, waving an emotional good-bye to the people shrinking in the distance as they returned the gesture.

I left the younger set to their business and checked in on Lulu, our driver, at the coachman stand.

Since Liza and Nana were riding on horseback, I couldn't see them from inside the carriage.

"Master, there will be a good deal of pedestrian traffic heading to and from the gate for a while, so I think we should take it slow."

"Sure. Drive safely."

Lulu spoke in a soft voice from the front of the carriage, her glossy black hair, light-blue dress, and warm-looking white shawl rippling in the breeze.

She was considered ugly by the aesthetic standards of this world, but from my point of view, she was more beautiful than any celebrity.

"Master, Nana and I shall lead the way."

I turned toward the voice and met Liza's dignified gaze.

"Make sure you give pedestrians the right of way."

"Understood."

The new leather armor I'd tailored for her in Sedum City and her traveler's overcoat obscured most of Liza's orange scales, a characteristic of her Scalefolk tribe. At most, I could catch a glimpse of her tail.

Her trademark black spear was evil-looking enough to draw attention, so she usually kept it wrapped in cloth. I'd improvised the weapon out of monster parts in the labyrinth beneath Seiryuu City back when I saved her.

It wasn't any stronger than an ordinary steel spear, but since Liza seemed to treasure it, I didn't try to stop her from using it.

Following a little behind Liza was Nana, a homunculus with a long blond ponytail.

She was wearing the same leather armor as Liza, but her ample chest was straining against it. Unlike Liza, she wasn't wearing a helmet, so her beautiful but expressionless features were exposed to the sunlight.

"Nana, don't try to let the horse take care of things. Don't force it."

"Master, your instructions have been registered, I report."

I gave some directions to Nana, who was still unskilled at horseback riding, and she responded in her usual robotic manner.

Without instruction from Nana, the horse moved to follow Liza in front of us.

"Satou."

Mia the elf emerged from the back of the carriage, waving a hand at me.

Her pale blue-green hair was tied into two long pigtails, and her pointed ears peeked out from behind them.

Since their kind didn't show themselves to humans very often, she usually hid her hair and ears under a hood to avoid any trouble.

Her short lime-green dress suited her childish appearance, and due to the chilly weather, she was wearing tights and a cardigan that matched Arisa's.

"Licorice."

As usual, the reticent Mia spoke to me in a single word.

She probably meant she wanted some thorn licorice as a snack.

I took out a jar from the Garage Bag, a magic tool that could hold far more than it appeared. When I opened the lid, a subtle, sweet scent wafted out.

I stuck a toothpick into a piece of the aloe-like, emerald-green substance inside and handed it to her.

"Aaah."

Mia opened her small mouth demandingly, so I went ahead and fed the thorn licorice to her.

"Yum." Mia smiled happily and put a hand to her cheek.

Given her appearance, it was hard to believe she was actually far older than me.

"Smells sweeeeet!"

"Like licorice, sir!"

Sniffing at the sugary aroma, Tama and Pochi hopped up from the back of the carriage.

Tama, with her pointy, furry ears and short white hair, rubbed her head against my hand like a real cat. She was a member of a rare race of cat-eared folk.

Pochi sat up eagerly, giving me puppy-dog eyes to match her dog ears and brown bob cut. Her tail mirrored her excited expression by wagging side to side.

She was from a race called the dog-eared folk, a rare presence in the Shiga Kingdom like the cat-eared folk.

Both of them were wearing their usual white shirts and poufy shorts. The outfits matched, except Pochi's shorts were yellow, while Tama's were pink. Their overcoats were the same color as their pants.

"Wait just a minute, all right? I'll give you some, too."

"'kaaay!"

"Yes, sir."

Tama sat next to Pochi, and they waited patiently together.

For elementary school–age girls, they have great judgment and manners.

I poked more toothpicks into the licorice and held out the jar to them.

"Aaah?"

"Aaah, sir."

The two of them opened their mouths like baby birds in an imitation of Mia's behavior, so I popped a piece of licorice into each of their mouths.

"Deliiish!"

"It's so sweet, sir. Pochi's happy, sir!"

Tama clamped the licorice between her teeth and stretched it, while Pochi expressed her joy by waving her hands and tail.

"Do you want some, too, Lulu?"

"Yes, please."

Since Lulu could hear the girls cooing happily, I offered her a piece as well.

Lulu shyly popped the licorice into her mouth, then smiled gracefully.

"Excuse me! Aren't you forgetting someone?"

Arisa showed up a little late to the party, so I gave her some candy as well. She was hiding her unlucky purple hair under a golden wig, and she was dressed like a princess in her dark-red cardigan and fluffy pink top and bottom.

"It's a bit sad to leave Sedum City, no?" Arisa chewed away on the licorice as she spoke. "Perhaps it's because we left after the festival?"

The festival had celebrated the triumphant return of the troops after they successfully drove the attacking kobolds out of the silver mines. We wanted to check it out, so we'd stayed about five days longer than planned.

"Festivals are greeeat!"

"It was fun to see everyone smiling, sir."

"Mm."

Between the parade of floats and portable shrines and the chance to taste festival-exclusive cuisine, it had been a very enjoyable couple of days.

This event had ended the day before, so we were finally resuming our journey to return Mia to her hometown.

"There are a lot of soldiers, aren't there?"

Lulu was right; there were indeed ten or so soldiers walking in formation on the main road.

This struck me as a little strange, so I opened the map to investigate. According to it, these men were conscripts from the villages of Kuhanou County.

"Injured."

"They must be coming back from the silver mines."

Mia's single word referred to the fact that most of the members of the group were sporting bandages or walking sticks; the wounded soldiers probably had to wait until they could move again before they were able to go home.

"Hey there, sweetie, wanna marry my son?"

"Those're some nice hips. Think you'd like to spend the night with me?"

"Idiot! If yer gonna compliment something, start with that rack!"

The men still had some life in them despite their injuries, as a few of them made vulgar comments about Nana as she rode past on horseback.

Nana only tilted her head, so at least she didn't seem anxious or uncomfortable.

"Ugh, those buffoons are infuriating!"

"Vulgar."

Although Nana was the target of the sexual harassment, Arisa and Mia were angrier to hear it from inside our vehicle.

"Perhaps I'll make them regret it with a taste of my Impossible Jail spell…"

"Please don't. Nana, we're trading places!"

Arisa was rolling up her sleeves and making to stand, but I had her sit back down and called out to Nana instead.

I switched roles with her and rode my horse side by side with Liza's. Sitting in a carriage is certainly easier, but horseback riding once in a while is nice, too.

I heard Arisa shouting something like "death to sexual predators!" in the back, but Lulu seemed to be keeping her in check, so I figured I could just let her be.

Once we passed the intersection of the main road and a path to the silver mines, there was far less pedestrian traffic, so I gave the horse back to Nana and returned to the carriage.

Mia could hardly stand to watch Nana's utter lack of skill with horses, so I had them ride together while the elf gave her brusque guidance.

"Watch the road."

"Mia, there was a squirrel in that tree, I report."

"Road."

"…Understood, I reluctantly report."

Nana seemed dispirited by Mia's scolding, though her face was as expressionless as ever.

I heard a soft "Achoo!" from Lulu in the coachman stand.

"You should wear this to protect you from the wind."

"Th-thank you."

I removed a fur coat from Storage and handed it to Lulu, then took over the reins for her so she could put it on.

"It's gotten colder than I expected."

"Yes, a chilly wind keeps blowing from the direction of those mountains."

The mountains Lulu referred to bordered the Muno Barony.

"Maybe it's because there's nothing to block out the wind here."

I looked past Lulu as she slid her arms into the fur coat and surveyed the main road.

As we neared the mountainous border, the vegetation had changed, and rocks and grasslands replaced the trees.

I'd heard from a merchant that the Muno Barony was colder than Kuhanou County, but I hadn't expected it to get this chilly.

I took a hand warmer out of Storage and infused it with a little magic power.

This was something I'd devised during our stay in Sedum City, a magic tool that resembled a silver electric pocket heater. I kept it inside a small purse so as not to burn anyone's skin.

"Lulu, wear this, too. I don't want you getting cold."

"Thank you very much... Ooh, it's so warm!"

Wrapping both hands around the device, Lulu pressed it to her cheeks to stave off the chill.

The expression on her beautiful face relaxed at the warmth.

I wish I could take a picture of this.

If we used that smile in advertisements, I bet shares of this little gizmo would rise 30 percent in value.

"Oh, I'm sorry. I didn't mean to leave the reins with you for so long," she said.

"It's all right. It was worth it, since I got to see your lovely smile."

I didn't mean to sound so flirtatious, but I also wanted to compliment her to ease her inferiority complex.

"Oh...but I..."

Lulu's face flushed bright red.

"Guilty."

Mia poked her head in between Lulu and me on the coachman stand, pouting moodily.

"Me! Do me next!"

Then Arisa appeared in short order, flailing her hand wildly in the air.

"All right, all right. You're cute, Arisa."

"Excuse me, that's not nearly as sincere as what you said to Lulu! Put more love into it!"

Arisa harrumphed and pounded my arm lightly, but there wasn't much power behind it, so I doubted she was all that angry.

Given the unexpectedly severe temperature, I took some time on our lunch break to mass-produce some earmuffs at Arisa's suggestion.

I accented each somewhat retro headband-style ear warmer with a colored ribbon so they wouldn't all look the same.

"Comfyyy!"

"My ears are happy, sir."

Tama and Pochi seemed pleased, despite normally favoring lighter clothes, and they kept coming over to show them off to me.

"You both look very cute," I told them, and they squirmed bashfully.

It was nice to have a journey peaceful enough for such a lighthearted exchange. Aside from one sighting of a distant pack of wolves, our trip was completely uneventful, and we reached the mountains by the time the sun started to set.

We proceeded along the narrow pass, and after about an hour without encountering any other people or carriages, we arrived at a fortress that also served as a checkpoint.

The gate of the fort was closed, but I could see a soldier in the fixture above the gate, so I approached.

"You there, with the carriage! What business do you have at this fort?!"

"We are humble peddlers, traveling to the Ougoch Duchy by way of the Muno Barony."

"...You're passing through the cursed territory?"

When I gave a polite response to the soldier, he gave me a dubious look.

"Don't you know this is a danger zone full of monsters and outlaws?"

"Yes, we are well prepared for it."

"Fine, then. However, we cannot allow you to pass through the checkpoint at night..."

According to the soldier, the air in the valley near the border was thick with venomous insects and vampire bats at night, so passage was forbidden for safety reasons. It was especially dangerous for horses, he said.

He suggested that we spend the night in the nearest village, but I'd seen a suitable spot along the path before, so we decided to spend the night there.

"Master, I have a request."

At the camp, Lulu approached me with a serious expression. She wanted me to teach her how to cook a delicious steak.

First, in order to find out what her weak points were, I had her try cooking one.

"Ahh, that won't work, Lulu. You can't keep flipping the steak or pushing it down with the spatula."

"Really? It smells good, so I thought this might be all right..."

Lulu looked discouraged, so I patted her head and explained.

"That delicious smell is the flavor coming out of the steak and burning. So it's better to only flip it one time so that the good juice won't come out."

I'd read that particular factoid in an article online a long time ago.

As a matter of fact, my "Cooking" skill had also taught me that it wasn't good to turn the steak over frequently, but I figured my explanation would be easier for Lulu to accept. Really, I doubted my second-hand summary was too far off.

Next, I taught her how to cook it step-by-step.

"If you listen closely, your ears will tell you when the timing is right."

"R-right!"

I explained that the sound of sizzling fat was a good indicator of the temperature of the frying pan.

I must have been getting closer while I was talking, because Lulu was bright red up to her ears. She looked so cute that I couldn't help whispering in her ear while I explained the techniques.

"Once you've prepared the meat and put it on the pan, you have to restrain yourself until the juices start to come to the surface."

"R-right, I-I'll restrain myself!"

The pitch of Lulu's voice was reaching new heights.

Whoops, looks like I went too far. I didn't want to cross the line into sexual harassment, so I backed off, but this just made her disappointed. It's hard to figure out what to do with adolescent girls.

As I affectionately watched her serious profile, I continued my culinary lecture.

After a few attempts, Lulu had gotten the hang of it, so I plated the steaks, including Lulu's failures, and made a Japanese-style sauce with the juices from the meat and soy sauce.

I figured if the failed steaks were still left over at the end, I'd take responsibility and finish them, but the beastfolk girls took care of them in no time flat.

Leaving the after-dinner cleanup to the other kids, I sat in the shadow of the carriage and started preparing magic-tool materials to create some appliances for warmth.

My plan was to make a heating device for the interior of our carriage. I figured a floor heater would be ideal so that we could use it while we slept.

I tried to employ the know-how I'd gotten from making the magic circuits.

I figured the best approach would be to fashion a slatted wooden frame and place a metal pipe containing the heating circuit inside.

My documents had nothing on how to make a magic battery, but I had pulled together a workable substitute for my hand warmer by combining the basic magic circuit, the anti-diffusion magic from the potion vials, and so on. I figured I could use that here as well.

It would work for only about three hours at a time at most, but it should be fine if I just had each night-watch replacement refill the magic supply.

I'd stocked up on wood and metal in Sedum City, so the work proceeded quickly enough.

Of course, without my many skills supporting me, I'd never have been able to produce a magic floor heater for a carriage in less than an hour.

I stowed the completed tool in Storage for a moment, then installed it in the carriage.

I gave it a try by infusing it with magic and lying down, and a gentle, pleasant warmth came up through the floor.

There was a bit of a draft, though, so I'd have to get everyone to help do some weather stripping later.

"What're you up to?"

"Making a heater."

Arisa poked her head into the carriage inquisitively.

"Warm."

"I never knew there was a magic tool like this. You're amazing, master!"

Following Arisa's lead, Mia and Lulu came in, patted the floor experimentally, and offered their impressions.

"I never imagined I'd find floor heating in this world." Sprawled out lazily on the floor to bask in the warmth, Arisa suddenly opened her eyes wide and closed in on me.

"*K-k-kotatsu*! Make a *kotatsu* next!"

"Why would we need a heated table if the carriage is already warm?"

"Aww, come onnn... Don't be like that! Pleeease, make a *kotatsu* next! Pretty please!"

Arisa's desperate pleading threatened to overpower me.

"Oh, Arisa, that's enough. Can't you see you're bothering master?" Lulu scolded Arisa gently.

At times like this, it was easy to think of them as sisters.

"Awwww. But *kotatsu* are the best things everrr... That's one bit of Japanese culture that I think we should spread to this parallel world."

I thought she was exaggerating a bit, but I didn't want to take the wind out of her sails.

Arisa gazed up at me with teary eyes, so I had no choice but to nod reluctantly.

"All right, all right. I'll make one when I have some time to kill, all right? But you'll have to make the blanket part yourself."

"Hooraaaay!"

Arisa leaped joyously inside the carriage. Her skirt flipped up past her navel, but she didn't seem to care.

"*Kotatsu*, good."

Mia nodded with quiet approval as Arisa rejoiced.

Right... I guess there was a hero hundreds of years ago who handed down some Japanese culture to the elves.

Arisa fervently explained the structure and virtues of a *kotatsu* to an attentive Lulu.

At this rate, she'd be asking me to cultivate mandarin oranges and make mochi. Since there was rice in the Ougoch Duchy, sticky rice for mochi shouldn't be a problem, but I had no idea where to get oranges.

I'll have to look for them when we get to a good trading city.

Now, putting that aside, I wanted to show off my invention to everyone else.

"This feeling is truly superb. It isn't quite as warm as a hot bath, but the temperature is excellent in its own right."

Liza gave me rave reviews with unusual passion.

It was popular with the other girls, too, of course.

Just as I'd predicted, the effect lasted only about three hours, but that was good enough.

It had gotten cold, so I planned to reduce the night watch to three shifts. I was planning on taking the graveyard shift, so as long as I refilled the magic supply before and after my watch, we should be able to keep warm all night.

For the night watch, each shift would include either Pochi, Tama, or me, since we three had heightened senses for detecting enemies.

The inside of the carriage was nice and warm with the combination of the floor heating and weather stripping, so everyone would be able to sleep soundly without a cold draft.

That evening, Arisa and I read a picture book aloud, complete with spirited reenactment for the others, so I gained the skills "Ad Lib" and "Ventriloquism," along with the title Lousy Actor.

I don't know who comes up with these titles, but I wish they'd stop giving me such insulting ones.

On the late-night shift with me, Arisa was shivering in the cold wind, so I decided to try using the Shelter spell I'd just learned from a Magic Scroll in Sedum City.

When I selected it from the menu, a transparent dome about ten feet around covered us.

"Ooh, it's not cold anymore. Is this a spell you learned in Sedum City?"

"Yep! …Oh, but this'll be a problem."

It was keeping out the wind well enough, but the smoke from the burning bonfire was accumulating inside the dome.

I guess this defense magic stopped air from flowing in or out of the barrier.

"Oh dear, you're right. If we'd nodded off without noticing, we might well have choked to death."

"Seriously. I'll cancel it for now."

I deactivated the Shelter spell, and the smoke escaped into the sky.

"Perhaps you ought to make a chimney?"

"I'll give it a try."

I took three rods out of the Garage Bag, stuck them in the ground, and wrapped cloth around them to make a simple tube about three feet tall.

Then I made a Shelter barrier that would intersect with the tube.

The tube stayed as it was. This was good, since I wasn't sure if the barrier would crush it or cut it off.

When I collected the cloth and rods, there was a hole where the tube had been.

Unlike Shield, you couldn't change the position of the barrier, so it wouldn't be usable on the move, but if I added a hole for going in and out like an igloo, it would likely come in handy for the night watch.

Like the heater, this spell lasted for three hours. Even when I used it from the magic menu, this didn't change. It was probably a precaution to make sure the people inside wouldn't suffocate.

The menu version seemed stronger than when I used it from the scroll, but I didn't know how much stronger, since both versions broke from a single punch. *Maybe I'll do a strength test with the help of the beastfolk girls in the future.*

By the way, Shelter wasn't the only spell I acquired in Sedum City.

I also got the Practical Magic spells Short Stun and Magic Arrow and the Earth Magic spell Pitfall.

On the day I'd gotten the scrolls, I went to the abandoned village near Sedum City late at night to test-fire each spell so that I would be able to select them from the magic menu later.

Just as when I used Fire Shot, the spells were fairly weak when I used them directly from the scrolls, but their performance improved by leaps and bounds once I used them from the magic menu.

The two attack spells could now fire up to a hundred and twenty shots at once, and even Short Stun, which was intended to be non-lethal, gained enough attack power to lay waste to a large tree.

Both of them consumed a base amount of ten MP, plus one point per every two additional shots.

In terms of efficiency, they were still no match for Fire Shot, which could melt a rock wall into lava with just ten points, but they'd be easier to use against monsters than my usual Magic Gun.

The Pitfall spell initially created a hole that was just four inches wide and four inches deep, but once I used it from the magic column of the menu, it could make a hole up to forty feet wide and deep.

This size could be altered in units of four inches, so the spell would have uses besides its intended purpose. Mainly, making holes to use as toilets or for throwing away garbage.

However, it didn't provide any way to fill the holes it created, which was a bit of an issue for me.

When I made a hole with Pitfall, where did the dirt go? The earth on the sides and bottom of the hole became hard as rocks, but if all of it had been compressed, the walls should be way harder than that. I had to assume that most of the dirt was disappearing somewhere.

I was somewhat intrigued, but not enough to go out of my way to do extensive research, so I figured I'd ask an Earth Magic expert or researcher if I met one.

While Arisa and I were chatting about the sillier points of magic, our night-watch shift flew by in no time at all.

The next day, we prepared to depart at early dawn and headed to the fort just as the sun rose.

"Hey, you're the guy from yesterday. I've heard that the Muno Barony is in such desperate poverty that the robbers from there have been coming this way instead. You gotta be careful, not just with bandits and soldiers but even with ordinary villagers."

"We will. Thank you for your advice."

Whoa there, you equated Muno Barony soldiers to bandits without even batting an eye, I mentally quipped. My verbal response was simply to thank the soldier for his kindness.

Apparently, there weren't any tolls to cross the barrier.

On the contrary...

"If you encounter any unreasonable demands on the other side of the fortress, you just run back here. Once you've crossed the border, our soldiers can come right to your aid."

"I appreciate your concern. If anything should happen, I'll be sure to take you up on your kind offer."

Thanking the soldier again, we started the carriage toward the barony.

While I drove, I thought back on the rumors I'd heard in Sedum City about the Muno Barony.

The territory had always been dangerous, but thanks to a famine that had been going on for the past three years, much of the population had fallen into slavery or turned to crime.

Not only had fraud and embezzlement by government officials become standard there, but the negligence of the soldiers meant that the main road was overflowing with monsters and bandits.

The border fortress that we'd be passing next would be just as bad, with scoundrels who would take all your cargo under the pretense of a "tariff" or kidnap women from nearby villages.

The reason we were leaving for the Muno Barony so early in the morning was to try to avoid these nasty soldiers.

Such disgraceful men weren't likely to go to work that early, and I knew there was no barrier on the Muno Barony side of the fortress.

I had some alcohol ready to use as a bribe just in case, but I figured if anyone approached us the wrong way, I could just have Arisa put them to sleep with Psychic Magic and get through.

Idle soldiers doze off on the job all the time, after all.

Once we came out from the fort on the Kuhanou County side, we found ourselves traveling along a narrow road wedged between steep cliffs on both flanks. It was barely wide enough for two carriages to pass each other, and visibility was quite poor.

After we continued through this ravine for ten minutes or so, we made it to the roughest part of the border.

Before us was a valley about a hundred feet wide and almost a thousand feet deep, along with a rope bridge just barely wide enough for a single carriage. The Muno Barony waited on the other side.

"Liza, Nana, pull back. Wait here with everyone else, please."

I called to Liza and Nana before they could cross on their horses ahead of us, and they returned to wait with the rest of the group.

"I'm going to make sure it's safe on the other side. If I tell you from over there to run, don't wait for me—just make a break for it, all right?"

"'kay!"

"Yes, sir!"

"…R-right."

Pochi, Tama, and Lulu were the only three who obediently agreed.

"Satou."

"You're not going to do something insane on your own again, are you?"

Mia and Arisa were anxious to stop me.

"Don't worry. I'll come back as soon as I've seen what the fort over there is like."

I patted their heads, then left Lulu as the coachman and jumped down from the carriage.

"Master, permit me to accompany you, I entreat."

"Forgive my presumption, master, but please allow me to join you as your guard."

Nana and Liza both wanted to come along, but I decided to minimize the number of people and bring only Liza. If anything did happen, I was confident she could take care of herself.

"All right, Liza, come with me. Nana, you wait here."

"Yes, sir!"

"Understood, I respond."

I took over Nana's horse, and Liza and I safely crossed the rope bridge.

On the other side was a plaza with enough parking space for a few carriages and a one-hundred-and-fifty-foot rock wall that blocked my view of anything beyond it.

Now, it was time to collect some information.

I selected **Search Entire Map** from the magic menu as a starting point to learn about the Muno Barony.

I'd known the area was big, but I was still surprised by how vast it was. Its strange shape made it hard to tell, but I'd say it was at least the size of Hokkaido. However, that was a rough estimate, since I didn't actually remember how big Hokkaido was.

The entire territory was relatively flat, and northwest of Muno City was a forest that covered about 30 percent of the territory. The rivers came together in a lake at the center of the forest, then continued on as one large river that flowed past Muno City toward Ougoch Duchy.

The main road connecting Kuhanou County and Ougoch Duchy ran along mostly level ground except for a few low mountains.

On the other hand, a range of much higher mountains bordered the barony.

Like Kuhanou County, this area's map also had a few blank zones of various sizes. The biggest one was located inside the large forest.

Now that I had a basic grasp of the geography, I moved on to investigate enemy presences and refined the search parameters on the map.

First I checked whether there were any reincarnations with **Skills: Unknown** like Arisa—none.

Next, anyone over level 50—also none.

Then, anything over level 30 that might be a threat to the kids—this time there were results.

Several targets fit my parameters. And the nearest one was in the fort in front of us.

The rest were pretty far away, so I suspended my search for now and brought Liza with me to get a closer look.

Following the path that cut through the rock face, we reached a desert slope.

The fort was in the middle of the barren region, and sitting atop the half-crushed structure was a hydra. Its four heads were rooting around underneath the rubble.

The cold, dry wind carried the crunching of huge teeth gnawing on something.

I checked the map, but there were no survivors nearby.

"Liza, take care of my horse, please."

Leaving Liza in charge of the animal, I started descending the slope.

The hydra's perch was about a thousand feet away from me as the crow flies.

This thing was level 44 and nearly twice as large as the one I'd seen between Seiryuu County and Kuhanou County.

"M-master, please forgive my arrogance, but I believe we really must retreat in this situation."

Liza stared, ashen-faced, at the enormous beast that would have been right at home in a monster movie.

"Don't worry. It'll only take a minute, so just wait here."

In order to ease Liza's worries, I decided to show her a bit of my real strength. I figured she could keep a secret, so it should be all right.

Once I was a bit farther away from Liza, I chose the Magic Arrow spell from my magic menu.

Since this was such a wasteland, I probably could have used Fire Shot without a problem, but since the spell moved at only about fifty-five miles per hour, there was a risk that the hydra would dodge it from this distance.

Thus, I chose the slightly faster Magic Arrow this time.

When I activated the spell, a menu popped up to let me select how many arrows to fire. I could choose any number between one and one hundred and twenty. Without hesitation, I chose the maximum.

A small red circle appeared on the hydra in my AR display, just like a target mark in an air-battle simulator.

However, since its heads were currently hidden, my attack might not be fatal.

I deliberately kicked one of the stones at my feet to draw the hydra's attention.

The monster reared its four heads and raised its bat-like wings in an intimidating posture.

When I concentrated on the four heads of the hydra in my mind, the target mark changed instantly to reflect my thoughts.

Fire.

I mentally pulled the trigger.

The spell consumed seventy magic points, and magic bolts the size of small spears appeared before me and fired at the hydra in rapid succession with a loud blast.

I wasn't sure if it was because of my high level and stats or some ability, but time seemed to slow until I was watching it frame by frame.

The first Magic Arrow was blocked when the hydra produced a red film around its body. Arrows two and three struck the membrane, the fourth pierced it, and the fifth arrow bore straight into one of the hydra's heads.

Before the impact could move the head away, the sixth and seventh arrows reduced it to pieces.

From the eighth arrow on, the only effect they offered was to splatter the remains of the head until nothing was left.

The arrows that had hit their mark continued on, pulverizing the dead trees, soil, and rocks behind them until the landscape was utterly transformed.

It was an overwhelming display of violence, as if I'd been firing a large-caliber autocannon.

After the one hundred and twenty Magic Arrows had finished annihilating the hydra's four heads and the mountain behind it, the flow of time around me finally returned to its usual speed.

Pressing a hand to my ears in case I'd torn an eardrum, I checked the log to confirm the death of the hydra.

Having lost all its heads, the rest of the hydra was flung backward, wrecking the remaining half of the fort. The ensuing tremors, thanks to its immense weight, reverberated through my stomach.

I covered my mouth with a cloth to protect my throat from the dust in the wind.

I returned to Liza, who was stunned speechless.

"It's over," I told her.

"Master, please forgive my earlier foolish remarks. While I certainly knew that you were strong, I had never imagined this degree of—"

I casually hushed Liza's dramatic display of surprise.

"Sorry, but could you keep that magic a secret from the others?"

"Yes, even if it costs me my life."

Okay, you don't need to take it that *seriously.*

"No, if your life is at stake for some reason, please just tell them."

I accepted the reins from Liza and rode the horse over to the corpse of the hydra.

From up close, the immense creature was truly stunning. If I'd run into it in my original world, I probably would've been eaten before I could even think to run.

Amid the reddish-brown stained rubble lay brutalized bodies and broken weapons.

Although I'd been told that this was a hangout of ne'er-do-wells, I still couldn't help feeling pity for their terrible deaths.

It wasn't quite enough to make me want to bury the bodies, but I could at least have a moment of silent prayer for them before leaving.

We carried on over the blood-soaked ground, dismounting in front of the fort that was now the tomb of the hydra.

Once I landed on the ground, the slight whiff of iron in the air became a stench.

I asked Liza to recover the monster's core, then retrieved one of the fallen swords at my feet and thrust it into the ground as a grave marker.

Then I pulled out a bottle of liquor to use for funeral rites—a far cry from its original purpose. I'd originally bought it in case I needed to bribe my way past this fort.

Sprinkling the liquid over the sword, I prayed for their souls to rest in peace.

While Liza was getting the core, I continued my investigation of the Muno Barony.

Returning to the search for enemies, I discovered a relatively high number of monsters level 30 and above.

In the mountainous area to the west-southwest of here, there were more hydras like the one I'd just defeated. My search had returned only one level-37 hydra, but on closer investigation, there were two more hydras of levels 29 and 24 over there, too.

The area was practically on the other side of the territory from where we were now. *So that hydra traveled all the way from there? I don't know what the cruising range of the average flying monster is, but they could be trouble.*

Not that I'd have any difficulty dealing with them, since I had an antiaircraft spell now.

Most of them seemed to live in the mountains far away from the highway or human habitations anyway, so we probably wouldn't encounter any.

I also found a single hell demon on the list. What's more, he was located in the lord's castle in Muno City. Most likely, he had employed a wicked plot that was responsible for the decline of this territory.

I examined the detailed information about the demon. He was level 35, a lesser hell demon like the eyeball I'd fought back in Seiryuu City. His race-specific inherent skills were "Flight," "Transformation," "Doppelgänger," and "Lesser Magic Resistance," while his general skills were "Psychic Magic" and "Ghost Magic."

This time, I searched specifically for hell demons and found three others. All of them were level 1, with the title Doppelgänger. They must have been created by the stronger demon's skill of the identical name.

These copies had the same inherent skills as the other demon save for "Doppelgänger," though they had only one general skill of either "Psychic Magic" or "Ghost Magic."

One was in Muno City, and the other two were in different towns. The one that had infiltrated Muno City was acting as a magistrate, among other things. I'd have to be careful of this guy.

Come to think of it, the demon in Seiryuu City was possessing a human...

Just to be sure, I searched the map for people with the status **Possessed** and found two knights.

There were higher-level knights to be found in the castle, but after a bit of comparison, I realized that they'd been chosen because they had the most crimes in their **Bounty** field. This made sense, since the guy being possessed in Seiryuu City was a villain, too.

Unless they posed a threat to my kids, I had no intention of deliberately setting out to defeat them, but it'd be another story if any of them got in our way like the hydra had. In that case, I'd use my full power to take care of them.

It'd be a huge pain if the lesser hell demon ended up summoning a greater hell demon and reprising the labyrinth incident in Seiryuu City, so I put a marker on all the demons and possessed knights so that I'd know if they went anywhere suspicious.

During our stay in the Muno Barony, I decided it'd be best to check the situation on the map at least twice a day, once in the morning and once at night.

If there were any signs of danger, we could make our move.

But, of course, the safety of the kids in my care came first.

As I finished my investigation of the demons, Liza returned.

"Master, I have recovered the core."

"Great, thanks."

I accepted the core and slipped it into a sack in the horse's saddlebag. It was deep red, about twice the size of a softball. Examining the grade, I found it was a very high quality.

"I'm going to take a little break. Do you mind calling everyone over?"

"Yes, right away."

After I gave instructions to Liza, I remembered the half-buried bulk of the hydra in the rubble of the fortress.

"I don't want to worry everyone, so let's keep this monster a secret."

"Certainly, sir."

Liza nodded meekly, then mounted her horse and left to summon the others.

After seeing her off, I went back to collecting information.

This time, I looked up the addressee of the letter I had been tasked to deliver for the old witch from the Forest of Illusions.

When I searched for giants, I found only one result. It was near the blank area in the large forest, so I guessed that the giants' village was probably in there.

The old witch's tower in Kuhanou County had been in a blank space, too, after all.

We could probably travel most of the way in the carriage, but if we wanted to travel on the side road leading into the forest, we'd have to take individual horses or go on foot. A peek with the map's 3-D display confirmed this suspicion. The side road was about a twelve days' journey away.

Next, I studied the distribution of people.

The population was awfully small. Though the barony was much larger than Seiryuu County, there were far fewer people. Muno City was the only place with over ten thousand people; the other towns and cities numbered only a few thousand at most.

There were several villages along the main road and the border, but most of them had only around fifty people.

And, consistent with the previous information I'd gotten about this place, many of the commoners' conditions read **Starving**.

The discrimination against demi-humans in the Muno Barony was so severe that there wasn't a single one in Muno City, and even the other towns and villages were entirely segregated.

Among the mountains more distant from the highway, there was a smattering of little settlements with less than a hundred demi-humans of the same variety.

In addition, there was an **abandoned mine city**, inhabited by kobolds, in the mountains near the west-northwest border. They belonged to the same clan as the ones that had hit the silver mines in Kuhanou County. The distance between the two was almost thirty miles, so I was impressed that they'd taken on such an expedition.

* * *

At any rate, the famine was even more severe than I'd expected.

If they could use this hydra as food, a lot of lives would probably be saved, like what they did with whaling in Japan after World War II...

Maybe it could be edible? The meat from the frog monster and the rocket wolves was delicious, and we might meet someone who knew how to cook it.

Each of the hydra's necks was as thick as a horse's body. I cut one into round slices of about three feet with the Holy Sword Excalibur and put them into Storage.

I stored the rest of the body, too, of course.

Suddenly, remembering what the hydra had been eating, I checked the details of the corpse in Storage. It was possible to remove the contents of the stomach separately.

Using the Pitfall spell, I made a hole about fifteen feet wide and deep.

I emptied the contents into my pit: the bodies of the victims from the fort. I knew I wouldn't want to see the state they were in, so I averted my eyes.

I moved away until I wouldn't be able to see what was inside the hole, offered another moment of silence for the victims, and left the fort.

> Title Acquired: Gravedigger

After descending the slope in front of the fort, I dismounted from my horse about thirty feet away and waited for everyone.

I took a deep breath of the dry air, then released it slowly, hoping to dispel the emotions that had settled over my heart like rust.

Having been in this parallel world for a while, I should have been used to encountering death by now, but it still just didn't feel good.

As Lulu and Arisa waved at me from the coachman stand, I returned the gesture as I tried to pull myself together and ran to meet the carriage.

◆

Once I met back up with everyone, I returned the horse to Nana and had Lulu drive while I soothed my heart playing old maid with the younger kids in the back using a handmade set of cards.

About two hours after we'd left the fort, Liza and Nana returned from their scouting mission.

"There are several men and women sitting on the side of the road some distance ahead, sir."

"Master, they did not appear to be hostile, I report."

The people turned out to be the head of a village, his granddaughter, and two other young serf women.

I had already seen that there weren't any dodgy creatures or robbers along our way, but I had sent them ahead because I didn't know what these four were up to.

"I wonder why?"

"Well, this gives us a chance to hear out what the locals have to say."

Brushing off Arisa's suspicion, I checked our food supply in Storage. Some of our lower-quality meat like bear or brown wolf could probably serve as a suitable payment for information.

I took over the coachman's position from Lulu and headed toward the intersection between the main road and the village road where the four were waiting.

When our carriage entered their field of vision, the man who was apparently the village chief leaped to his feet and hailed us with a wave and a yell.

His granddaughter was on my radar, too, but I couldn't see her. She must have been hiding in the shadows.

"Can we help you with something?"

"I'm the chief of the village over yonder. You're a peddler, ain'tcha?"

While I exchanged introductions with the leader, I reviewed their information.

My AR display said the man was forty-three years old, but he looked like he was in his sixties. Just as his **Starving** condition implied, he was gaunt and rather pale.

Despite the cold, he wore no coat over his filthy-looking tunic.

The serf girls, who were in their early twenties, were probably freezing as they sat on the side of the road. They wore nothing but simple sack dresses of unbleached cloth, and their feet were bare. Furthermore, the dresses were so short that the girls were in danger of flashing their underwear just by walking normally.

Strangely, they seemed better nourished than the village chief. They were certainly skinny, but they didn't have the **Starving** condition.

After we finished our introductions and standard chat about the time of year, we finally reached the meat of the conversation.

"See, there's something we'd like you to buy."

"You don't mean those serf girls, do you?" I asked.

The village chief shook his head.

"No, no. Come over here."

"Sure."

The man's granddaughter crawled out from a little hollow off to the side of the road. She was gaunt, like the others.

She was wearing what appeared to be her grandfather's coat, and the hem dragged along the ground as she approached.

"What I want you to buy is my granddaughter. She's still young, but if she grows up anything like my daughter, who was the most beautiful girl in the village, she's sure to be—"

I cut him off there.

"You want to sell your own granddaughter into slavery?"

"If she stays here in the village, she'll starve to death, like as not. The soldiers at that fort might kidnap or kill her…"

The village chief averted his eyes bitterly.

So the stories I heard in Kuhanou County weren't just rumors.

"By my reckoning, she'd be better off getting bought by a kindly seeming merchant such as yourself."

Personally, I think it's best for a family to stay together even if they're poor, but then again… I've never been starving to death.

The chief was eyeing the healthy-looking faces of the younger kids as they were peering out from the carriage.

"Please buy me, Mr. Merchant."

The chief's granddaughter spoke very clearly for such a young girl. Her expression was solemn, and it looked so desperate that I was a little intimidated.

"Please! If the village can buy rations with the money, so many young children will be able to make it through the winter…"

The girl folded her hands in front of her face pleadingly.

Arisa was gazing at me with wide eyes, but I had no intention of buying this child.

"I'm sorry, but I have plenty of slaves."

Really, they're more like family than slaves anyway.

My flat refusal left the chief's granddaughter in despair, and she lowered her head miserably.

At this, one of the serf girls who'd been watching with great interest stood up.

"Chief, is it our turn to negotiate?"

"…Go ahead."

The two serfs removed their tattered clothing, exposing their naked bodies. They were so emaciated that it was more painful to watch than sexy.

"Mrrr, lewd."

"E-excuse you!"

Arisa and Mia leaped out of the carriage to cover my eyes.

"S-so cold!"

"Yes, it's especially cold today."

Through Mia's and Arisa's fingers, I saw the two women hunch over for a moment, shuddering in the frigid air.

Well, yeah, that tends to happen when you take off your clothes outside in the middle of the winter.

"Mr. Merchant, wouldn't you like to buy yourself a good time?"

The older of the two serf women struck an odd pose as she launched her sales pitch.

"The price is one copper coin, or you can fill this pouch with grains and potatoes."

"Ah, of course, meat is welcome, too! It doesn't have to be anything as fancy as rabbit or bird. Any meat will do just fine, even rats or monsters," added the younger.

Monster meat, huh…?

Perfect, now I can find out what kind of meat is edible.

"Monster meat?"

"Yeah, insect monsters are usually pretty bad, but legs from crickets and grasshoppers and the like can be quite tasty—"

"There's a shortage of food around here, see. We're not forcing the serfs to eat monsters or anything."

The village chief cut in with an excuse.

"They eat wyvern in Seiryuu City, too. I've had some before, so I'm not going to judge," I reassured him, and he patted his chest.

Admittedly, I might have wrinkled my nose at it before we tried that rocket wolf meat, but not anymore.

"I don't need any slaves or 'good times,' but there is something else I'd buy," I said.

"Something else? I'm not sure what else you're hoping to buy from a remote village like ours…"

"What I'm looking for is information."

"Information?"

I nodded. "I want you to tell me anything to do with the current situation in the Muno Barony."

"I'm just a simple farmer. All I know is what goes on in our village and the ones nearby."

"That's good enough. I can offer you brown wolf meat in exchange for the information."

I saw the two women hugging each other with joy through the cracks between Mia's and Arisa's fingers.

Just put some clothes on before you catch a cold, please.

What I learned from the chief about the village and the surrounding area was that things were in bad shape.

Since they'd had poor crops for the last three years, they'd depleted all the edible wild plants and tree nuts in the area, which caused the wildlife to retreat deep into the mountains, and, because of all the monsters, sending people out to forage farther away only led to casualties.

Most of the monsters around here were level 10 and up, so they were probably too strong to take down with farming tools.

"We sold some of the girls from the village to a slave trader early in the fall, so we were able to stock up for winter with that money, but…"

"Did some thieves show up or something?"

Judging from his hesitation, I guess it had something to do with the government, but I figured an indirect question would prompt him to explain more easily.

"No, most of the thieves around here are just penniless young folk from neighboring villages. They're not so heartless as to steal our stores for winter."

"Of course not!" one of the women interjected. "Those thieves are our best customers."

"Unlike those soldiers in the fort, they even give you food afterward," the other added.

So that was why they didn't have the **Starving** status condition.

"I heard they were heading to the next territory over because there's no one to steal from here."

"Yeah, they said they were going to a far-off town 'cause of the recent fighting in the silver mines."

I thanked the serf women for their report, then returned to my conversation with the chief.

"Was it monsters, then?"

"If that were the case, we'd have just given up and accepted it. But it was a tax collector... He took almost a third of our winter reserves, saying it was a wedding gift for the baron's daughter."

The village chief heaved a weighty sigh.

I don't think 30 percent of the winter food stores for sixty people is a contribution for a wedding gift. It sounded more like a tax collector had taken an unofficial extra share to keep.

"You didn't appeal or anything?"

"If we did, they'd demote the whole village to serfdom."

"That can't be right."

"It's true. Haven't you heard about Tonza Village? They made the whole settlement into serfs, and now no one lives there."

I searched the map for the name the chief had mentioned, and sure enough, all of the village's former inhabitants were now slaving away in the vicinity of Muno City. So the story was true.

Even if you took into account that a hell demon was probably behind all this, it was a cruel predicament.

I was a bit curious now, so I pressed for more information.

"Do you know who the baron's daughter is intended to marry?"

"According to that tax-collecting scoundrel, it's some hero."

A hero?

I searched the map, but there was nobody with the Hero title. *This guy must be a fake.*

"Say, village chief. How old might this baron's daughter be?" Arisa leaned in and interrupted after listening to the conversation.

"I believe he has one nineteen-year-old and one twenty-four-year-old."

"Is that so? Thank you. Pardon me for interrupting."

Apparently satisfied by the chief's reply, Arisa retreated into the horse-drawn carriage.

"I'm sure the fee he took was poppycock, but the part about her getting married is true," he continued. "I heard it from another village chief, too."

"I see. Thanks. I'll get your payment together, so wait a moment, please."

I climbed back into the cargo area of the carriage, then withdrew the wolf meat from Storage via the Garage Bag. Of course, touching raw meat would contaminate my hands, so I'd placed the pieces in waxed waterproof bags within Storage before taking them out.

Since there were about sixty villagers, two pounds for each person should be enough.

I removed two bales of rice, too, and set them down in front of the chief.

"O-oh? But this is so much..."

Peering into one of the bags over the chief's shoulders, the two women shrieked with joy. The chief's granddaughter was overwhelmed and celebrated by flailing her hands in a rather bizarre manner.

I decided to add two more bags of the same size.

The village chief toppled backward onto his rump in shock.

It might have been a bit more than necessary for the information, but I decided to treat it as a chance to get rid of some of my surplus stock.

Once we had started on our way again, I gave the reins back to Lulu and spoke to Arisa in the rear compartment. It turned out the other kids had been so quiet because the trio was fast asleep.

"Why did you ask about the baron's daughter's age earlier?"

"I wanted to find out whether the hero was real or not."

I tilted my head in confusion. "How would that question help?"

"Remember how I told you that I'd met a hero before?"

I nodded, then grimaced at the recollection. Generally, I tried to keep the memory of being pushed down by a naked little girl buried in the deep, dark recesses of my mind.

"Why are you making a face?"

"Forget it. Just go on," I brusquely prompted, so Arisa crept closer to me and plopped down.

"You see, that hero actually had a Lolita complex."

"...What?"

I stared at Arisa in surprise.

She responded by closing her eyes and puckering her lips together in a kissy face, so I pinched her nose.

"Owie! Goodness, you could stand to be a bit nicer to me. Let's see... I met Hayato Masaki, the hero, in the castle of my old homeland. When he saw me, he shouted in this weird voice, like, '*Yes* Lolita! *No* touching!' Until a woman in his retinue smacked him."

Arisa winced a little at the memory.

Who are you to judge? You're the one going after a kid.

I almost muttered this aloud, but I resisted, since it would distract from the main issue.

"I see. So based on that, you know the hero must be fake?"

"That's right. Want to hear more about him?"

"Eventually, but not right now."

It was enough for the moment to know that there wasn't a hero in this territory. Further information about this weirdo could wait until I had lots of time to kill.

In the evening, we passed another village and exchanged food supplies for information as we had with the first one.

We didn't learn anything new this time, but since what they told us was similar to what we'd heard from the first village's chief, it at least added credibility to his account.

I still had brown wolf and bear meat stores, but at the rate things were going, it'd run out before long.

Since the young serf women from the first village had mentioned eating monster meat, I decided to try sampling the hydra from this morning before dinner.

I took a round slab of meat out of Storage via the Garage Bag and placed it on top of the folding table.

Everyone else, who'd been preparing for camp, turned at the sound.

Tama and Pochi in particular were staring at the meat with great excitement.

"Master, is that by any chance...?"

"I don't know if it's edible, but I figured I'd try it once."

Noticing from the color that the meat was from the hydra, Liza was asking me with astonishment.

My "Analyze" skill had told me there wasn't any poison, so I figured it should be fine. Just in case, I'd wash the blood out before cooking it.

Liza offered to cut it into smaller pieces for easier cooking, but she seemed to struggle with it.

"Is it hard?"

"Yes... I can scratch the surface of the skin, but I can't quite cut through it."

Wow, I bet I could use the skin to make pretty good armor or something, then.

I borrowed a knife from Lulu, who was practicing next to Liza, and used it to butcher the meat. Trying to force an ordinary kitchen knife through the skin would likely chip the blade, so instead I sliced off a test piece from around the hole of the esophagus.

Since the serf girls had said it was tasty, I decided to sample the rear leg of a grasshopper-type monster, too. This was one of the monsters I'd slaughtered with a halberd in the Cradle incident.

Its exoskeleton was harder than a crab's shell, so I took a steel one-handed hatchet out of Storage and hacked off a four-inch piece.

I then chopped this in half lengthwise so it'd be easier to eat. Inside was fibrous black meat with green streaks from the tendons. I'd been hoping it would be white, like crab meat.

I sprinkled some salt onto the leg and the hydra meat, then arranged them on top of a wire mesh screen and set it over the fire. I went light on the seasoning because I wasn't yet familiar with the flavor.

Lulu watched intently from off to the side, trying to memorize the technique. Her eagerness to learn was admirable.

Taking care to give Lulu as good a view as possible, I started cooking under everyone's watchful eyes.

Once it was done, I transferred it to a dish with metal tongs I'd purchased in Sedum City.

First, it was time to try the small cut of hydra meat.

It was hard to eat it while Pochi and Tama gazed up at me with their mouths open wide, but I couldn't give them any until I was sure it was safe.

Feeling a little guilty, I popped the hydra nugget into my mouth and chewed it.

This is actually really good.

It tasted like a cross between rabbit and poultry. The flavor was bland, like chicken, but also gamier than the light eel-like taste I'd sort of expected.

I preferred the rocket wolf, but if I came up with a good sauce and cooking method, this could certainly make a delicious meal.

I checked my log but didn't see anything abnormal.

Next I picked up the leg. It looked like grilled crab, except for the color, but it smelled grassy, sort of like freshly cooked green onions.

I cut the meat into chunks the size of imitation crab.

Stabbing one onto my fork, I examined the color. Holding it up to the fire and inspecting it, I saw that cooking it had darkened the meat further. Putting it into my mouth took considerable courage.

Resolutely, I plunged it into my mouth—and it was like rubber.

The taste itself wasn't that bad, but I couldn't say it was delicious. The green streaks were strangely bitter, so it would probably be better to remove those before cooking.

It would work in a pinch, but I had no desire to add it to my regular diet.

Just to be sure, I checked the log again, but this was safe, too.

"Does everyone else want to try some?"

I didn't really need to ask; I was met with a chorus of *yes*es, so I let everyone else have at it.

Arisa narrowed her eyes, Tama's ears and tail stood up straight, and Pochi waved her hands and tail around happily.

"Mmm! I'm rather afraid to ask what kind of meat this is, but it's delicious, so I'll let it slide."

"'liiish!"

"Meat is just the best, sir."

Arisa, Tama, and Pochi gave the thumbs-up to the hydra meat, although Tama's review was some strange word that Arisa had taught her. Most likely, she was trying to say *delish*.

"It really is delicious," Liza commented. "What method of preparation would suit it best, I wonder?"

"Ahh…that was really good. It's sort of like rabbit, so maybe a stew?" Lulu suggested.

"Skewers would be an excellent choice as well, I advise," Nana added.

"Stew sounds excellent, too," Liza said, "but since it's so big, I think it might be nice to stuff it with vegetables and steam it."

"Doesn't that seem a bit too extravagant? It sounds like something you'd have at a festival feast."

After downing the hydra meat and smacking their lips, the other three excitedly brainstormed different cooking methods.

Liza's suggestion of steaming it sounded good to me. We had more than enough ingredients to spare, so I wanted to try it sometime. I'd have to request it from her later.

For now, it was more important to look after Mia, who was sitting alone outside the mosquito net looking cross.

Elves couldn't eat meat, so I felt bad for her.

"Mrrr."

"If you puff up your cheeks like that, they'll never go back to normal."

"Satou."

I poked Mia's inflated cheeks, then held out some dried fruits wrapped in a handkerchief.

I had dried them myself after I purchased the fruit in Sedum City.

Lulu had befriended the maid at the inn we'd stayed at and learned the recipe from her.

"Yum."

"What do you think we should make with these?"

"Hmm."

While carefully eating her snack with both hands to make it last as long as possible, Mia knotted her brow in contemplation.

I'd never been one for dried fruit, so all I could think of was putting it in yogurt or cereal. I passed to Mia the task of figuring out a recipe.

Next, we continued our taste test with the insect legs...

"Springyyy?"

"The meat man has a good mouthfeed, sir!"

"Yes, it has a very nice mouthfeel. If we could successfully deal with the bitterness, it would be even more delightful."

The beastfolk girls enjoyed the texture of the insect meat, but it received a lukewarm reception from everyone else.

"We'd have to either cut around these hard streaks or slice it more thinly."

"Ugh, gross! It might be better as ground meat, but the taste wouldn't be worth all the effort."

Lulu shuddered at the unpleasant flavor but considered possible cooking methods nonetheless. Arisa, too, offered suggestions for improvement as she wrinkled her nose.

"Master, I would like to rid my mouth of this taste, I entreat."

Nana found the astringency particularly unpleasant and tugged on my arm with all the distress her unchanging expression could muster.

"We'll have dinner soon, so you'll have to wait till then."

"Your instructions have been registered, I report."

I handed Nana a glass of water as I chided her.

So the insect legs were a failure, but a 50 percent win was good enough for me. The hydra had been quite tasty, and if nobody had any stomachaches or anything in the morning, I figured we could start testing out the edibility of various monsters once a day.

At any rate, tonight's main dish was a stew with copious vegetables and a rabbit we'd bought in Sedum City.

Lulu was on cooking duty tonight; her abilities had already started to surpass Liza's, even though the Scalefolk girl had the "Cooking" skill. I was eagerly anticipating her future as a chef.

Leaving the others in charge of cleanup, I opened the map to check the situation around the camp.

I'd noticed earlier that an undead-type monster had popped up on my radar, so I examined the details. It probably wouldn't come out in daylight, but it might start to encroach on us later in the night.

Along the main road were a few abandoned villages where more undead were prowling about: skeleton monsters with single-digit levels, ghosts around level 10, and wraiths approximately level 20.

As we always did before bedtime, I tossed some monster repellent powder onto the fire.

Apparently, the smoke from the powder worked on undead monsters, too: The ghost on my radar retreated to a certain distance away. After that, it made no attempts to approach.

Since our safety was secured, I glanced over to help with cleanup, only to find that they were just about finished.

"Do you need something, master?"

"Not really. You can just relax."

Liza asked me as a representative for the group, so I assured her that they didn't need to do anything else.

The advance guard—the beastfolk girls and Nana—started training in a field near the campsite with wooden swords and spears, while Arisa and Nana sat across from each other at the fire and began discussing ideas for spells I should invent.

Lulu changed into trousers and started doing some yoga-like exercises on a mat near the fire. Arisa had apparently taught her.

I thought stretching was a good idea, since there weren't many opportunities for exercise while traveling by carriage. In fact, I wished Arisa and Mia would exercise once in a while, too.

Once everyone had set about their business, I sat near the mat and arranged my supplies for magic-tool crafting.

I was planning to make a *kotatsu* next, per Arisa's request.

A *kotatsu* big enough for eight people wouldn't fit into the Garage Bag, so I planned to make four two-person *kotatsu* that could be linked together.

Step one was briskly assembling the table portion with timber bought in Sedum City.

It was harder than the slatted wood frame I'd made before, but thanks to my "Woodworking" skill, the construction went surprisingly well.

I designed it so that the legs and the heater would be detachable.

Creating a safe heating element proved pretty difficult. I covered it with wire mesh so that clothes and such wouldn't touch it, then installed a wooden frame so nobody would get burned on the hot mesh.

I'd originally bought the mesh for cooking meat and fish, but I had plenty to experiment with.

That should prevent any injuries. Then I envisioned Arisa or Pochi kicking the wooden frame, so I rounded the edges to ensure it wouldn't hurt their feet.

Next, I whipped up a heating circuit for the *kotatsu*. With this setup, you would have to stick your head under the *kotatsu* to supply magic, but since creating a cable to run outside would be a pain, I left it as is. I could always just keep an eye out for cable components next time we reached a big city and craft one without too much effort.

Now to make a top for the table…

There was a large rock on the other side of the carriage about five feet around, so I used the Holy Sword Excalibur to slice off four slates less than half an inch thick.

Holy Swords really are something else. The surfaces of the slates were as smooth as if they'd been carefully polished. I couldn't put them into the Garage Bag at this size, so I cut them down to the dimensions of the *kotatsu*.

I decided to make the table portion easy to disassemble for storage, too. I have to say, making screws without any tools was a little annoying.

"Arisa, it's done."

"What? You made it just now? It hasn't even been two hours."

"That's because I used some things I already had instead of starting it from scratch."

Secretly feeling a bit proud of myself at Arisa's surprise, I set my handiwork on top of the rug.

Then I reached into the Garage Bag I'd brought along with me, pulled out the quilt Arisa had made yesterday, and placed it between the heated table and the slate on top to complete the job.

When I let some of my magic power flow into the heating circuit inside, a soft, gentle warmth radiated from the *kotatsu*.

I told Arisa and Mia that it was ready, and they immediately shoved their feet under it.

"Aaaah! No winter is complete without a *kotatsu*."

"Mm. I want oranges."

It sounded like they had mandarin oranges in Mia's elfin village. I'd have to remember to pick some up when we brought her home.

Finishing her pseudo-yoga, Lulu toweled herself dry and eyed the new contraption curiously. Her hair, damp with sweat, clung to her skin in a way that bordered on sexy. *Once she becomes an adult, she'll probably be dangerously attractive.*

"So this is a *kotatsu*?"

"Yeah. You can try it, too."

At my recommendation, Lulu delicately slid her feet under the blanket and looked pleased.

Now the vanguard group had paused their training to approach curiously.

"Is this another magic tool of your creation, master? How very wonderful. I look forward to using it on night watch."

"*Kotatsuuu?*"

"It's warm inside, sir."

Tama and Pochi stuck their heads under the quilt, sniffing around and patting the device studiously.

"Master, this is too small for everyone to use, is it not? I inquire."

"Don't worry. There are three more of them."

I pointed at the other *kotatsu* a short distance away, though some assembly was still required.

Before long, the vanguard team called off their training, and instead I ended up leading a practice session on how to put together and take apart the *kotatsu*.

Once everyone could handle that, I had them try supplying it with magic, but Lulu and the beastfolk girls couldn't quite manage it.

Lulu and Liza had used the Tinder Rod before, but it automatically absorbed magic when you pressed the switch. This was probably harder.

"It's all right. You'll be able to do it sooner or later."

I comforted the kids who hadn't been able to do it and readjusted the night watch shifts accordingly.

After all, if nobody on a particular shift could supply the magic, the heating would stop, and they'd get cold.

That evening, I was on the late-night watch with Nana.

Since there weren't any animals or monsters around that would harm us, I decided to do an experiment I'd been meaning to try for a while. Just to be sure, I asked Nana to use her Foundation Magic spell Sonar to keep an eye on our surroundings.

I went outside the igloo-style Shelter wall and began some prep work.

This time, I wanted to attempt forging a Holy Sword with the instructions I'd gotten in Sedum City.

Arisa's hint had helped me decode the cipher, and the resulting text was a guide to making "blue," a special circuit liquid for creating Holy Swords, and then using that to create the special blade.

The blue seemed doable enough, but the sword itself required special casting equipment and the help of various magic experts, so that wasn't feasible right now.

However, the process bore a close resemblance to the one for making demon blades described in Trazayuya's documents, so the liquid itself could probably be used for other magic tools. I fished through Trazayuya's documents and found a guide to making Holy Stones that I could try instead.

These were the elf version of the barrier posts I'd seen keeping monsters away from villages. According to the documents, the effect radius was about half that of the barrier pillars.

There were several types of Holy Stones to choose from, so I picked the easiest kind, which had an effect only when it was infused with power.

I did a search in Storage to make sure I had enough material on hand.

All right, let's give this a try.

First, I'd need to make the blue.

The materials were similar to those used for making the circuit liquid that was needed for crafting normal magic tools, but blue's stabilizer was powdered gold and gems, and dragon powder was required instead of ground-up cores.

Dragon powder seemed to be particularly rare. Once I'd figured out the recipe for blue, I'd immediately checked at all the magic and alchemy shops in Sedum City for it, but none of them had any.

Fortunately, I'd found a vial of dragon powder while exploring the labyrinth under Seiryuu City with the beastfolk girls, so I wouldn't even have to mess around with the scales I'd plundered from the Valley of Dragons.

Following the instructions, I began the formulation and transmutation.

It was more difficult than I'd expected. If I lost focus at all, the dragon powder would start vibrating strangely, as if it was about to separate, so I had to keep constantly adjusting the flow of magic.

Come on, Satou. Concentrate!

After dozens of what felt like very long seconds, the blue was finished.

> Skill Acquired: "Precise Magic Manipulation"

Good thing I pulled it together and focused. It would be a shame if the finished blue deteriorated, so I moved it safely into Storage for now.

Next, I prepared a thin stone slate to use for the magic circuit of the Holy Stone. I'd utilized a similar one when I made the *kotatsu*.

With a sharp metal rod, I carved the lines of the circuit diagram–like design into the stone—then cleaned the dust and dirt off the surface with a cloth.

Then, in Storage, I filled the precision carving rod with the liquid blue. The tool was like a pen with a slim opening, used for depositing circuit liquid into the finely detailed grooves of the design.

Since the characteristics of items in Storage didn't change, I took advantage of this to keep the blue fresh while I created my circuit.

The blue seemed to harden faster than the normal liquid. This made it easier to trace the intricate pattern, but without my Storage system, I think it would've been ridiculously difficult.

I completed the task and poured some power into my handiwork.

Since the circuit was so delicate this time, I moved the magic with the same precision as sorting grains of salt with chopsticks.

Using the "Precise Magic Manipulation" skill I'd just gained, I was able to move less than one point of MP at a time, down to two-digit decimals. As I did so, a faint blue light began rising from the circuit.

It was similar to the glow of a Holy Sword.

The color of this light was probably why the liquid was called "blue."

Normally, the light was red-based, so it was easy to differentiate between the types of liquid.

Just as I'd added about one point of magic, the Holy Stone's core began to work. I kept slowly increasing the supply of magic until the circuit was completed, about five points.

A pillar of blue light appeared around the slate, about three feet wide and twenty feet tall.

At a glance, it seemed to be a simple beam, but if you examined it from different angles, you could see the circuit pattern repeating over and over again.

Nana emerged from the Shelter igloo, where she'd been keeping watch.

"Master, the monsters shown by my Sonar magic have suddenly disappeared, I report."

I shifted my gaze to the radar occupying a small corner of my field of vision.

Sure enough, the monsters around the edges of the display were gone.

"This light pillar has a monster-repelling effect."

"Master, according to my information library, only Holy Swords emit a blue magic light such as this, I report."

Expressionless, Nana tilted her head as she regarded the pillar.

"Yeah, this uses the same material as a Holy Sword."

"I see... It is quite pretty."

Nana nodded without looking away. She seemed to be entranced by it.

I left her to it for now, since I wanted to investigate the performance of the light pillar.

On the map, there were no longer any monsters within a third of a mile of us. They had been driven away and were now huddled in a neat ring around the area of effect.

I looked at my log, too, and found that a few ghost monsters had been destroyed when I activated the stone. The insect types were still around, and only a few skeleton monsters had been defeated, so my circuit was probably particularly effective against undead-type monsters that had no corporeal form.

Makes sense, since this is part of a recipe for a Holy Sword.

The effect range of a blue-based Holy Stone was a little less than the three-hundred-foot radius of a barrier post, but it was still ten times more than that of a Holy Stone made with normal circuit liquid, according to my documents.

Since the range of our go-to monster repellent powder was partially dependent on the wind, I was glad the Holy Stone had such a good radius. The problem was this exceedingly conspicuous pillar of light. At this height, it was probably visible from the nearby villages.

I tried using "Magic Manipulation" to reduce the Holy Stone's strength by making myself part of the circuit, much like how I'd supplied Nana with power before. I let the magic flow through it and me, gradually lessening its power inside.

My plan was to temporarily remove all the magic and then try again, but...

"Master, the light has disappeared, I report."

Though she was still expressionless, Nana's announcement sounded vaguely crestfallen.

"Would you like to try powering it?"

"Yes, master."

At my recommendation, Nana eagerly approached the stone and started pouring magic into it.

It was probably more difficult than usual because of the delicate circuitry; a few beads of sweat appeared on Nana's forehead.

She got the hang of it soon enough, though, and the stone started emitting a pale-blue light. This time, the pillar maxed out at around six feet in height.

"That's enough, thanks."

"Understood."

Nana seemed a little out of breath, so I handed her a handkerchief to wipe the sweat from her brow.

According to her status, Nana had expended about 3 percent of her MP.

Judging by the information Arisa had given me before, Nana should have about seventy points total, meaning that this had cost her almost twenty times as much magic as me. Given the size of her pillar, the difference was probably greater.

Clearly, my magic efficiency was rather unusual when it came to tasks like this.

Since I could do it with essentially no loss at all, the ratio seemed way too different. My guess would be that a single point of magic could have different densities or something like that. It seemed likely, especially considering the size of our respective results.

Incidentally, the Holy Stone stayed in effect until morning with the magic Nana supplied.

With a few experiments during the night watch, I discovered that interrupting the light or covering it with a Shelter wall didn't alter the effect.

I'll have to make a cylinder with a light-shielding curtain tomorrow so that we can put the Holy Stone inside it and ward off monsters that way.

I still had a huge stock of the inferior monster repellent powder, but I figured there would be a use for that eventually. Holding on to it wouldn't cause any trouble, so I squirrelled it away in a corner of Storage for now.

As I reviewed the map before bed, I noticed that the demon's doppelgängers had been reduced from three to just one.

In exchange, the demon himself had changed from level 35 to 37. Apparently, creating a doppelgänger meant losing one level, and that level was recovered when the doppelgänger returned to the main body.

If the thing possessing the knight was another doppelgänger, it was probably best to assume that the hell demon's real level was at least 40.

Kid Bandits and a New Village

Satou here. Every time I watch the treasure-hunting TV show **Hidden Cash in Your Home,** *I can't help thinking,* Their taxes must have been murder that year. *But then, my taxes are bad enough as it is.*

"Take this, sir!"

Pochi's short sword stabbed at the leg of the thieves' boss.

"Don't underestimate me, little girl!"

The boss raised his ax high overhead to crush her.

"Mrrr."

"Hiyaaah!"

At that moment, an arrow from Mia's short bow and a stone from Tama struck the man's arms, disrupting his attack on Pochi.

"Grr, that's enough out of you, you—"

Even as he staggered back, the boss tried to intimidate us, but then Arisa's Psychic Magic spell Mind Blow came out of nowhere.

The man lost consciousness immediately and slumped to the ground like a puppet whose strings had been cut.

Once Arisa's magic had knocked out all the thieves, we stripped them of their weapons and tied them up with rope in the middle of a meadow near the main road.

"So what're we going to do with these fellows?"

"Well, what would people normally do in this situation?"

I didn't know the answer to Arisa's question, so I responded with one of my own, about the standard practices of this world.

Since all the bandits we'd met so far were ordinary villagers without a bounty to their name, we'd just knocked them about a bit, disarmed them, and sent them scurrying away with the help of my "Coercion" skill and Arisa's Fear Magic.

"If they have caused trouble, the usual practice is beheading. If you bring the head of a thief to a town or city guard, you will receive a reward for their extermination."

Liza was the one who answered my question.

That's a pretty violent way to handle things. I'd prefer a method that's a bit more peaceful, if possible.

"What if they haven't caused any trouble?"

"Then one generally brings them to the city alive. In that case, the thieves will be sold to slave traders as criminal slaves, and the person who apprehended them will receive half the price in addition to the reward."

So in the latter case, the city increases their labor force in addition to protecting the peace. This probably worked because of the "Contract" skill.

"Should we bring them back to the town we passed by earlier, then?"

"No, let's just dig a hole and toss them in it."

The bounty columns of the guards in that town had just as many outstanding major crimes, like sexual assault and murder, as the thieves did, so I didn't want to go there. They could drum up false charges to take away our carriage or cargo or, worse, try to do something to the kids.

"All of them?"

"Yeah. I have a spell that'll make it easy."

As proof, I used my Pitfall spell to create a hole under the thieves that they wouldn't escape from easily.

Now that our safety was secured, I dismissed the Shelter wall that was protecting Lulu and the carriage.

I'd asked Lulu to look after our horses and vehicle while we took care of things, but now she was wearing a dispirited expression.

"Are you all right, Lulu?"

"Y-yes…"

Such a gentle girl was probably shocked to see people wounded in battle.

As she sorted through our spoils, Tama found something of interest and brought it over to me.

"Gabo fruuuit?"

In Tama's hands was a root vegetable, about the size of a fist, that looked like a red miniature pumpkin.

To my memory, gabo fruits made up for their gross taste by being nutritious and easy to cultivate, so it was no surprise that they'd be grown in the Muno Barony.

However, since they were a favorite food of goblins, they were only supposed to be grown in cities or other walled-in areas.

Checking the town we'd just passed, I found that they were being raised in huge quantities. According to the map, about two-thirds of the area of the town had been converted into fields.

Normally, this wouldn't be too surprising in a territory as plagued by famine as this one; still, I couldn't help but suspect that there was more to it, since there was a demon masquerading as a magistrate.

Searching the map for goblins, I found five or so small settlements of demi-goblins in the large forest near Muno City. Each settlement was comprised of only thirty goblins or so, and they weren't close together, so I concluded that they probably weren't being bred deliberately.

What's the difference between a goblin and a "demi-goblin," though?

Since "demi" usually referred to some kind of subspecies, it had to be a particular subspecies of goblins. Monster subspecies would be strong, but they were all only between level 1 and 3, so they wouldn't pose a problem for us.

At any rate, that was probably enough information about gabo fruits and demi-goblins for now.

I put the sorted loot in Storage, and we left that area behind us.

After another two days of travel, we began our sixth afternoon since entering the Muno Barony.

This time, we encountered a troublesome band of thieves.

"Oh? It's those kid bandits we heard about a while ago."

"…Yeah, seems that way."

Five young girls were lying across the road, blocking the carriage's path.

I get that they're trying to stop us and all, but even recklessness should have its limits.

"Don't move! There are ten shooters aiming at your horses from the woods."

A young boy emerged from the forest, threatening us in a cracking, prepubescent voice.

Liza stopped her horse in front of the kid bandits to guard the carriage, while Nana moved to protect Lulu and me in the coachman's stand.

Of course, the boy was bluffing. I had already determined with a map search that they didn't have any bows or slings. They were holding stones, but we could easily handle a few kids throwing rocks at us.

I warned Liza and Nana not to act unless things got dangerous.

"Give us some food if you value your lives!"

The boy's brash request might have sounded impressive if it weren't for the debate that followed.

"Yeah, especially your potatoes!"

"Shouldn't we tell them to give us jerky instead?"

"I wanna try some bread."

"Anything is fine, as long as it isn't weeds."

"Shut up, you dummies!"

"Takes one to know one, dummy!"

"Just be quiet!"

As the peanut gallery chimed in with their requests, the whole mood was ruined.

I didn't mind giving them food, but I'd like to get the road cleared first if possible.

"Private Pochi, Private Tama, you're in charge of getting those little girls out of the street. Don't hurt them, though, okay?"

"Aye-aye, siiir!"

"Roger, sir!"

Tama and Pochi gave a military-style salute they'd learned from Arisa, then jumped out of the carriage.

I got down as well, picking up one of the kids who was blocking our path and gently tossing her toward the children in the woods. The other kids scrambled frantically to catch her.

As I looked for the next kid, I noticed Pochi and Tama had neglected their road-clearing duties in favor of plopping down next to the girls and peering into their faces.

"They look hungryyy."

"Rumbly tummies, sir."

Tama and Pochi rummaged around in their pockets and started

feeding the girls whatever scraps of dried meat and baked goods they could find.

"Meat?"

"It's yummy!"

"Thank you."

The young girls raised a little cheer in unison.

Then Pochi and Tama noticed me watching them. With a few shifty glances, they quickly hustled two of the girls off to the side of the road. One of the remaining two panicked and hurried after them into the forest.

"No fair! What about us?"

"I wanna eat meat, too!"

In the woods, the kids started bickering among themselves.

"Get alooong?"

"Y-you mustn't fight, sirs!"

Even though they'd caused the conflict in the first place, Pochi and Tama were doing their best to mediate.

I thought I'd call them back and get the carriage moving, but one girl was stubbornly staying in the road, refusing to take the hint.

She looked like she could be in middle school, but the AR display told me that she was the same age as Lulu, so technically she was a teenager.

"Are you going to head back into the forest yourself, or would you prefer me to throw you?"

Despite my slightly harsh words, the girl remained facedown and unmoving in my path, as if nothing on earth could budge her.

I started to lift the prone girl by her girdle but had to stop partway through.

Her hand was stuck in a root that was embedded in the road. Yanking her up would probably hurt her, so I took a knife from my belt to free her.

"L-let go of Totona!"

The apparent leader came rushing out of the woods with a club in hand.

Ignoring him, I cut the root that had trapped Totona, lifted her up from the road, and hefted her over my shoulder.

Liza made to move toward the boy frantically waving his club, so I stopped her with a motion of my hand.

Just as he swung at me, I plucked it out of his grip and knocked him down with a gentle push from my foot. This dazed him for a moment, so I picked him up by the belt and tossed him into the woods toward his friends.

I threw the girl Totona in after him.

When I returned to the carriage, Arisa handed me a meal that she'd taken out from our bag of holding, so I placed it on the side of the road.

Kids though they were, they'd still attacked us, so we gave them some of the more unappetizing rations.

As we resumed our journey, Liza made Tama and Pochi kneel in the carriage as she scolded them.

Apparently, slaves were strictly prohibited from giving away their master's belongings without permission.

I didn't think it was a big deal, since it was only snacks, but I'd entrusted Liza with their education. I didn't want to undermine her, so I decided to reassure them later.

Mia was riding Liza's horse in her stead.

As the lecture continued in the background, I opened the map to check out the next leg of our journey.

First, we would cross the river ahead and proceed west on the road bordering the large forest on the other side. We'd reach the back road that led into the heart of the forest in about three days. Since the side road seemed too narrow for the carriage to traverse, we'd have to procure more horses in the town near the forest.

The more pressing problem, however, was the mysterious militia of old people on the bank of the river.

They'd probably come from the nearest village to fish, but the lack of young people among them struck me as a bit odd.

"Are you worrying about those children from earlier, by any chance?"

Arisa sat down next to me, acting rather like a counselor.

"No, now I'm worried about this elderly army."

"...Elderly?"

Surprised, Arisa tilted her head with a confused expression.

It was a cute gesture coming from a little girl, but I would never hear the end of it if I said as much, so I kept that to myself.

"Yeah, elderly."

I patted Arisa's head as I repeated the statement.

After the encounter with the kid bandits, our carriage traveled on for about two hours until we arrived at the riverbank.

The elderly group that I'd detected before was still there.

They weren't even fishing in the river—there were just eight or so of them keeping warm around a fire.

In fact, the river was almost completely dried up, with only a few pathetic trickles of water in the middle, so I guess fishing would have been impossible.

Since the river looked like it had once been fairly wide, an earthquake or something must have changed its course.

The elderly group noticed us, but they made no move to react.

At first glance, they looked homeless, but camping out in such a dangerous land would normally be suicide.

I was a little intrigued, so I stopped the carriage on the opposite side of the road from them and brought Liza with me as an escort to go make contact with them.

As a peace offering, I'd brought a bottle of liquor and some smoked bear meat.

I'd figured out during my Item Box test in Sedum City that I could create a sort of smoke box inside it, which was how I'd made this smoked meat.

Unfortunately, since there was nowhere for the smoke to escape, most of the meat had gotten over-smoked and developed a strange taste and smell. This smoked bear meat was one of the few successful results.

"Hello there. The sunshine is warm today, isn't it?"

"Oh-ho, a merchant, is it? What business might you have with an old man like me?"

When I spoke to the man who seemed to be the leader, he gave me a surprisingly polite response.

The other elderly folk were ordinary enough, but this person projected a degree of status.

On top of being level 13, he had the skills "Etiquette," "Calculation," and "Penmanship." Perhaps he had once been a civil official in the service of some noble.

"Please pardon me for intruding. We stopped our carriage to refill our water supply in the stream and happened to notice all of you here, so I simply thought I would come and greet you."

It was a lame excuse, but they probably wouldn't mind.

Before the leader could respond, the other old people all started talking at once.

"Awful polite, aren'tcha? Just think of us geezers as a coupla rocks by the roadside."

"S'true. We can't even admire the river till we go home to heaven anymore."

"And if we return to the village, we'll just be a burden on our sons an' daughters."

"If we're meant to sell our grandkids, I'd rather the gods just take me right here."

"But yer always welcome here if ya got some food?"

"Boy, if I ever eat another meal, I might just float up to heaven with happiness."

"Ain't that the truth."

I guess instead of abandoning their elderly on mountains like in those old folktales, they abandon them at rivers here?

"Now, now, don't make that face. It's all right," an old woman chimed in, eyeing me with concern.

I have the "Poker Face" skill, so she shouldn't have been able to guess my feelings from my expression, but something about my aura must have given it away.

"Right. We left th' village on our own so there'd be less mouths to feed."

"An' if us geezers get outta the way quicker, then maybe those poor gals won't have to sell themselves."

"Yeah, 'specially since the chief was sayin' there ain't been many merchants buyin' slaves lately."

So without anyone to buy their daughters, now they were sacrificing their elderly?

Apparently, monsters rarely attacked near this river, so they were simply waiting here quietly for their lives to run out. They didn't know why this place was safe from monsters.

The map showed the remains of a fort on the mountain behind the riverside camp, so maybe that was why.

"Well, I brought this as a sign of friendship."

I handed the wine and smoked meat over to the leader.

He distributed it right away to the other old folks, who were practically mad with glee.

You would never guess that their statuses read **Starving** and **Overworked** from this display of energy.

"Oh-ho-ho, it's booze, I tell ya, booze!"

"What a heavenly smell, sonny!"

"How many years's it been?"

"Oh-ho, there's some nice meat here, too!"

"C'mere, sir merchant, why don't you 'n' your lovely guard there join us by the fire?"

"Looks like we'll get to make one more good memory afore we die."

"'S it all right for us to eat this 'fore them kids come back?"

A few of these comments were a little morbid, but overall everyone seemed happy.

That last remark from one of the old ladies was probably in reference to the kid bandits we met earlier.

"We still have extra supplies, so I'll give you some more before we go."

"Well, that's awful kind of ya. Now, have a drink!"

I accepted the little teacup of alcohol offered by one of the old men and knocked it back.

"Oh-ho, the boy can drink!"

As I shared a few rounds with the elderly folks, I had them tell me rumors about the area and such.

According to them, the kid bandits were serf children who'd been driven out of a nearby farm village to reduce the number of mouths to feed.

Since I didn't end up needing a guard, I sent Liza back to the others to have them set up camp. We'd planned on resting a little way up the stream on the other side anyway, so it wouldn't be a big deal to do it here instead.

I asked Liza to prepare enough wheat porridge and a stew of sinewy meat and potatoes to feed a large number of people. My reasoning was that the old folks didn't normally eat much, so the wheat porridge would help with digestion while the stew would fill them up. The sinewy meat would take longer to chew and feel especially satisfying.

This would involve peeling a lot of potatoes, so the younger kids were helping with that as well.

"…One time, I was surrounded by skeleton monsters, and I thought for sure I was a goner—"

"This ol' story again?"

The leader's face was red from the liquor as he started to speak, and another old man interrupted him.

"Was this back when the territory was a marquisate?" I asked.

"Yes, that's right. Back then, undead monsters were springing up all over. It was like they were rising from the shadows of buildings."

"You must've been lucky to survive."

"Well, strangely enough, the monsters only attacked nobility or soldiers who attacked them first."

So the Undead King Zen hadn't attacked people indiscriminately.

"But the real danger came after that."

"What happened?"

"The marquis burned down the whole city to get rid of the monsters."

"…That seems excessive."

"It was indeed… Huge flaming shells rained down on the city, burning up monsters and citizens alike. That was the real hell on earth…," the leader said in a trembling voice. It really was amazing that he'd survived such a calamity.

"Then was the current Muno City rebuilt after that?"

"No, I wasn't in Muno City at the time."

Apparently, the one who'd abducted Zen's wife wasn't the marquis himself but his younger brother. Thus, Zen had attacked the city where the marquis's brother was serving as viceroy.

"Still, any weapon used to burn down an entire city must have been truly terrible."

"Yes, the Magic Cannon in Marquis Muno's castle was inherited from an ancient empire."

"An ancient empire?!"

So it's an ancient empire this time? Now there's a key phrase. My fantasy-obsessed middle school self would be swooning right about now.

I wonder if this Magic Cannon is different from the one in that anti-dragon defense tower Zena showed me back in Seiryuu City?

"Oh yes, before the Shiga Kingdom was founded…"

To summarize the leader's somewhat tedious explanation: The

ancient civilization in question was an orc empire that had existed before the Shiga Kingdom was founded, stretching from then–Muno Marquisate to present-day Ougoch Duchy to the south.

And with the Magic Cannon installed, Muno City was on the front line of the battle between the demon lord that ruled the Orc Empire and the hero of the Saga Empire.

...Wait, so this Magic Cannon could be fired in the city?

It probably used a mana source for power, but if it could attack a city that was dozens of miles away, it sounded like my Meteor Shower spell.

"However, the Magic Cannon is gone now. The Undead King was said to have destroyed it when he killed Marquis Muno."

By the time the leader's captivating tale was finished, the sunset was casting long shadows over the camp.

"Hey, geezers, we brought some food."

"It's not weeds today!"

Covered in leaves and spiderwebs, the kid bandits came tumbling out of the woods behind the fire, where I was sitting with the old folks.

"Hey, it's the guy from before!"

"You didn't come to take back the food, did you?"

"He got here ahead of us!"

The other kids spotted me among the elderly and crowded anxiously behind their leader.

Can't they see we're having a relaxed little banquet over here?

"Oh, masterrr, dinner is all ready!"

"Have Liza bring it over, please. Let's eat together."

I'd already discussed this with the old folks' group, so the kids were the only ones caught off guard.

Liza and Nana carried a large pot over to us and placed it beside the bonfire.

I'd made a whole bunch of wooden bowls during our stay in Sedum City, so there would be enough for a group of this number.

Even after the old folks and my own party had served their portions, the kid bandits made no move to line up for food.

"You don't like wheat porridge?" I asked. The boy in front was still radiating hostility, so I addressed the girl next to him instead.

"Nuh-uh, I love it."

"Then come eat with us."

Despite my invitation, the children were still guardedly keeping their distance.

"Come on now, children, eat with us."

"Have a seat already, sonnies."

When the old men held out bowls of porridge to them, they finally gave in to temptation and timidly accepted some food.

"Y-yummy!"

"It's not weeds at all!"

"Whoa, somethin' else smells good, too."

"There's meat in this stew over here!"

"For real?"

"You're right, it's meat!"

With a rather strange comment among their cheers, the children began devouring the meal gleefully.

"Make sure you chew thoroughly before you swallow, or your stomachs will pay for it later," Arisa advised.

"This little lass is right, you kids better chew up good. We may never get to eat like this again, y'know."

"Don't say such dark things in the middle of a meal, fool!"

The old guy followed up with an ominous remark, but the old lady next to him whacked him in the head.

Just then, Pochi, who was the first to clear her plate, started a war with a single sentence.

"Seconds, please, sir!"

The young bandits jolted with nearly audible tension at the word.

As the one eating closest to the pot, Nana nodded expressionlessly and doled out more food to her.

Having already finished their food, a few of the young boys gnawed on their spoons a little as they enviously watched Pochi receive seconds.

"No need to be modest, you lot. If you want more, then go and get some," Arisa said to them, noticing the situation.

As soon as they heard her, the children who'd already finished their food rushed up to Nana.

The other young boys and girls who hadn't finished yet started wolfing down their food. A few of them started choking in their haste, and the older folks chided them to "chew yer food up right."

"No need to rush if you want seconds. There's plenty more," I said, excusing myself.

We might run out of what we'd made at this rate, so I headed to the kitchen area by the carriage to make more food.

Lulu and Liza rushed over to help, and I used the Garage Bag to take some hydra meat out of Storage, cutting it into bite-size pieces and putting them on skewers.

At this point, it would probably be best to make two per person.

"D'ya need any help, then?"

"U-um, excuse me, but if we can help at all..."

"We'll help!"

An elderly lady, the girl Totona, and a younger girl who seemed to be her sister came over to help out.

Thanks to the three extra pairs of hands, preparing the meat skewers for cooking took less time than I'd expected.

Figuring we might as well serve them freshly cooked, I returned to the bonfire with a tray of meat skewers on wire mesh.

"Yaaay!"

"Meat skewers, sir!"

Smelling the meat skewers as they started to cook, Tama and Pochi waved their arms overhead with joy.

The children who were eating their second helpings nearly dropped their spoons as they stared at the meat skewers Lulu was cooking.

Mia, always a light eater, moved to an area where the smoke from the meat wouldn't bother her and started playing the lute.

Her joyful songs matched the atmosphere.

The shouts of delight from the children as they feasted on the skewers mingled with the music of the lute underneath the starry sky.

The children grew drowsy after they'd eaten their fill, so they began filing into a large ditch next to the bonfire.

I wondered how deep it was and peered into the hole. It was only about six feet, enough for the nine children to be concealed as they huddled together inside.

To ward off the wind, they put a mat woven from grass or something similar over the hole. The old folks had a sleeping pit of their own.

This looked terribly cold, so I offered them some brown wolf and bear furs that I'd been stockpiling in Storage.

We shared a meal together as friends. It should be all right for me to meddle just a little.

"Hey, Mister Merchant."

"What is it?"

One of the boys approached me, the one who'd tried to protect Totona with a club. According to the AR display, he was her younger brother.

"This is for the food. And to make up for attacking you earlier today."

The boy held out a smooth, wood-carved object. It looked like three two-inch wooden cubes, each connected to the other two.

When I accepted it from the boy's hands, it was heavier than I'd expected.

According to my AR display, it wasn't wood at all but a metal called Damascus steel. Upon closer inspection, there were several reddish streaks that might've been joining points.

With the help of my now neglected "Analyze" skill, I learned that it was an all-purpose **Magic Key Apparatus**, but I had no idea what kind of lock it might be for.

"Did you make this yourself?"

I didn't think he had, but I figured it was a good prompt to find out where it came from.

"No, I found it on the mountain."

"What's that, sonny? I toldja never to go up there!"

One of the old men jabbed a finger at the mountain and scolded the boy in a spray of spittle.

Wondering if there was a dangerous creature up there, I checked the map.

There hadn't been anything there during the day, but now the ruined fortress was full of thirty or more monsters like skeleton soldiers and a wraith.

The skeleton soldiers were around level 10, but the wraith was level 25.

In particular, the latter had the hereditary skills "Paralysis," "Fear," "Kin Control," and "Life Drain." It was even able to use Ice Magic.

Even if these things appeared only at night, it was alarming to think such dangerous monsters were so near these elderly folks and small children. There were also wild boars roaming the mountain, one of which was level 15.

"Is there something living on that mountain?"

This time I spoke to the old man who'd scolded the boy.

"The vengeful ghosts of nobles appear there at night. And during the day, a huge boar we call One-Eye wanders around there."

"A large boar might be a good source of food, though."

"Sure, if we could kill it. Three former soldiers once went into the woods to hunt ol' One-Eye, and only one came back alive."

The old man heaved a sigh.

So they regarded this boar as the master of the mountain, then.

We were getting low on boar meat anyway, so I decided we could pay a visit to the ruined fortress to help level up my kids.

The next day, we rode the four horses up the path leading to the fort ruins. We left the carriage down at the foot of the mountain.

Today's missions were wild-boar hunting and exterminating the monsters at the fort.

My plan was that I would defeat the dangerous-looking wraiths with my magic or a Holy Sword, and the other small-fry monsters would serve as EXP for my kids.

Incidentally, the pairs on each horse were Nana and Pochi, Liza and Arisa, Mia and Lulu, and Pochi and me.

"Rest in peeeace?"

Sitting in front of me, Tama pointed toward a cliffside near the mountain road.

"What is it?"

"There's booones."

I followed Tama's finger to something like an old rag caught in the rocks partway up the cliff, and sure enough, I could see flashes of white.

Nearby, I also caught a glimpse of what seemed to be a knife handle. As I squinted at it, an AR display popped up that read **mithril dagger**.

Ooh! I wasn't expecting to find that classic fantasy metal in a place like this.

"Tama, take the reins for a minute."

"Aye!"

I left Tama in charge of the horse, told the others I was going to recover the deceased person's belongings, and headed down the steep slope.

Once I reached the outcropping, I stored the bleached skeletal remains and items trapped in the rocks. Thank goodness I didn't have to touch things to put them in Storage.

Inside the satchel I'd found, there was a sturdy case with a number of books inside and a lever-like object made of the same material as the device the young boy had given me yesterday.

The books had some disturbing titles. There were two larger volumes, *Magic Cannon: Noble Blood Maintenance Guide* and *Magic Cannon: Noble Blood Operation Guide*, and three smaller ones that seemed to be ciphers of some kind.

These had to be connected to the Magic Cannon that the old folks' leader had been talking about last night.

The lever I'd found was apparently a Magic Cannon Control Stick, so the Magic Key Apparatus the boy had given me yesterday must have belonged to this person, too—perhaps a member of the aristocracy connected to Marquis Muno.

These seemed like important, top-secret materials, but since the Undead King Zen had destroyed the Magic Cannon some twenty years ago, they were probably nothing more than collector's items now.

It was still morning when we arrived at the ruins on the summit. The trip up had taken about two hours.

This former stronghold was larger than the fort at the border had been; it had probably fit two or three hundred people while it was still standing.

The steel portcullis had fallen, blocking the entrance.

Even with the combined strength of all four members of our advanced guard, it wouldn't open.

Well, it *was* the main gate of a fortress, after all.

While everyone was focused on the portcullis, I hopped over the outer wall and turned the crank to open the gate.

As I crossed the wall, I felt myself breaking through some kind of barrier.

I stared at the spot where I'd felt the barrier, but I didn't see anything. Unlike the barrier of the Forest of Illusions in Kuhanou County, this one seemed to have disappeared completely when it was broken.

We took a light lunch of warm soup and bread in the courtyard, then explored around the perimeter of the fort.

Most of it was overrun with weeds, but Pochi and Tama eagerly took up their tools and quickly cleared a path. We arrived in the rear garden area.

There, a few defenseless orange birds were pecking at some feed.

"Preeey!"

"There are eggs here, sir!"

The reason I'd steered us straight toward the backyard was that I'd noticed these birds on the map.

Just like the chickens in modern Japan, these birds couldn't fly very well.

They were slow-moving, too, so Tama and Pochi could catch them easily.

The orange chickens were all large and plump, enough to hide Pochi's face after she caught one. The eggs were a normal size, though, no bigger than your typical large chicken egg.

"Geh!"

"What is it?"

Heading toward Arisa's fed-up voice, I found an area full of fresh parsley.

"Oh, parsley?"

"Who're you calling parsley?! I won't let anyone call me a parsley at this age! The least you could do is marry me until I become an adult, even if it's just a common-law marriage, master!"

Arisa growled like an angry dog, frowning and jumping at me.

Lulu, who was nearby, widened her eyes in surprise at her sister's behavior.

What, does "parsley" mean an unmarried single woman or something? I've never heard anyone say that before, but it sounds like something from a girls' manga.

"I'm serious! And Lulu's my sister, so you should marry both of—"

"Yeah, yeah. I'll consider it if you're still single in ten years, all right?"

Arisa seemed to be heading toward an inappropriate comment, so I hurriedly cut her off.

"Really? It's a promise, then!"

Arisa pumped her fists in a pose more befitting a triumphant athlete than a little girl, then dashed away.

"…How nice…"

My "Keen Hearing" skill alerted me to a tiny murmur from Lulu. I looked down and saw an earnest expression on her lovely face.

If she kept staring at me with those beautiful features, I worried I'd be tempted to set foot on the dark path of the lolicon.

Maybe that's why I said such a stupid thing…

"Master, could I also…?"

"Sure, Lulu. If you're single in ten years, too, I'll marry you along with Arisa."

"Yes!"

I got carried away and gave her an irresponsible reply. A hint of guilt needled my heart at the sight of such a huge smile on Lulu's face.

Bigamy did seem to be allowed in this country, but I didn't know if I'd still be in this world in five years, never mind ten.

I had arrived here suddenly, as if this were a dream; it wouldn't be too surprising if I returned just as abruptly as waking up from one.

Besides, it wasn't as though I didn't have any attachments to my home world. Even if I was fated to stay here for good, I'd want to send letters to my friends and family first at least, so I was planning to go to the Saga Empire once everyone's future plans were settled.

Well, I probably don't need to worry about this too seriously right now.

If magic existed for summoning and sending people back, surely I could develop magic to allow me to move freely between the worlds within ten years.

Besides, there was no way Arisa and Lulu would stay single for ten years.

Oblivious to my innermost thoughts, Lulu pressed her hands to her cheeks and mumbled to herself.

"Hee-hee… A bride, huh?"

Miss Lulu, stop it with the heart-melting smile while it's just the two of us, please.

I nearly gave in to desire for a moment, but I managed to hold out by calling on my sense of reason.

"Master, if you'd like, please come over here and look at this."

Luckily, a call from Liza saved me from drowning in Lulu's pinkish aura. I headed toward her with Lulu in tow.

After passing through an arch of withered roses, we found a water fountain among the sea of weeds.

"We suspected that there may be a trap, so nobody has approached it yet."

"Good thinking."

After praising Liza's cautiousness, I investigated the fountain.

My "Trap Detection" skill wasn't reacting at all, and I didn't see anything on the map that looked like a trick, either.

"…I think it's safe."

After I gave my verdict, Liza proceeded toward the fountain as an advance scout, her spear still at the ready.

"Weeding brigaaade!"

"We'll do our best, sir!"

Tama and Pochi popped up immediately and hacked away at the flora in the hall leading to the fountain. They were very efficient.

"Satou."

Mia tottered over to us through the arch, her arms full of vegetables.

"Is that broccoli and celery?"

"Mm."

They were a little different from the varieties I'd seen in Japan, but they were definitely some species of the familiar vegetables.

Apparently, they'd been growing in the same corner as the parsley.

"Maybe we should make a broccoli stew for dinner, then," I suggested.

"Great."

Mia gave an excited little nod.

The beastfolk girls caught three goats that were on the other side of the fountain, and Nana held a little orange chick in the palm of her hand with delight.

There were persimmon and plum trees growing in the backyard. The persimmons were sour, but I collected some of the fallen ones, figuring I could dry them out.

For a place that was supposed to be a den of undead monsters, this area was quite peaceful.

Clonk…clonk…

With a fully armed Liza leading the way, we strode into the entrance hall of the fort.

Tama and Pochi walked behind Liza, followed by Nana, Arisa, and Mia, and I brought up the rear.

The entrance hall contained a stairwell leading up to the second floor, where light leaked in through a window. It was the sort of place where balls might have been hosted.

Since the undead appear only at night, we'd decided to explore the fort during the day before the real battle at sunset.

The skeletal remains of a number of soldiers were strewn about the entrance hall.

Once night had fallen, these would probably begin to move.

I should probably put them in Storage in the daytime, then cremate and bury them later.

Glancing over, I saw that Lulu looked very anxious. Arisa and Mia seemed a bit nervous, too.

"Don't be scared. It's perfectly safe during the da—"

As I attempted to reassure them, the loud bang of a door slamming shut interrupted me.

At the same moment, specks of black appeared on the window and soon blotted out all the light from outside.

Shrieking, Mia and Lulu latched onto me.

With the aid of my "Night Vision" skill, I could see our advance guard team warily keeping watch in the darkness.

I took my Magic Lamp out of Storage and supplied it with some MP to illuminate the room.

"Kweh-heh-heh… Foolish vandals. You know not your place, daring to enter the secret base of the revival of the house of Marquis Muno."

I couldn't see the source of the voice. There was nobody on my radar but us.

Checking the map, I determined the enemy was one of the wraiths I'd noted last night. It was on the underground third floor of the fort. It hadn't shown up on my map when we first arrived here, so I had no idea where it came from.

It was probably using a speaking tube or some occult-type means to make its voice reach this room.

"Prepare to become the cornerstones of the revival of the marquis's house, at the hands of our faithful soldiers!"

Sure enough, as the wraith spoke, the skeleton soldiers that had been lying on the floor arose.

There were only three in this room, but more were approaching from other rooms, too.

"These enemies are strong, so take each of them on in pairs. I'll handle the last one."

"Understood!"

"Aye!"

"Yes, sir!"

"Orders registered. Switching to combat-doll mode."

The four members of the advance guard promptly took action.

I've never heard of this so-called "combat-doll mode" before, though.

Arisa was snickering at my side, so she must have taught Nana some weird phrase. Of course, there wasn't actually any change in Nana's status information.

Once I'd taken out my target with a rock to the head from Storage, I watched over the advance guard's battle.

The skeleton soldiers' movements were jerky, but they attacked with fast overhead strikes. Those kinds of blows might kill you instantly if you let your guard down.

While Pochi parried the heavy sword attacks with her small buckler, Tama aimed at the leg joints with her short sword.

Since Tama's attacks were so light, a single direct hit wouldn't destroy anything. Still, she persisted, and the fourth attack finally broke the joint.

The skeleton lost its balance and toppled over, and the two girls finished it off in a flurry of strikes.

Nearby, Nana managed to use her shield to parry an attack from a skeleton soldier wielding a large ax. With the help of her Foundation Magic technique Body Strengthening, she managed to keep up with her opponent, if only barely.

Luckily, Liza was on the scene, shattering the skeleton's bones with a few rapid jabs of her spear. She appeared to be using the blunt end, not the tip.

When the dust settled, all three of the skeleton soldiers in the room were defeated.

The health gauges of the two shield users had declined slightly, but no one had any noticeable physical wounds.

There were more soldiers heading toward us from the other rooms, so we could probably take care of healing later.

All three of the beastfolk girls had reached level 14 as a result of this battle. Each of them received a new skill: "Strike" for Liza, "Thrust" for Pochi, and "Enemy Detection" for Tama.

However, they wouldn't be able to use these freely until they'd had a proper rest so that their bodies could adapt to the new skills.

Even so, it had been a closer contest than I'd expected, so it might be wise to fortify the battlefield and make fighting a little easier.

With that thought in mind, I set about creating a barricade.

I wrapped a few poles in cloth and cast the Shelter spell to create a lattice for defense. It was a dome with an entrance and some smaller holes for attacking.

This would keep the rearguard safe while we fought.

Next, I thought I should do something about the lighting.

The Magic Lamp was illuminating the members of my party from behind, so their own shadows would hinder them as they fought.

"Mia, can you light the room?"

"Mm."

Mia cast a new spell I'd developed.

"...■■ **Bubble Light** *Hotaru Awa!*"

Several spheres materialized, like faintly glowing soap bubbles. The only problem with this spell was that the MP cost was high, since I'd used code from a Light Magic spell.

When I checked in on everyone now that the room was lit, I noticed that Lulu was wearing a dark, brooding expression.

Maybe the sight of the attacking skeletons scared her?

"M-master. I-is there anything I can do to be of help?"

Lulu clasped her hands in front of her chest, her voice trembling as she spoke.

Right... She had looked like she wanted to say something after we took care of those professional thieves, too.

I was glad that the normally shy Lulu had spoken to me of her own volition, but I couldn't put her on the front lines without any kind of training.

While I contemplated how to convince her of this, she pleaded with me further still.

"I—I want to be useful like everyone else!"

"You don't need to worry about that. You're already useful, Lulu."

That was the truth. I couldn't have her believing she was useless.

Just before I could explain that everyone had their own roles, Arisa tugged on my sleeve. I looked over my shoulder at her.

"Master. Perhaps Lulu could try one of those Magic Guns you used before?"

"Oh yeah, I forgot about those."

We decided to give Arisa's proposal a try. With that, Lulu should be able to participate in battle from a safe distance away.

I put the Magic Lamp on the floor, took out the spare Magic Gun from Storage, and handed it to Lulu. As a precaution in case of friendly fire, I put it on its lowest power setting.

"Aim this toward the monster. Then pull this bit—it's called the trigger—and a Magic Bullet will come out from the end of the barrel."

"R-right!"

I gave the Magic Gun to the nervous Lulu and had her do a test fire at a random pillar.

Her first shot completely missed.

"Lulu, you don't need to be so tense. Try to relax."

I moved behind her and put my hands over hers to demonstrate how to pull the trigger.

"Gently, like this. All right?"

"R-r-r-r-r-riiight…"

Hmm? Lulu's face was so red that steam was practically coming out of her ears.

Right. I'd forgotten, since she'd gotten used to me lately, but Lulu was still pretty uncomfortable with men.

"Sorry, sorry. I was too close."

I stepped back, and Lulu gave a despairing little "Ah…"

If I was a pubescent boy like my current appearance indicated, I might have fallen in love with that voice.

However, since I'm around thirty years old on the inside, the majority of what I felt toward Lulu was the protectiveness of a guardian.

So, although she was looking up at me with a strangely sexy expression, I remained deliberately serious and had her do another test fire.

She took to the Magic Gun faster than I'd expected, and after a few more tries, she had the hang of it.

However, since Lulu's magic ran out after just two shots, she had to depend on potions to recover it.

Arisa and Mia wanted to use the Magic Gun, too, so I let them practice while Lulu was taking a break.

With our newly established barricade, the next battle was much easier.

Lulu, Arisa, and Mia took turns using the Magic Gun to attack the

skeleton soldiers, then finished them off with spears or stones. Any time one of the soldiers tried to attack with a long weapon, I forcibly yanked it from their grasp.

During the third round of this tension-free, almost gamelike battle, Liza's spear started producing a red light.

It always happened just as she landed a powerful strike, so maybe it was a visual effect to indicate that a skill had been used?

Liza's MP gauge had decreased slightly, so magic was involved.

We had a bit of time until the next enemy's arrival, so I took down the current Shelter wall and put up a new one.

Then I decided to have Liza show me her technique again before the next battle.

"Liza, can you show me that last spear strike again?"

"The last strike?"

Liza repeated the movement despite her puzzlement, but this time there was no red light like before.

I took out a spear from Storage by way of the Garage Bag. I'd gotten this one during the Cradle incident, and it had a similar design to Nana's rapier.

I tried to re-create Liza's movement with the spear.

Of course, it didn't make a red light, and it didn't even cause a powerful sound like Liza's did.

It was probably because I was taking care not to put a hole in the floor with my excessive strength, but still, my little *fwoosh* was disappointing compared to the loud *boom* that Liza's attacks normally produced.

"That was an excellent thrust."

I was a little embarrassed to have Liza compliment me on such a weak attempt.

"Pardon me, master, if I may."

Unable to watch any more of my repeated failures, Liza stood behind me and put her hands over mine on the spear to explain.

"When you land a thrust, it's best to flick your wrist to rotate the spear on impact, like so. Keep a loose grip on the spear, then tighten it the moment that you strike. I'll demonstrate slowly, so please pay attention to my fingers and wrist."

Liza demonstrated the timing for me with her hands on mine.

I could see why: It was difficult to understand this from a verbal explanation.

Once Liza stepped away, I tried it out for myself.

Yeah, that's better.

"Impressive as always, master. You've taken the main point to heart with just one demonstration."

"Only because you're such a good teacher, Liza."

It was true that her teaching was excellent, but the reason that I'd been able to learn so quickly was probably that I had a maxed-out "Spear" skill.

I tried it a few more times to memorize the sensation.

Now my thrusts looked much closer to Liza's, but I still couldn't produce the red light from my spear.

I probably needed a different skill for that.

The clattering of bones from across the room announced the arrival of two more skeleton soldiers. I had everyone take a strike so that they'd all gain EXP before I finished off the enemies.

I struck the first one in the skull, sternum, and spine in three rapid-fire attacks.

> **Skill Acquired: "Thrust"**
> **Skill Acquired: "Strike"**
> **Skill Acquired: "Pierce"**
> **Skill Acquired: "Consecutive Attacks"**

Just like that, I gained all sorts of skills.

I put skill points into them and activated them, then defeated the second skeleton.

Sadly, I still couldn't get my spear to shine.

Maybe Liza had learned some new trick that she hadn't acquired as a skill yet?

She had used up some magic, and the red glow was identical to that of a charged magic tool, so magic had to be related somehow.

"Master, a newcomer has arrived."

"I'm good now. Take it down the same way as before, please."

"Understood."

I left Liza in charge of directing combat, then tried inserting some magic power into the steel spear.

It felt strange. If I had to put it into words, I'd say it was most like pouring water into a pipe that was clogged with clay and full of holes.

It was hard to get the magic to go through, and even when it did, it leaked straight out like a sieve.

Oh right. I did read in a book about magic tools that iron has a magic-diffusing effect.

When I forced some magic into it, it lit up red for just a moment, but an instant later there was a dry *crack*, and the tip of the spear split.

Nobody but Tama seemed to notice the sound amid the clamor of battle, so I quickly switched it out with another spear of the same design in Storage and pretended nothing had happened.

As for Tama, I gestured, *Don't tell a soul.*

In return, Tama signaled *Okay* with a hand.

Then I decided to borrow Liza's spear after the battle and try the experiment again.

"Liza, could you lend me your spear for a minute?"

"Understood."

Liza handed the spear over to me reverently, and I accepted it and lightly put some magic into it.

I didn't want to overdo it and break the spear, so I was very careful to use a small amount.

It was far easier to infuse this spear than the steel one, and a faint red light emitted from the joints of the spear.

I tried adding a little more magic. This time, I faintly sensed something sticking. It was the same feeling as when I first tried to replenish Nana's magic.

Remembering that time, I finely adjusted the strength of the magic flow, clearing the pathway of magic through the weapon as I had with Nana's body.

> **Skill Acquired: "Magic-Tool Tuning"**
> **Title Acquired: Tuner**

This must've paid off, because now the tip and other parts of the spear were glowing after just a single point of magic.

When I swung the weapon, it left a beautiful trail of red light.

> **Skill Acquired: "Dance Performance"**
> **Title Acquired: Dancer**

This didn't seem like it'd be useful in combat, since it would let my opponents read the trajectory of the spear, but it might be nice for some kind of dance performance.

"I-is that Spellblade?" Arisa murmured.

"So that's what Spellblade looks like? Wonderful. Master, I had no idea you were able to use such an art. It takes countless years for master martial artists to grasp."

Liza melodramatically heaped on the praise.

"Is it a famous art?"

"Well, I think each territory only has two or three people who can use it. Still, if you went to the royal capital of a large kingdom like Shiga, I'm sure there'd be dozens."

Liza's hyperbole had me thinking that this was some amazing ability, but I guess it wasn't all that rare.

…Or maybe it is? If you're going by people per territory, it'd certainly be rarer than "Item Box" or "Analyze."

"Should I not use it in front of people, then?"

"Perhaps not. I've heard that nobles consider it a status symbol to employ knights with the ability, so if people find out that you can use it, you'll be in high demand."

So using it in public would seal my fate, huh?

I thanked Liza and returned her spear, then tried doing it with the steel again. It didn't go well, though, maybe because I didn't have the skill for it.

Clearly, weapons made with monster parts like Liza's spear were well suited to Spellblade use.

I would guess that the Holy Swords and sacred blades in Storage would work even better, but it would be silly to test that out here.

After twenty skeleton soldiers, their assault was over, so now it was our turn to attack.

However, a situation arose that made me wonder if we should retreat instead.

Lulu wasn't looking too well.

"Lulu, are you all right?"

"Oh, don't worry about me."

Arisa hovered over Lulu with concern as she sat on the floor.

"Maybe she has level-up sickness."

"Really?! So that's not just an urban legend...," Arisa said with surprise, and I nodded.

Lulu had gone from level 2 to level 6 in the battle and gained four skills: "Casting," "Shooting," "Driving," and "Cooking." The other kids hadn't leveled up at all.

The "Casting" skill seemed to be a result of her having practiced magic with Arisa a long time ago. I was really very jealous.

After a moment of discussion, we decided that I would carry her on my back. It would be dangerous to leave her alone here, after all, and she'd be safest if she stayed close to me.

It was then that I made a new discovery.

Although not much time had passed since we'd first met, Lulu's chest had grown. She had been an A cup before, but now she'd definitely crossed well into B-cup territory.

She is in her growth spurt, after all. Let's hope this trend will continue as she gets older.

As I cheered her on in the depths of my mind, we arrived safely at the underground third floor, in front of the room where the wraith was lurking.

Along the way, we'd defeated six more skeleton soldiers that tried to stop us. They were a bit stronger than the ones on the upper floors, but there was nothing else of note about them.

Since the wraith in this room had a Paralysis attack, I decided to make anti-paralysis potions for everyone.

It was a pretty simple recipe, so I blanked out my name and produced them easily.

All right, now we're ready to go.

"Finally, it's time for the boss battle!"

"The boss can use Ice Magic, so I'll head in first and take it out. The rest of you, wait a bit before you come in after me. There are four stronger skeleton soldiers in there, too, so I'm leaving those to you."

"Understood."

"Seriously, Miss Liza? We can't just let him charge in there on his own!"

"Arisa, master can defeat a single wraith with ease, I report."

Arisa was the only one opposed to my strategy.

"I'll be fine, all right? You don't need to worry about me unless the enemy's a greater hell demon or something."

"Greater...?"

I gave a joking reply, then had everyone evacuate to some distance away from the door.

"Master, please use this, at least."

Liza handed me her beloved spear.

"I believe the spear you currently have will not allow for effective Spellblade use. Ideally, I would prefer to accompany you, but I understand that I am not nearly strong enough to do so. And if I can at least offer you my spear—"

"All right. I'll borrow it for a minute, then."

I accepted Liza's spear and handed her the steel one instead.

I had planned on using a Holy Sword to get the "Spellblade" skill once I got inside, but I didn't want Liza's kindness to go to waste, so I accepted her loan gratefully.

"Kweh-heh-heh... So you have come to seek your own deaths, foolish vandals. The great house of Marquis Muno will..."

When I entered the room, the wraith started giving some kind of speech, but I didn't really care enough to listen.

The hall had a high ceiling, like an audience chamber. At the far end was a throne, upon which sat a skeleton dressed in the tattered remains of aristocratic clothing.

The semitranslucent wraith was superimposed on the skeleton, and its pallid complexion most likely bore a faint resemblance to what it had looked like in life.

And four skeletal guards in full-plate mail flanked it.

Still ignoring the wraith's speech, I approached the throne briskly, powering up Liza's spear as I did so. I was careful not to use too much magic, lest I accidentally break it.

"...And so, with the house of the marquis buried under this land..."

I was only about fifteen feet away, yet the wraith was still just pontificating.

It was probably controlled by an obsession it had had when it died.

Once I got the "Spellblade" skill, I figured I'd exorcise it with a divine blade. If I used a Holy Sword, it was more likely to obliterate the soul than send it to a peaceful rest.

With a firm step forward, I swept out the spear for an instant, creating a trail of red light.

My "Strike" and "Thrust" skills activated, and the momentum carried me into a powerful attack through the wraith's soldier into the empty space beyond.

The moment the glowing red tip of the spear touched the wraith, it vanished away, leaving behind a ripple like a single drop of black paint on the surface of a lake.

> Skill Acquired: "Spellblade"

...Oops. Was that too strong?

Just then, either I got too distracted or I messed up by using unnecessary skills, because Liza's spear started vibrating strangely.

Oh crap.

It must have been reaching its limit. Red streaks were starting to appear on the black surface of the spear, like it was about to crack.

I hurriedly drew the magic back out of the spear. This time, I was careful not to remove it all at once.

It could break like a hot cup that'd been doused in cold water too suddenly, and I didn't want that.

The spear was still tinged with magic, but the strange vibration had stopped. I tried swinging it a few times. Luckily, the balance hadn't changed, and the red streaks didn't seem to have left any cracks or scratches on the surface.

The red streaks closely resembled the hardened circuit liquid of magic-tool creation.

Since this spear was made from monster parts, maybe it was exposed to the same components as monster cores, or even made up of a crystallized version.

After a quick appraisal of the spear, I realized its performance had greatly improved.

I didn't exactly remember what its stats had been originally, but I was pretty sure it had been similar to the steel spear, and now it was nearly seven times stronger.

It still didn't compare to my Holy Swords, but it was an unusual increase in performance.

Its name had even changed, from **Black Cave Cricket Spear** to

Magic Cricket Spear. I had to wonder what the naming standards were exactly.

It was being treated as a completely different item from before the transformation, as the name of its creator had changed to a blank.

I must have forgotten to change my name back after I created those anti-paralysis potions before.

> ### > Title Acquired: Magic-Spear Smith
> ### > Skill Acquired: "Imbue Magic"
> ### > Skill Acquired: "Weapon Enhancement"

The kids entered the room, following Liza.

"Oh my. Is it over already?" Arisa asked.

"Yeah, I guess so." I noticed that the plate-mail-clad skeletons had collapsed to the floor, their bones scattering everywhere.

I guess when their master perished, the underlings disappeared, too.

"I'm sorry, Liza. Your spear looks different now."

"...Is this a pattern, not cracks?"

Surprised, Liza stroked the surface of the Magic Cricket Spear.

Then she slowly swung it in the air a few times experimentally.

"Perhaps it's my imagination... But it's as if my senses travel all the way to the tip of the spear now, even more so than before."

With that comment, she gave a more powerful strike, and the red streaks lit up in response.

"I see! Could it be that you've remodeled it so that I might learn to use Spellblade?"

I wanted to correct her misunderstanding, but she seemed so happy that I couldn't bring myself to tell her.

The next morning, I would end up confessing that I had almost broken the spear and meekly apologize.

"Wait just a minute! There's a hidden door over here!"

Arisa pulled back the tapestry behind the throne and beckoned to me.

According to my "Analyze" skill, the coat of arms on the tapestry belonged to Marquis Muno.

My "Trap Detection" skill was sounding the alarm, so I had Arisa pull back while I disarmed the snare.

Then I stepped into the hidden room. For some reason, there were two slimes in the corners of the room, so I disposed of them and put the remains in Storage.

After ensuring there were no more dangers, I called the others into the room.

"Wooow!"

"So shiny, sir!"

"How very remarkable."

"Whoa, what is this?!"

Everyone entered the room and exclaimed with surprise at the piles of treasure.

There was a heap of what must have been ten thousand gold Shigan coins, statues made of precious metals, and jewelry on display.

Along the walls of the room, there were piles of boxes full of equipment. Mithril weapons were lined up on beautiful display stands. The objects wrapped in oiled paper were probably paintings of some kind.

There wasn't a single rusted item or speck of dust in here.

The slimes had probably been for cleaning and rust removal. I should've captured them without killing them.

I told the kids that they could look at whatever they liked, and everyone began searching the room.

Pochi and Tama ran around the mountain of gold coins, Liza asked my permission before inspecting the weapons, Mia examined the silver musical instruments with an inscrutable expression, and Arisa scooped up gold coins with both hands, cackling something about filling a bathtub.

Everyone seems to be having a great time.

As for myself, I discovered a magic satchel like the Garage Bag wrapped in oiled paper in the corner by some wooden boxes.

It was stuffed with books and documents. Most of it was territorial tax revenue reports and information on a proposed mining site, but there were some intermediate and advanced spell books, too. Sadly, there weren't any scrolls.

The bag itself was about the same size as my Garage Bag, but its capacity was far less. Still, even ten cubic feet of space was pretty impressive.

As I put the Lesser Garage Bag in Storage, Nana appeared in the doorway, carrying Lulu.

"This is amazing."

"Is it a treasury? I inquire."

"Looks that way."

Marquis Muno's family must have hidden away this treasure for the revival of their house. But from what I'd heard, it didn't seem like any relatives of Marquis Muno were around anymore, so it was probably fine for us to do as we liked.

It'd be a good reward for exterminating that wraith.

After I told everyone to let me know if they wanted anything, I joined in on exploring the items.

> Title Acquired: Grave Robber
> Title Acquired: Treasure Hunter

I acquired a rather insulting title in the process, but I ignored it as I rummaged through the loot.

"Master."

Liza beckoned to me from the back of the room. Enshrined there was an egg-like object the size of a truck.

The AR display called it **Magic Cannon: Noble Blood**. The very same weapon of mass destruction that the older man had told me about. If the corpse we'd found in the mountains had gotten here alive, a new massacre might have taken place.

"What could it be?"

"Probably some kind of magic tool. Can you check those weapons again and see if there's anything we can use? I'll take care of this."

"Understood."

Once Liza had gone to the other side of the room, I put the Magic Cannon in Storage and created a Magic Cannon folder for it and all the related items and materials.

It was best to lock away a dangerous thing like this. As long as it was in my Storage, nobody should be able to misuse it.

It was our tenth morning in the Muno Barony, three days after we'd defeated the wraith.

We were still staying in the fortress.

"Perhaps the children and the elderly could live here somehow?"

After Arisa made this remark, we had called the old folks and the young bandits and started fixing up the fort.

I wasn't very enthusiastic at first, but once we started, it reminded me of making a secret base as a kid. I ended up enjoying it, reliving a bit of my childhood.

We repaired the broken well and fixed up one of the barracks to a habitable state, then gave the old folks some cloth and fur that they could use to mend their flimsy clothes.

Next, we dug a field in the courtyard so that they'd be able to grow food starting in the spring. For produce, I gave some gabo fruit to the leader of the elderly. They were the same ones I'd confiscated from the thieves before.

We had the kids teach us what wild grasses were edible and collected them while the beastfolk girls and I went wild-boar hunting.

Aside from the edible wild grass, we collected an abundance of gourds that bore a resemblance to winter melons. They weren't good to eat raw, but they would likely work well in stew or stir-fry. Mia was very pleased.

As for the immediate food supply, we all worked together to make smoked food and dried meat in large quantities. I took the monster meat out of Storage, but I told everyone that we'd hunted in the mountains.

To ensure their safety, I placed a normal Holy Stone in the center of the fort. Since the leader of the elderly group had a relatively high level, he should be able to supply it with magic.

I made a wooden frame around the Holy Stone so it'd look like it was part of the original fortress, which landed me a few shady skills like "Disguise" and "Destruction of Evidence."

Then, after we stayed three days to make sure that the undead monsters wouldn't be resurrected, we decided to depart from the fort.

Before we left, we held a memorial service with the kids and old folks for the bones I'd found in the mountains. This wasn't so much to mourn the dead as it was to ensure that they wouldn't come back again.

Then just as we were saying our farewells to the fortress, the children called out to stop us.

"Umm, Mister Merchant? This is a thank-you gift from all of us."

The girl Totona's little sister handed me a small pouch.

Inside was a collection of beautiful pebbles that they'd gathered by the riverbank. It was most likely the children's treasure. The mix even contained real gemstones and ore.

I reached for one stone from the collection and gave the rest back to them.

"I'll take one, but you should hang on to the rest of them, all right?"

"Okay!"

The girl hid bashfully behind her older sister.

After receiving words of thanks and farewells from the old folks and the kids, we descended the mountain.

We'd stayed a little longer than planned, but since we weren't in any particular rush on our journey, it wasn't a big deal.

Our carriage took us past the riverbank where the old folks had been encamped and across a sturdy stone bridge. Then, at the crossroads with the main road on the other side, we changed our path to follow the dried-up river.

Sitting on the warm carriage floor, I rolled the pebble I'd gotten earlier between my hands.

"There were much prettier gems in that bag. Why'd you choose such a plain one?"

"It's a treasure to me."

Arisa peered at the pebble in confusion, so I gave a somewhat pretentious response.

This opaque red pebble was called a "Serpent's Blood Stone," and it was used as raw material in alchemy.

Like the dragon powder I'd bought in bulk in Seiryuu City, it was one of the components of a universal antidote. I was still missing other materials, so I couldn't make one just yet, but it couldn't hurt to have it on hand.

Apparently, Totona's little sister had found it in the dried-up river along the main road.

After I did a map search for **Serpent's Blood Stone**, I found that there were a large number in the dry riverbed.

Thus, we took a little detour to collect the stones and camped out nearby for the night.

The barbecued wild boar we ate that evening was exceptional.

Forest of Giants

Satou here. In my twenty-nine years of life, I've never once thought that I want to become the kind of person who saves people. I've led a life totally free of aspirations toward being some hero or savior, but apparently, I can't get away with that in a parallel world.

It was our fourth day since leaving the fort and our fourteenth day in the Muno Barony.

A lot had happened in the past four days.

Starving villagers attacked us three times. We handled these encounters in the usual way, so there was nothing much of note about this.

Real professional bandits came after us, too. They must've robbed some knights or something, because the two leaders were decked out in impressive full-body armor, armed to the teeth, and mounted on warhorses.

This was good luck for us, since we needed more horses to enter the large forest. We acquired both their horses after we'd taken care of them.

In addition, though the river along the highway was dry downstream, it provided us with plenty of water once we got farther upstream.

While we were camping out by the river, fish monsters like flying eaters and kelpies attacked us.

The danger didn't stop there, either: While she was drawing water in the river, Pochi got bitten on the butt by a piranha-like fish.

It wasn't poisonous or anything, but since it wasn't a monster, I was slow to deal with it.

A magic potion fixed her up right away, but Pochi still stayed away from the water for a while after that.

I continued monitoring the demon in Muno City; he had increased the number of doppelgängers from one to eight, and they were all ambling through the towns and cities.

Occasionally, the demon himself would wander into the blank area under the castle, but he would soon return to the map with his HP and magic depleted.

The City Core was probably located somewhere in there, so my guess was that he was trying and failing to seize control of it.

During my observations, I noticed something troubling: The demon was able to trade places with his doppelgängers instantaneously. Luckily, the switch cost a lot of magic, so he probably wouldn't be able to pull that off too frequently. If I had to defeat him, I would need to dispose of the doppelgängers first.

Another item of note was the group of demi-goblins I'd learned about before.

There had been only a few settlements the first time I checked, but their number had increased. Two days ago, the total population had swelled to more than ten times what it had been before.

However, most of them were level 1, so the population was soon halved as many of them were eaten by nearby monsters and beasts. At this rate, there wouldn't be enough of them left to pose a threat to the count's army before too long.

At the moment, we were taking a lunch break on the dry riverbed near the intersection between the main road and the side road into the forest.

Liza and Nana were preparing the kitchen area, Mia and Arisa were setting up the quilt and *kotatsu*, and Lulu was washing the vegetables in water I'd collected.

Tama, Pochi, and I were taking care of our horses, old and new.

It was getting cold, so I thought hot pot would be a good lunch for today. The ingredients were meat from a two-headed bird that had attacked us along the way, a generous helping of mushrooms, and cabbage.

The village we'd visited that morning had been growing a lot of cabbage, so I'd traded a quantity of our food to get some.

It was a bit smaller and yellower than the cabbage I'd eaten in Japan, but the AR display said it was **cabbage**, so there was no argument there.

Pochi and Tama had finished caring for the horses, so I put them in charge of plucking the feathers from the wings of the double-headed bird after it had been bled out.

They put the carcass in a large bag so that the feathers wouldn't fly everywhere and set about plucking with great focus. The creature was considerably larger than both of them, so de-feathering it was difficult work.

Once the *kotatsu* was set up, Mia went to help prepare the vegetables, and Arisa supplied magic to warm up the space under the table before coming to consult with me over how best to season the hot pot.

"I think miso should be good for the seasoning, but the problem is how to make the broth."

"True enough. We don't have kelp or dried bonito flakes, either…"

We'd gotten miso and soy sauce at a high-class food store in Seiryuu City, so those were no trouble.

If anything, I regretted not buying any rice at the time. Usually it wasn't a big deal, but I didn't want to have hot pot without rice.

Well, there was supposedly plenty of rice in the Ougoch Duchy, so I'd just have to remember to stock up there.

Liza tilted her head as she watched the two of us.

"Master, couldn't we simply boil the bones of the double-headed bird to create the stock?"

Oh right. I guess that's how Liza makes the stock for her stews.

Since we were making hot pot, I'd gotten all hung up on having a Japanese-style stock.

"Yeah, let's go with that for now." I nodded sagely at Liza, as if I'd known it all along.

Arisa looked like she wanted to say something, but I pointedly ignored her.

"Dooone!"

"Master, the wings are all plucked, sir!"

Tama and Pochi gleefully held up the featherless bird for my approval.

"Wow, it's totally plucked clean. Great job!"

"Aye!"

"Thank you, sir."

Pochi giggled and wagged her tail with gusto as I patted her head.

When I petted Tama, her tail stood upright, and she pushed her head against my hand.

As I doted on the two of them, Liza set about separating the meat, bones, and guts of the bird.

This bird's internal organs were actually ingredients for a stamina recovery potion, so instead of eating them, I stowed those away.

I put the pot on the fire with some water inside, then added the bones that Liza had extracted to boil up the stock. It started smelling a bit strange, so I added some herbs to improve the fragrance.

Nana was in charge of scooping out the meat and scum that came off the bones, since she was particularly good at repetitive tasks. Her face was too expressionless to read, but she appeared to be enjoying herself.

Because the stock would keep indefinitely in Storage, we ended up mass-producing it in two large cauldrons.

"Chicken dumplings! I want chicken dumplings, too!"

Arisa waved her hand in the air insistently.

I guess that is a hot-pot staple.

"Good idea. Do you know how to make them, by the way?"

"Huh? Don't you just mix minced chicken with other stuff and roll it into balls?"

…Yeah, that "other stuff" is the part I'm asking about. It's fine to make requests and all, but I wish she'd remember how to make the things she's asking for once in a while.

Given what I'd learned on my journey, flour and eggs would be a good bet for holding the filling together.

As Mia intently sliced mushrooms into thin pieces, I worked nearby to mix the minced chicken with flour and the orange chicken eggs we'd gotten in the fortress.

Thanks to the help of my "Cooking" skill, I was able to make a respectable filling for dumplings. The skill system was so handy.

I put Arisa in charge of mass-producing the dumplings. It was her request, so I figured that was the least she could do. Technically, we could've just dropped the filling directly into the soup in spoonfuls, but shaping it into dumplings ahead of time was how my family always did it.

Lulu and Liza separated the bird meat into the portion we'd have tonight and the portion we'd save for later. It was too much to eat all at once.

The absence of an earthenware pot took away from the traditional hot-pot image a little bit, but we just poured stock into our usual stew pot and then added the other ingredients, from slowest- to fastest-cooking.

Finally, we added the duck-like meat of the double-headed bird and put the lid over the pot.

All that was left now was to wait for everything to cook through, but just then, a dot appeared on my radar that indicated a normal person.

The map informed me that it was a nineteen-year-old, level-2 woman with no skills. Her condition read **Hungry**, one step below the **Starvation** status.

At first I thought she was out foraging for wild plants, but one look at her name told me that something else was afoot.

The girl's name was Karina *Muno*. The daughter of the current Baron Muno.

What was she doing all alone in a forest full of beasts and monsters?

Maybe she was running away from her engagement to the fake hero.

The whole thing smelled like trouble. I was tempted to just leave it alone, but I wouldn't be able to handle the guilt if I let this girl wander aimlessly in the woods by herself.

So what should I do now...?

"Bubbliiing?"

"Smells good, sir."

Unaware of my dilemma, Pochi and Tama sat near the pot, their excitement rising at the scent of the simmering ingredients in the air.

It'd still be a while before it was ready, though.

Checking my radar again, I saw that the young woman had stopped moving, and her status condition now read **Unconscious**.

She didn't seem to be injured, but her magic and stamina were running low. She didn't even have any magic-based skills, so what could've depleted her MP?

Now I certainly couldn't abandon her. *I guess I'll have to go to the rescue.*

"Something else just came up, so I'll be right back. Sorry, but can you come, too, Pochi and Tama?"

"Aye-aye, siiir!"

"Roger, sir."

The two kids wiped away their drool and threw up a salute. According to them, this was called the "yessir!" pose.

"Master, if you are planning to exterminate a monster, please allow me to come along as well."

"Master, permission to depart?"

Liza and Nana reached for their weapons, but that wouldn't be necessary.

"No, no, I'm not going to fight anything. I think someone's in trouble nearby, so I'm going to go help her."

With that, I headed into the forest with Pochi and Tama in tow.

Unlike the wooded area we'd walked through so far, this area was full of thick undergrowth that made it difficult to walk. Visibility was poor, too, thanks to the dense trees.

We must've been downwind of the camp, because the scent of the simmering hot pot was tickling my nostrils.

As a result, there came a chorus of grumbles like an animal's growl from the two beastfolk girls' tummies.

"Hungryyy?"

"Stomach Man isn't very patient, sir."

"Well, the hot pot should be ready by the time we get back, so let's just look forward to it, shall we?"

"Aye-aye!"

"I'm excited, sir!"

As we conversed, we reached the area where the girl was supposed to be.

"Something's heeere?"

"It's shining, sir!"

Just as Pochi had said, the girl was inside a cocoon-like barrier that glowed a pale white. Perhaps it was a trick of the light, but the barrier appeared to be made up of shiny oval scales.

She didn't have any skills that would do this, so the barrier was probably coming from the object on her wrist that was gleaming blue.

The woman was wearing a thin cloak and high-laced leather boots suited for horseback riding. I couldn't see it well under the cloak, but her dress looked fit for a noblewoman.

Her dark-blond hair spilled out from her hood, and behind it I could see a glimpse of a face that wouldn't be out of place in a French film.

She was no match for Lulu, but her features were on par with Arisa and Mia for good looks. To be perfectly honest, she was a beauty.

"Don't touch it, all right? It could be dangerous."

"Rogerrr."

"Yes, sir."

Pochi and Tama reluctantly dropped the twigs they'd been using to prod at the cocoon.

Well, I could hardly rescue her if she was protected by magic. *Now what?*

I touched the barrier experimentally, and the area gave a little jingle like a clear bell. The scalelike segment fell away.

"Is it just for appearances, then?"

"Haaard?"

"It's solid, sir."

Pochi and Tama disagreed with my comment. I'd told them not to touch it, so they'd settled for whacking it rhythmically with their sheathed short swords.

I put a stop to that and took apart enough of the barrier to retrieve the woman inside.

"Who are you?"

The solemn, masculine voice seemed to come from the direction of the girl's mouth.

For a second, I wondered if I'd rescued a drag queen, but the beauty's lips hadn't actually moved a bit.

The voice had come from somewhere lower.

I slipped my arms underneath her and laid her down faceup.

Magic.

Something unbelievable appeared before my eyes.

"You are surely no ordinary man, if you broke my barrier so easily."

The same voice as before reached my ears.

Magic.

Even though I knew this was reality, I couldn't believe what I was seeing.

"I shall ask once again. Who are you?"

Yes, it was the sort of sight one only expects to find in two dimensions.

Magic.

∗   ∗   ∗

Magic breasts. Before my very eyes was a pair of breasts that surpassed all imagination. A phrase like *huge knockers* wouldn't even begin to do them justice; they were like a pair of rockets.

"Answer me, boy!"

The man's voice, now a little annoyed, repeated sharply in my ear.

Whoops, I guess I got a little distracted. I thought this only existed in fiction.

A silver pendant with a blue gem inlay flashed at her chest.

This must be where the voice is coming from. According to my AR display, it was some kind of magic tool. If it had appeared in a game, it would probably have been called an "Intelligent Item."

But instead of speculating further, I addressed the pendant directly.

"Oh, pardon me. I've never seen a talking object before, so I was startled."

"Very well. My name is Raka, and you need not speak formally to me. O mighty one, I must beseech you to protect my mistress."

This "Raka" thing had five functions: Perceive Demon, Perceive Malice, Perceive Mightiness, Bestow Strength Enhancement, and Bestow Pain Resistance. It was classified as a legendary artifact.

Given the color of the glow when it spoke, I wondered if it was made with the same blue used to create Holy Swords.

"Should you really be entrusting this to some random person in the forest?"

"I possess a feature called 'Perceive Malice.' I do not detect any malicious intent from you. I must now sleep for a time to store up magic power. Please take care of Lady Karina."

"All right, leave it to me."

I nodded reassuringly, and the blue light disappeared from the pendant with an air of relief.

"All right, let's go back."

"'kay!"

"The hot pot is waiting, sir!"

I beckoned to Pochi and Tama, who were poking at Miss Karina's chest with strange expressions, and slipped my arms under her back and knees to lift her up. (The so-called "princess carry.")

She was surprisingly heavy, considering that she was only a bit taller than me. Or maybe it just felt that way because of the extra weight from her breasts.

When I adjusted my grip to improve the balance, those rockets shifted against my chest.

I walked back to the camp at an easy pace. This was only out of concern for the fainted young lady's comfort, of course. There was no ulterior motive at all.

"Welcome back, master!"

"Thanks."

Arisa greeted me as I pushed my way through the thickets back to the camp.

The other kids stopped setting up the tableware on the *kotatsu* and ran over to me, too.

"So that's the lost person—it's another woman?!"

"Mrrr..."

Arisa and Mia pouted, probably noticing Miss Karina's good looks or impressive chest.

With a pang of reluctance as her chest parted from mine, I laid Miss Karina down on the furs that Liza and Nana had spread out on the ground for her.

"Boy, what a rack. Think they're fake?"

"They are the genuine article, I report."

"Hey, Nana. Even if you're both girls, that's still rude."

I whacked Nana on the top of the head before she could brashly squeeze the unconscious woman's chest.

Meanwhile, Lulu removed Miss Karina's hood to pluck the leaves out of her bangs and wipe the dirt from her face.

"Curlyyy?"

"It's all wavy, sir."

This time, Tama and Pochi were prodding at the blond strands that had escaped from her hood.

"So not only does she have huge boobs, but she's a blonde, too? That's too many distinctive character traits by far! If she's one of those cute hot–cold types on top of all that, my seat as the rightful first wife might be in danger!"

"Mrrr, danger."

Mia nodded seriously in agreement with Arisa's absurd remark.

...Who are you calling a "first wife"? I don't want to hear about this again for at least another ten years.

"I doubt she's going to wake up for a while, so we might as well eat for now," I suggested, and everyone's stomachs growled in unison.

Trying to encourage them all through their embarrassment, I put some magic into the simple stove heater inside the *kotatsu* and placed the two pots on top. We'd elected to use two so that everyone would be able to reach easily.

As soon as I lifted the lid from the pot, the aroma of stewed duck spread through the air.

Mmm, that smells great.

I didn't have much time to savor the smell, though, or the drool from Pochi's and Tama's mouths would drown us all.

For some reason, I ended up in charge of doling out everyone's food, so I made sure to scoop a good variety of veggies, chicken meatballs, and meat into each bowl. Mia's helping only included vegetables, of course.

With Arisa's "thanks for the food!" as our usual signal, we began to eat.

"You all can help yourself to seconds from the pot, all right?"

"Hottt!"

"The meatballs are fighting back, sir."

Tama and Pochi stuffed their cheeks with meatballs, then widened their eyes and puffed rapidly as the piping-hot broth burned their mouths.

"It's quite delicious."

Liza nodded in satisfaction as she chewed on a bone-in chunk of the double-headed bird.

"Every ingredient is equally delicious, master, I commend."

"The cabbage really soaks up the flavor of the broth... It's delicious! Your cooking really is amazing, master."

Each time they sampled another ingredient, Nana and Lulu piled on the praise.

But really, it's my "Cooking" skill that's amazing, not me.

"Gourd."

Mia used her chopsticks to pick up a piece of the gourd, which resembled tofu, and chewed on it blissfully.

This was a recent favorite of hers.

The gourd had a totally different flavor from the winter melon I'd eaten back in my world.

The cabbage here tasted wilder than I was used to, as well, so it was probably best not to assume that any vegetables were the same in this place. I figured the best approach was to cook with lots of different ingredients and learn about them as I went.

"Yum."

Noticing Mia's pleasure, the other kids, who'd been reluctant to try the strange-looking vegetable, started to taste it as well.

"No more than ten meatballs per person, you two!" Arisa decreed to the beastfolk girls as our self-proclaimed hot-pot magistrate.

Tama and Pochi, who'd both been reaching to take meatballs from the pot, stopped at once. They must have been going for their eleventh ones.

Furtively, I slipped the two meatballs I'd saved for myself into their bowls.

"Yaaay!"

"Thank you, sir!"

"Goodness, you're going to spoil them."

I smiled in response to Arisa's motherly scolding and popped a ripe mushroom into my mouth instead.

"Something smells good..."

A half-delirious mutter came from Lady Karina's direction.

Putting my dish down on the table, I approached her.

"You're awake?"

"A-a man?!"

The half-asleep young woman leaped to her feet and aimed a round-house kick in my direction.

Really, I think shrinking away or at most a slap in the face would be more appropriate to this situation...

I didn't even bother trying to dodge. Considering that she'd fainted from hunger not long ago, it was obvious where this was going.

"O-oh, I'm dizzy..."

Miss Karina looked about to faint again, so I caught her and gently led her toward the dinner table.

The young woman flailed around in my hands, but it was easy to keep her in check in her weakened state.

"...U-unhand me."

As if she were a totally different person from the forceful individual of a few moments ago, Miss Karina flushed bright red and trembled in my arms.

Maybe she's androphobic?

"Please calm down. Raka asked me to protect you."

"…Mr. Raka did?"

At the name, she stopped resisting.

You use "Mr." to refer to your own equipment?

"That's right. I am Satou, a merchant."

"M-my name is Karina. Karina Muno, the second daughter of Baron Muno."

Apparently either shy or nervous, Miss Karina stammered a bit through her self-introduction.

Still, it seemed awfully risky to openly reveal that she was the daughter of the baron, given the current situation in the territory. Maybe she had some purpose for doing so?

"So you're a noble, then, Lady Karina?"

I guided Miss Karina toward the *kotatsu*, offering her a seat between Nana and Lulu. She started to sit, but stopped when she saw Tama and Pochi.

I thought at first that she was reluctant to sit near beastfolk, but there was something strange about her behavior.

"Animal-eared folk… Could it be that you are a hero, perchance?"

Miss Karina whirled to look at me again, her voice rising like an excited child's.

"As I said before, I'm just a humble peddler," I replied as my mind searched for an explanation for her surprise.

Presumably, "animal-eared folk" referred to dog-eared folk like Pochi and cat-eared folk like Tama, perhaps among others.

Come to think of it, Nadi from the general store in Seiryuu City had mentioned that the first hero had animal-eared folk in his party.

Most likely, Miss Karina knew this and had jumped to the conclusion that I might be a hero.

The young lady's stomach was growling, so I put some food into a bowl and held it out to her. I assumed that she couldn't use chopsticks, so I handed her a fork and spoon instead.

"I don't know if this will suit the tastes of a noble such as yourself, but you ought to eat something first."

"It smells lovely. I've never seen cuisine like this before."

At my suggestion, Miss Karina cut her meat into bite-size pieces and lifted a morsel to her mouth.

Unsurprisingly, the baron's daughter's table manners were very refined.

Her eyes widened, and she covered her mouth with her hand as she began chewing vigorously. She must have liked it.

After gulping it down, she finally opened her mouth to speak.

"I-it's incredibly delicious!"

"I'm glad it suits your tastes. There's plenty more, so please help yourself."

Miss Karina nodded with a slight pink blush to her cheeks, then happily returned to her meal.

Watching her elegant etiquette, Arisa and Lulu immediately began eating more politely as well. *I feel like it's a little late for that now, but do whatever you want.*

Ideally, noodles and rice gruel went best with hot pot, but since we had neither of those on hand, we'd made wheat porridge with broth from the pot instead.

"Hooraaay."

"So full, sir."

Having eaten their fill, Pochi and Tama flopped onto their backs and sighed contentedly.

But Liza wasted no time in assigning their next task.

"Now then, we must begin cleaning up."

"Rogerrr."

"Yes, sir."

The pair bounced to their feet and, along with the other kids, carried the dishes.

While they were busy with that, I decided to ask about Karina's situation.

Lulu brewed some tea, so I offered Miss Karina a cup.

"Please, have some tea."

"Oh my, this is blue-green tea, isn't it?" Miss Karina accepted the cup happily.

Perhaps because we'd shared a meal, she'd relaxed toward me enough to have a normal conversation.

"Why, it's been two years since I last had blue-green tea."

Two years?

That seemed strange; it wasn't as if they couldn't import anything here.

"How delightful… Between this and that truly delicious meal, you must be rather wealthy."

"Really?"

I was wealthy all right, but the ingredients for the food were mostly things we'd bought locally, so they didn't cost any more than the average person's meal.

"But of course. That was a more luxurious meal than what they serve in the castle."

"Are you sure? We didn't use any particularly valuable ingredients."

As far as I remembered, the meal we ate as guests at Count Seiryuu's castle was much more extravagant.

"Our territory is in the midst of a famine. If the baron was to indulge in luxury at a time like this, he could hardly face the common people. Thus, our meals at the castle have consisted mostly of bean soup and sweet potatoes."

I was impressed that she could cultivate such a large chest on that kind of diet, but she seemed to be telling the truth.

If the lord of the land was really that honorable, then the only explanation for the corruption of the top bureaucrats and soldiers must have been that the hell demon was plotting something behind the scenes.

"Incidentally, what were you doing out in the forest?"

Miss Karina looked a little embarrassed as she opened her mouth to speak.

"I had hoped to speak to the giants that live deep within the forest to borrow their aid, but I'm afraid I lost my way. I thought it best to leap to the top of a tree, but..."

She must've used Raka's Bestow Strength Enhancement function, then.

Charging into unfamiliar territory without a map struck me as a reckless strategy, though.

"What did you want to speak to the giants about?"

"I had hoped to request their help in defeating a hell demon," Miss Karina replied in a clear voice. "The demon has disguised himself as a magistrate and a fake hero, and my father and elder sister are completely fooled. And so, Mr. Raka and I set out into the forest in the hopes of meeting a giant that could defeat the demon."

She seriously thought the giants would take on a demon just because some random stranger asked them to?

Not only was she overly honest; this young lady was extremely sheltered.

"Lady Karina, you've said too much."

Raka woke up to offer some blunt advice.

"So you're awake, Mr. Raka."

Miss Karina's pendant blinked blue as it spoke. "Forgive me, but I must request that you keep what you've just been told a secret."

"Sure, I won't tell anyone."

Raka's request was easy enough to accept.

"You have my gratitude, mighty one."

Raka had called me "mighty one" when I first found them, too. He probably knew I was strong because of that Perceive Mightiness function, although I wondered how much specific information it gave him.

"Mighty one?"

"Indeed, you are mighty. I do not know what level you might be, but you are strong enough that my lady Karina could not defeat you even with my Strength Enhancement."

"In that case, perhaps this gentleman could defeat the—"

"Do not ask the impossible of him, Lady Karina. He may be strong, but he is still a human being. The only humans who possess the power to defeat a demon are those chosen as heroes or a select few who do not conform to the common understanding."

My "Poker Face" skill let me respond with a simple smile, but inwardly I was puzzled.

The demon in this territory was only a level-40 lesser hell demon, wasn't it?

The giant I'd seen on my map was above level 30, so I couldn't help thinking that he was exaggerating a bit...

Maybe his "Perceive Demon" skill just enabled him to detect a demon's presence, not determine what class it was.

After all, it seemed able to judge "mightiness" only in relation to Lady Karina's strength.

"Sir Satou, if you are a traveling merchant, do you perhaps know where the village of giants might be?"

"I've never been, but I have a rough idea of how to get there."

"I-in that case, is there any chance you might be able to guide me?"

Lady Karina clasped her hands together pleadingly in front of her incredible chest, which was terribly persuasive.

I was about to nod involuntarily, but then Arisa cut in.

"A thank-you would be nice."

"Yes, of course, I will certainly reward you with payment."

Lady Karina misunderstood her statement, and Arisa raised her eyebrows.

"No, no. You still haven't even thanked my master for saving you when you were collapsed in the forest, have you?"

"Ah…" Lady Karina was speechless.

As I'd suspected, she must have simply forgotten.

"I-I'm terribly sorry. I sincerely thank you for your aid, Sa— Um, sir."

Quickly changing her attitude, Lady Karina held the ends of her skirt in a very noble curtsy.

Behind her, Tama and Pochi immediately imitated her gesture by pinching the ends of their wide pants.

Her arms still folded, Arisa nodded self-importantly. She'd be a good mother when she grew up.

"Oh, don't worry about it."

I stood and bowed. I'd seen a young nobleman do this in a movie once.

> Skill Acquired: "Etiquette"

"As for your request, we happen to be heading to the village of giants anyway. Would you like to join us?"

"Are you sure it's quite all right?"

"Yeah, one more person is no big deal."

I sort of made a unilateral decision, but none of the kids raised any objections.

There were a select few who seemed a bit threatened by Lady Karina's bust measurements, but at least they were willing to accept the traveler herself joining our party.

◆

"Kyaaaaah!"

Miss Karina leaped into the air with a scream and then tumbled along the ground until she crashed into a tree.

It was the kind of pratfall that would be the envy of any young comic actor, but thanks to Raka's scalelike barrier, she was completely unharmed.

When the advance guard team had begun their training after the meal as usual, Miss Karina had announced that she wanted to participate, too. However, she couldn't control herself very well under the influence of Raka's Strength Enhancement, and instead she kept crashing and burning.

Since she hadn't changed out of her dress to participate, the skirt kept flipping up to reveal what was underneath in an extremely unladylike fashion.

However, since she was wearing long drawers, the standard undergarment in this world, there wasn't much to get excited about.

"Karinaaa?"

"Are you all right, ma'am?"

Tama and Pochi hurried over to Miss Karina where she lay tangled upside down in the roots of the tree and peered at her face with concern.

The two weren't very good at remembering titles, so Miss Karina had given them permission to simply call her by her first name.

I called out to Lulu, who was watching the training with Arisa and Mia.

"Lulu, could you lend Lady Karina some of Nana's spare clothes?"

"Yes, of course."

I would've suggested Liza's or mine, but I thought the chest might be too tight on Miss Karina's figure.

Accepting the clothes, Miss Karina said a few words to Lulu and turned her back to her. Apparently, she couldn't undress without help.

Lulu immediately started assisting her, so I quickly spun around.

I wished they'd be a bit more modest about doing this with a guy around.

"What's this? You're not going to enjoy the show?"

"Arisa..."

Mia, always sensitive to this sort of remark, shot Arisa an accusatory glare.

When they were done with the process, I turned back around.

The shirt was about to burst open at the chest. There wasn't enough fabric to cover everything, so the bottom edge of the shirt was hiked up, exposing her navel.

Embarrassed, Miss Karina vigorously yanked the hem lower, which only dragged her breasts down in an uncomfortable-looking manner.

"Satou."

"If you like boobs so much, get a load of this!"

Arisa and Mia had noticed my eyes wandering, drawn like magnets, and the two girls latched on to obscure my vision.

Arisa's bony chest pressed against me rather painfully.

In the end, while my view was being blocked, Miss Karina changed into Nana's loose pajama shirt.

I made sure to mentally file away the spectacular sight from earlier, though.

Really, it's a pity that my menu doesn't have a screenshot function.

"Sa— Um, you aren't going to participate in the training?"

Miss Karina walked over to me, still catching her breath.

The combination of her sweaty brow and breathless voice was pretty sexy. I would be tempted to make a pass at her if she weren't the daughter of a baron.

She kept starting to call me by name, then getting embarrassed and sticking with "you" instead.

"Liza said the strongest member of the group is you, Sa— Um. Perhaps you'd be so kind as to have a bout with me?"

"Sure, I can do that."

I stood up and headed over to the dry riverbed where the girls were training.

Along the way, I picked up a pebble and gave it a toss.

Not at Miss Karina, of course.

The pebble made direct contact with a half-horse, half-fish kelpie that was starting to emerge from the water in the mostly dry riverbed, and the creature disappeared with a small geyser.

Pochi and Tama, who'd noticed the kelpie, lowered their wooden practice swords with an air of relief.

"Now, shall we get started?"

I smiled brightly at Miss Karina, who was still stunned by the sudden sequence of events.

"V-very well... Here I go, then!"

Although her movements were clearly amateurish, she came at me with an immediate high jump kick.

The move was something out of a fighting game, but since I'd seen her use it in her training with the other girls, I was able to avoid it easily enough.

Still, she was fast. Her speed was on par with Pochi's.

"Hmph! You may have dodged that one, but I'm just getting started!"

Miss Karina left tracks in the riverbed as she skidded to an abrupt halt, then kicked up a cloud of dust as she attacked me a second time.

This time it was a flying roundhouse kick, but I crouched to avoid it.

Looking up, I saw that the momentum was carrying her magic breasts around in a dynamic dance as if they were separate creatures entirely.

"Goodness, your movements are simply too smooth!" she complained.

I was frankly concerned that she might tear the ligaments in her chest, but she didn't appear to be in pain, so maybe Raka's Pain Resistance or Strength Enhancement functions were coming into play here. In the back of my mind, I sang the praises of whatever pioneer had created Raka. What a wonderful piece of equipment.

Miss Karina punctuated her frustrated shout with a dropkick, so I dodged to one side.

Since all her attacks were so dramatic, it was easy to avoid her as long as I didn't become distracted.

Still, we wouldn't get anywhere if I continually dodged them, so I decided to take one of her assaults head-on.

This time, Miss Karina was charging at me with an elbow strike, so I caught the blow with one movement and killed her momentum as if I'd caught her in cotton.

It was a rather heavy strike, on par with Liza's spear. I wouldn't have expected this much strength from a level-2 opponent.

Apparently, Raka's Strength Enhancement added about five levels. I guess an artifact like that was bound to give some pretty amazing buffs.

I was impressed, but now that her momentum was gone, it was easy to toss her aside.

Miss Karina rolled away on the riverbed with a cute little squeak.

With the protection of Raka's white defensive barrier, landing on the rocky surface of the riverbed wouldn't harm her at all.

Still, she seemed too dazed to stand, so I walked over to her and offered my hand.

"Are you all right, Lady Karina?"

"I-I'm perfectly fine!"

Avoiding my hand, Miss Karina scuttled to her feet suspiciously.

I was a bit hurt, but with her flustered state and trembling voice, it wasn't so much that she disliked me specifically as that she was overly conscious of men in general. She had doubtless led a sheltered life; maybe she was just afraid of germs.

She made no effort to change her tactics after this, and instead continued to throw herself at me with straightforward attacks and special moves, which I dodged or parried.

At some point, it became less like a training match and more like a drill.

"Lady Karina, you won't be able to beat an opponent who's good at dodging if you just keep using such bold techniques."

"Master's right, ma'am! You have to break down their defense with smaller moves, then finish them off with a big move, ma'am!" Pochi complemented my advice.

I think Liza taught her something along those lines before.

"Small moves?"

Miss Karina was clumsier than Pochi; she tried to use feints and foot sweeps, but these were so obvious that her defense was even more full of holes than before.

Clearly, someone like me who always relied on skills had no talent for training others.

"Sorry, Liza, but would you mind taking over to teach her for me?"

"Please leave it to me, master."

I handed my role as instructor off to Liza and went back to observing.

"Lady Karina, Pochi and I will give a demonstration fight. We will start out without using any small moves and then incorporate them later. Please examine Pochi's movements closely. Pochi, please fight with slower movements than usual, so that Lady Karina can follow them."

"Yeeesss, sssiiirrr!"

You don't actually have to talk more slowly, too, Pochi.

The pair's dance-like training performance imparted to Miss Karina the importance of small moves.

They continued training for about an hour with more practice battles, ending only when nobody could stand any longer.

They might catch colds if they stayed all sweaty, so I used the kettle-style magic tool to prepare hot water and had them wipe themselves clean. Of course, this took place inside an igloo-shaped Shelter wall to ward off the wind.

"Is that a magic tool that boils hot water?"

"It is. They don't use these in the castle?"

"A maid told me that hot water is restricted to mornings only because of the high cost of firewood, so I suppose they mustn't have used such a thing."

Sounds like a rough life.

Still, if the maid considered even firewood to be expensive, the demon or some bureaucrats must be embezzling most of the tax revenue.

I charged up the floor heater in the carriage, and as I worked, I could hear the others' happy voices as they washed up with the hot water.

I realized with a bit of regret that I should've made an open-air bath at the river's edge. I'd have to make sure to do so when we came back from the giants' village.

Once everyone was refreshed, I made a bed for myself out of the *kotatsu* and put everyone to sleep. From inside the carriage, I heard a cry of "goodness me, the floorboards are warm!" from Miss Karina.

I didn't like being left out, but I figured I couldn't share a bed with a baron's daughter.

Since I'd taken an interest in strengthening equipment, that evening I sat next to the kids on night watch and read through Trazayuya's documents.

Apparently, making this kind of equipment required just as much complicated setup as Holy Swords, but I did notice something while reviewing the materials.

All these processes seemed to involve a good deal of trouble in preventing the magic circuit from collapsing during forging or casting.

Since it seemed like I had the means to make the magic circuit that was the first step for all this, I used the Holy Sword Excalibur to cut a wooden practice sword in half and tried carving the circuit into that.

I didn't get any skills or titles, but I was able to make an imitation Magic Sword easily enough.

It was much easier to infuse the magic wooden sword with energy than it was an ordinary wooden sword.

Complicated circuits would be impossible, but it was easy enough to incorporate simple circuits like these for strength or durability improvements.

I completed two swords that evening: the wooden Magic Sword and a wooden Holy Sword. When they were charged up, the former emitted a red light while the latter emitted a blue one.

I went out and found a ghost-type monster on which to test the wooden swords and discovered that both of them exhibited the same level of power as the mithril sword I'd found in the fortress.

On my way back, I tried them on an ordinary monster, but they both broke apart. They'd be useful only on monsters without a corporeal form, which wouldn't be affected by ordinary weapons.

They were good conductors of my "Spellblade" skill, however.

This wasn't particularly useful to me, since I could use "Spellblade" even with sticks or my fingertips, but it might come in handy for training the advance guard.

By dawn, I was able to complete three new wooden Magic Swords for the girls to use for skill practice.

It was the morning of our fifteenth day in the Muno Barony.

After warming ourselves up with some soup, we set off into the large forest, which was shrouded in a chilly morning mist.

Incidentally, I stowed our carriage away in Storage from a slight distance so that nobody would notice. At the very least, I was confident that Raka and Miss Karina hadn't noticed during her exuberant departure.

We were riding down the side road on six horses.

Nana and Liza each rode solo on the warhorses we'd confiscated from the thieves; Miss Karina rode on one of the horses I'd bought in Sedum City, since she was an experienced rider, while Arisa and I rode the other.

Finally, the two horses we'd first bought with the carriage in Seiryuu City carried Mia and Lulu on one and Tama and Pochi on the other.

Tama didn't have much riding experience, but Effie and Rye, the carriage horses, were strangely intelligent. They followed her orders carefully, crossing fallen trees and avoiding ruts as if their riders were veteran jockeys.

"There are rather more obstacles and inclines than I expected."

"Normal."

Mia responded to Arisa's complaints indifferently.

Most likely, she was trying to say this was normal for a forest path.

"Master! Look, sir! It's prey, sir!"

Pochi had spotted a mountain bird through the trees.

That would work for lunch, I supposed. Taking a short bow out of the bow holder beside the saddlebag, I took aim and shot the bird down.

"Hooray! Sir!"

Pochi hopped off the horse that Tama was steering and zipped over to the fallen bird like a hunting dog.

"A fine shot. It appears that it's not only your martial arts skills that are first-class, hmm?"

"Only because I had a good teacher."

I patted Mia's head as I replied to Miss Karina's admiring words.

To hide her embarrassment, Mia started playing a reed pipe as her cheeks turned pink.

Our first day ended without any monster encounters, and we camped on the bank of a small river.

We took out the necessary tools from the Lesser Garage Bag I'd found in the fortress and started setting up camp.

Since we would have to use it in front of Miss Karina and Raka pretty often, I'd decided to start using the one that I'd be less reluctant to part with in case the noble demanded that I hand it over.

However, this was an unnecessary precaution.

"Oh? I see you have a magic bag. There used to be several of those in our home, too."

When we took out the quilts and *kotatsu* from the Garage Bag, her response was nonchalant.

The family of Baron Muno had sold their Garage Bags to raise money, but they were apparently not an uncommon magic tool amid large merchants and wealthy aristocrats.

"Oh, gracious! This desk is warm on the inside!"

Instead, it was the *kotatsu* that caught her by surprise.

"Karina, c'meeere."

"This is the warm part, ma'am!"

Miss Karina stuck her head inside the *kotatsu* along with Tama and Pochi, gazing at the red light of the magic circuit inside.

"Mind your manners," I chided them, though I also had to note that Miss Karina's waistline was just as sexy as her chest.

The ever-mischievous Arisa chose that moment to pat Miss Karina's bottom, so the young noblewoman banged her head on the underside of the table and let out a shriek.

Fortunately, Arisa apologized as soon as Miss Karina emerged red-faced and teary-eyed, so I wasn't subjected to any false accusations of being a pervert.

"Karinaaa?"

"Karina, you can help, too, ma'am!"

The sheltered Miss Karina was sitting in the *kotatsu* as the rest of us set up camp, but Tama and Pochi grabbed her arms and pulled her out.

"Y-you would dare imply that I should do the work of servants?"

"Yeees!"

"No work means no food, ma'am!"

The concept of going without food elicited a dramatic expression of shock from Miss Karina, and she hastily participated in setting up the campsite with helpful direction from Pochi and Tama.

We'd had sandwiches that we'd prepared that morning for lunch, so I had Lulu assist me in preparing baked mountain fowl as the main dish for dinner.

"Master, I've prepared the meat. Is this about right?"

"Yeah, that's perfect. I can always count on you to do a thorough job."

I accepted the prepared bird from Lulu, stuffing the cavity with herbs and boiled eggs where the organs had been removed.

After applying a soy-based sauce to the outside, I put the bird in a magic steam oven that I'd made in Sedum City. The bird was quite large, so it just barely fit.

"Since we can't see inside, we'll have to rely on the outside temperature of the oven and the sound of the meat to figure out how long to cook it."

"…It's started to get warmer."

Lulu held her hand over the square oven with a serious expression.

"There's no sound yet."

This time she pressed an ear to the oven as she gave her report.

"Please don't put your face against the oven, Lulu, or you might get burned."

"R-right. I-I'm sorry!"

Even if she did burn herself, it could probably be cured with a magic potion, but to allow Lulu's lovely features to be marred even for a moment would be a massive loss for the world at large.

After a while, steam began to rise from the oven, along with a pleasant fragrance.

Pochi and Tama stared excitedly at the steam, along with Miss Karina.

As I watched the three of them, even I started getting impatient for the food to be finished.

By the time Mia and Arisa returned from collecting herbs, dinner was ready.

We were lucky that it was finished before Pochi's and Tama's drool flooded the campsite.

Pretending not to see the small trickle that threatened to escape from Miss Karina's half-open mouth, I placed the steamed bird on a large platter on the table.

Liza was in charge of carving it and serving the meat and vegetables onto everyone's plates.

"Thanks for the food!"

On Arisa's cue, everyone else chorused, "Thanks for the food!" and dinner began.

"'Thanks for the food'?"

"You see, where I come from, we…" Arisa started in with a lengthy explanation in response to Miss Karina's question, but I was more interested in the steamed meat, so I paid her no mind.

The flavor was light and not very fatty, on par with high-quality baked teriyaki chicken. A bit underwhelmed, I took a bite of the thinly cut vegetables instead.

That's delicious.

The fat from the mountain bird and the flavor of the vegetables mingled beautifully with the subtle taste of the sauce.

Combining the vegetables with the chicken made for even better flavor. I added a bit of pepper, since it was a little light on seasoning, and was rewarded with a downright heavenly piquancy.

From now on, any mountain birds would take top hunting priority.

I shared my discoveries and pepper with the rest of the group, and together we went to gourmet paradise.

After dinner, Miss Karina attempted to take on the task of washing dishes; however, after she'd broken her fifth plate, Liza demoted her to safer work like wiping down the table with Arisa.

Arisa, incidentally, had previously dropped and broken plates due to her weak grip, while Miss Karina had broken them by grasping them too strongly.

*　　*　　*

The next day's journey was also peaceful but by no means boring.

"Wow, what a view!"

"How wonderful."

Next to Arisa, Lulu breathed a graceful sigh.

On the second day of our journey, the path took us to a sheer cliff, where the stream we'd camped by yesterday turned into a waterfall, creating a rainbow.

Inside the forest, we saw a mysterious pyramid-like building, some stone ramps that reached toward the sky like a galactic railroad, and other strange structures.

The pyramid looked like it was the ruins of an ancient temple. It was fairly distant, but it contained facilities for astronomical observation, so it might be worth a visit on our way back from the forest giants' village.

Stronger monsters had started to appear on my radar in this area, so at night, I sneaked out to dispose of the giant serpent and the frightening basilisk with a gaze that could turn us to stone.

Of course, I left any solitary monsters that might be good for battle training.

"Humans, humans, and sometimes elves! Humans, humans, and sometimes something else!"

On the afternoon of our third day in the forest, we encountered a singing tree with flowers shaped like trumpets.

The lyrics were a bit strange, but apparently, certain dilettantes in the royal capital would pay big money for a tree like this. I had no desire to transport it, so I left it alone.

As we advanced deeper into the forest, we found plenty of rare plants, particularly those that could be used for potions or magic tools.

Among others, we found mana-infused element stones, including earth stones from the cliff and water stones that we found at the bottom of a clear spring.

The water stones were used to make magic tools like the Well Bag that produced fresh water.

We met a few monsters along the way, but they were only small-fry, so I used these opportunities to have the girls practice cooperating in battle. Plus, Miss Karina could experience actual combat.

"Karinaaa! Look uuup!"

"Hmm?"

A level-3 monster called "crawling ivy" that came down from the trees entangled Miss Karina.

It did possess weak paralysis poison, but unless it jumped you while you were alone, it wasn't a particularly scary monster.

And since Miss Karina had Raka's protection, it wouldn't be much of a threat.

"How impudent!"

Miss Karina used the power from Raka's Strength Enhancement to tear the crawling ivy to shreds and toss it to the ground.

Liza delivered the finishing blow with her magic spear. There were more crawling ivies lurking about in the trees like snakes, but they were quick to flee when one of their number was destroyed.

"Are you injured?"

"I-I'm quite all right."

I approached on my horse, and Miss Karina hurriedly backed hers away.

Aside from battle and meals, Miss Karina's aversion to men still hadn't changed. She reminded me of a particularly guarded cat, so I didn't really mind.

After that, the third day of our journey ended fairly uneventfully.

I didn't see any strong monsters that night, so I headed to some unexplored areas and collected more element stones, like earth, water, and wind stones.

These were essential components of certain special magic tools and potions, but they were hard to find even at alchemy and magic-tool shops. I collected about three hemp bags' worth.

I would've liked to find lightning stones and fire stones, too, but I wasn't able to get any of those this time.

As I hunted for these materials, I saw several dots on my map in the mountain range at the western edge of the Muno Barony. They belonged to people I'd met before—Nana's sisters, who we'd parted with in front of Seiryuu City.

The tomb of Zen's wife that they were headed for was deep in the mountains there.

It would've been nice to see them again, but they were too far away, so we wouldn't be able to meet this time.

We'd probably see them again sooner or later anyway, in Labyrinth City at the least.

"Beeear?"

"It might be a boar man, sir."

Just before noon on the fourth day, we spotted a brown animal on a cliff along our path with its back turned to us.

Abruptly, the creature fell over sideways.

"Nap tiiime?"

"I don't think so, sir! There was a monster behind it, sir!"

Sure enough, there was something that looked like a metal armadillo.

My AR display indicated that it was a level-20 monster called an armored rat, with the skills "Charge" and "Shock Absorption." It was about the size of a small pickup truck.

"All hands, dismount and assume combat positions. Arisa and Lulu, please take care of the horses."

At Liza's shout, everyone got down from their horses and prepared for battle.

It must have heard her voice, because the monster rolled up like a pill bug and rolled down at us from the top of the cliff.

Mia and I fired at it with our short bows, but the cheap arrows simply bounced off the armored rat's hide.

...But this was enough to throw off the armored rat's rotation, and it crashed into a big tree nearby and teetered over.

Arisa, who had muttered the Balance Jamming spell, flashed a peace sign in my direction. I showed my appreciation with a thumbs-up.

"Now's our chance! I'm going in, Mr. Raka."

Without waiting for Liza's signal, Miss Karina shot over like an arrow.

"Lady Karina, stop!"

"Please stay back, Lady Karina!"

Raka and Liza both cried out to stop her, but with the speed granted by Raka's Strength Enhancement, Miss Karina was practically on top of the armored rat already.

In a flash, the creature unrolled itself and knocked Miss Karina away. She soared up into the air, crashing through a few bushes along the way.

It was a clean hit that would normally be enough to cause serious injury, but thanks to Raka's powerful defense, Miss Karina didn't take a single point of damage.

I'd have loved to equip all my kids with an exceptional item like that. *I wonder if they're sold anywhere. I'd even take one for ten thousand gold coins.*

While I was distracted, the group steadily dealt damage to the armored rat. Tama and Pochi distracted it, Nana defended against it, Karina got blown away repeatedly, and Liza struck with her Magic Cricket Spear.

…I'm not sure Miss Karina's role was much help, but since she was still only level 4, there wasn't much else she could do.

"Everybody, fall back! Mia's going to use a spell!"

On Arisa's signal, everyone backed away.

"…■■■■■ *Balloon Kyuubouchou!*"

Mia's spell rapidly vaporized the green blood that had accumulated at the monster's feet, knocking it over.

Miss Karina was too slow to escape, though, and Mia's magic launched her away along with the monster, straight onto a branch of a large nearby tree.

"Mrrr?"

Mia looked bewildered by the unexpected result.

"Now! Go on the offensive!"

The armored rat scrambled to get back up, but Arisa hit it with a Psychic Magic spell, Mind Blow, to knock it unconscious for just a moment.

Once it stopped moving, the vanguard team was on it in an instant with their swords and spears to finish it off.

Miss Karina gained a level as a result of this battle and acquired the skill "3-D Maneuverability." I detected a hint of irony, but at least it was a useful skill. There'd be no sense in complaining.

The girls had taken a liking to Miss Karina's corkscrew locks, so I made a magic curling iron to style their hair.

"Twirlyyyy?"

"So curly, sir!"

The kids had great fun rolling the ends of their hair.

I'd started making it on the first day Miss Karina had arrived, but it was difficult to maintain a temperature that wouldn't burn the hair, so it'd taken several tries until I finally completed it on the fourth day.

I'd kept my effort secret from everyone, though.

It was my job as their "master" to work only in the shadows, after all.

That night, I defeated a chicken-shaped monster called a cockatrice that used a petrifying breath and collected the plants and small animals that it had turned into stone.

The cockatrice meat that we sampled the next morning was delicious.

Then came the fifth day. Soon after we set out, we arrived at what I'd noted on my map as the most difficult terrain in the forest.

"Now that's quite a gorge," Arisa commented.

"The river at the bottom of the ravine appears to be flowing at a very high speed, I report," added Nana.

"If one were to fall, the chances of survival certainly seem unlikely," said Liza.

Behind the three, the other kids tried to peer at the bottom, too, but I stopped them, since it seemed dangerous.

"Perhaps we should take a detour?"

"It's all right. There's a bridge up ahead."

I knew this because I'd built it after hunting the cockatrice last night.

We rode the horses a little way, and a log bridge came into view.

"Th-this thing is the bridge?"

"That's right." I nodded at Arisa.

"So…you're saying you want us to cross this?"

Sitting in front of me on our horse, Arisa paled.

It was nothing but a plank held up by two logs, so crossing it would require some courage.

"No, no, no. Aaabsolutely not. Let's just take a detour with a few days' extra travel. All right?" Arisa's eyes filled with tears.

In order to prove that it was safe, I took the lead and moved toward the bridge.

"See? It's fine."

"Nooo—!"

Since Arisa's scream was bound to frighten the horse, I cut it off by covering her mouth.

Arisa had apparently lost the will to complain and instead pressed her forehead limply into the horse's mane.

"Tama, please don't be so bold, sir…"

"Don't worry—be happyyy!"

Tama was the only one to follow me, but since Pochi was on the same horse and therefore shared her fate, she was protesting desperately.

"Tama, take the reins."

"'kaaay."

I left Tama in charge of the horses and went back across the bridge.

It would probably be fastest for me to ride the rest across myself.

"M-master…"

"It's okay to close your eyes if you're scared."

"V-very well."

Liza hung on to my back as I brought her horse across. Surprisingly, she was afraid of heights.

Next, I took Lulu across.

"M-master, even if I close my eyes, it's still too scary…"

"You can sit sideways and hide your face in my chest, then, all right? Just focus on the sound of my heartbeat."

"R-right!"

I can't say I minded having a trembling girl clinging to me desperately in this situation. It certainly stimulated my protective instincts.

As I rode across the bridge with Lulu, Arisa chewed on her fingers.

"Jealshhh…"

Was she trying to say she was jealous?

"Want to take another round trip, then, Arisa?"

"I-I'll pass, thanks."

I was only joking, but Arisa shook her head rapidly with a deadly serious expression.

"This is very dangerous, Satou. People can't fly, you know? They don't have wings, after all. So elves can't fly, either, you know. It's true."

Next, Mia expressed her fear with an unusually verbose explanation as I carried her across the log bridge on my back. Finally, I rode the last horse with Miss Karina, and our journey over the ravine was complete.

It was hard to ignore the charms of Miss Karina's magic breasts, but I somehow made it through.

Then, at last, we arrived at the blank area on the map.

"Waaall?"

Tama turned her horse away to the side, reaching out and patting an invisible wall as if in pantomime.

Arisa, who was riding with Lulu, extended her arms to mimic Tama's movements.

"Oh my, you're right."

"It's strange, sir. I don't see anything, but something's there, sir."

The other kids also explored the invisible barrier. Even Miss Karina joined in.

The sight of them patting the wall and tilting their heads in puzzlement was adorable.

I turned my horse to the side and reached out, too, but I didn't feel anything.

When I stared for a moment at the spot everyone was hitting, an AR display reading **Mountain-Tree barrier wall** appeared.

It was probably the same sort of barrier I'd found at the border of the Forest of Illusions.

What was "Mountain-Tree," though?

Had we come to the wrong place...?

When I moved my horse forward, I felt a slight sense of discomfort, but I was able to advance without resistance.

A lukewarm wind tickled my cheek, but I barely noticed that compared to the unusually enormous tree that had suddenly appeared in the distance.

Wondering if I'd been teleported, I looked over my shoulder to see the others all gesturing wildly and flapping their mouths open and closed. They looked desperate, so they were most likely seriously worried about me, not just playing around.

The barrier must have been blocking their voices.

I hadn't been able to see that giant tree from the other side, either, so maybe it could block images, too.

For the time being, I selected **Search Entire Map** from the magic menu to acquire information about the area beyond the barrier, then headed back to the other side.

"Don't go disappearing like that! You gave us a fright!"

Arisa took the lead and castigated me for worrying them.

I was appreciative that they'd been concerned about me, but it was more important to determine whether the area on the other side of the barrier was safe.

As the girls ranted at me, I started investigating the information I'd gained.

Firstly, I learned through my menu information that the large tree beyond the barrier wall was called **Mountain-Tree**. It seemed to be the same size as the Cradle where Mia had been kidnapped.

And the village of the forest giants, where I was supposed to deliver the letter, was at the foot of that tree.

The population of the area was concentrated in the forest giants' village. There were only ten of them altogether, the strongest of which was level 39. The average level was 31.

There were other giants besides the forest giants, too.

There was another race called little giants, which averaged around level 20. The name seemed a little self-contradictory, but I assumed they were just small by giant standards. There were about a hundred and twenty of them.

There were also nearly a thousand demi-humans of diverse races living here. About 40 percent were birdfolk, 50 percent were various beastfolk, and the remaining 10 percent were fairyfolk.

The fairyfolk were mostly brownies, gnomes, and spriggans, but there were three kobolds, too. I hadn't gotten to see the ones in Kuhanou County, so I'd have loved to meet one this time.

There were a lot of mythical creatures inside the barrier, too.

There were several herds of unicorns, plus some creatures called gjallarhorns. The Holy Sword of the same name was probably modeled after these creatures, or made from them.

There were more creatures living in the top of the large tree, including several elder sparrows like the one the witch had ridden.

At any rate, there didn't seem to be any dangerous creatures with a high-enough level to pose a deadly threat to the kids, so that was a relief.

Once I'd confirmed that it was safe, we all moved to the opposite side of the wall.

For some reason, the others were able to pass through normally if I led them by the hand.

I was worried that Mia would be upset when she saw the Mountain-Tree, but she must not have seen the Cradle from the outside for the most part. She didn't react.

"Who are you really, Sa… You?"

Miss Karina observed me seriously. As usual, she was too embarrassed to say my name.

"The barrier might have let me through because I have a letter for one of the giants of the village."

I avoided her question with an arbitrary answer, but I wasn't really sure why I was able to pass through the barrier, either.

Instead of worrying about something I didn't understand, I was better off figuring out what path we should take.

The village was about twelve miles away as the crow flies, so it should take only a day or two on horseback.

Suddenly, a green human figure emerged from one of the old trees in front of us.

"Oh? Well, if it isn't that human."

"Hey. Thanks for your help before."

The figure that had appeared was the dryad who'd helped me get around in the Cradle.

She was beckoning to me, so I approached. As before, she was naked, but I didn't care, since I'm not interested in little girls.

"Mrrr, go away." Mia stepped between the little girl and me, spreading her hands as if to protect me. "Drain." She gave a monosyllabic warning.

Most likely, she was trying to say that the dryad would suck up a lot of my magic.

"Oh my. Don't be rude, child."

Child was probably referring to Mia. She did have the title Child of Bolenan, after all.

I rested a hand on Mia's head, then spoke to the dryad.

"So, did you need something?"

"Yeah, the chief of the forest giants asked me to find out who trespassed on the barrier. If it's you, though, I'm sure I can just take you to the village. The youngling there can come, too."

I didn't mind going alone, but if I left the other kids here, they'd probably get lost. They wouldn't be able to reach the forest giant village.

I didn't know what the forest giants were like, but since they were friends of the kindly old witch, it was probably pretty safe to trust them.

"Wait a minute. Would you mind taking all of us there?"

"Sure, sure. But I don't have quite enough magic power for that, so you'll have to give me some of yours."

Without waiting for my response, the dryad placed her hands on my cheeks, smacked her lips onto mine, and started absorbing my magic.

Since there were children watching this time, I intentionally helped the magic along.

This had the desired effect, as the dryad released my mouth after just a few seconds.

"You've gotten better at this, human."

Her remark sounded like praise for a worthy opponent, but in reality, we were just transferring magic.

So I'd appreciate it if you would take your fist out of your mouth and stop staring up at me, thank you. Don't whack my stomach or give me jealous glares, either!

"All right, here goes!"

With that, mushrooms popped up from the ground to surround us, giving off spores that glowed a pale green.

"A fairy ring."

Just as Mia mumbled somewhat nostalgically, we were teleported away.

"Dryad! Who have you brought here?!"

The dryad faced a shrill interrogation as soon as we arrived.

There's no way a forest giant would sound like that, I thought as I looked up. Above, I saw a group of forest giants as tall as buildings, but on a stand next to their chairs was a tiny old man hopping up and down. According to my AR display, the little man was a brownie.

My map informed me that we were now in a hall located in a hollow near the base of the Mountain-Tree.

The hall was about seventy feet high, and its radius was about one hundred and fifty feet. The walls were the bare wood from the tree, and a lamp near the ceiling shone with a gentle white light.

The giants, as tall as small mountains, were sitting in enormous chairs installed directly into the wood walls.

Perhaps because they were so high up from where we were standing, their faces were shadowed, making their expressions hard to read. They were sitting so still that it would be easy to mistake them for statues.

"Answer me, dryad!"

"They're humans."

"That's not what I mean. I'm asking you who they are!"

"Oh, I dunno. Besides, I'm not gonna listen to anyone except that kid Stonehammer. *He's* the master of this mana source."

"BOH-YAH, MEEROH."

One of the giants muttered something to the dryad, and my body trembled with the vibrations. His voice was incredibly deep.

I had no idea what he said, though. All I could tell was that the giant's words sounded somewhat Elvish.

Maybe their language was related.

> Skill Acquired: "Giant Language"

Oh, so he was speaking the common language of giants, not a forest giant–specific language.

I went ahead and raised the skill level to five so I'd be able to understand their words.

The giant looked down and opened his mouth, and the bass rumbled in my stomach as his low voice filled the hall. He was facing this way now, so it reverberated even more strongly than before.

"WHO ARE YOU? WHAT IS YOUR PURPOSE IN THIS VILLAGE?"

When the giant was done speaking, the brownie nearby translated into Shigan.

"I AM SATOU, A TRAVELING MERCHANT. THE WITCH OF THE FOREST OF ILLUSIONS ASKED ME TO DELIVER A LETTER TO YOU, WHICH IS WHY I HAVE COME HERE."

With the help of my "Amplification" skill, I replied to him in giant language. I took care to speak slowly to match their speed.

"W-was that…giant language?"

"Yes, Sir Satou seems to be quite knowledgeable."

"Goodness, is there anything he can't do?"

I heard Miss Karina and Raka talking behind me.

The other kids were surprised, too, but their reactions weren't as dramatic as Miss Karina's.

"OH-HO, SO YOU CAN UNDERSTAND US? HOW SPLENDID. LET US SEE THIS LETTER FROM THE WITCH."

Just as I'd thought, no matter what world you're in, speaking a new acquaintance's language always gives a good impression.

The giant lowered his enormous hand at a ponderous speed, like a heavy machine, and I put the letter onto his palm.

The characters were probably too small for him to read, so he placed the brownie on his shoulder and had the letter read aloud to him. Since it was a personal letter, I switched off my "Keen Hearing" skill so as not to eavesdrop.

Before long, the letter was finished, and the forest giant looked back down in my direction.

"IT SEEMS YOU HAVE COME QUITE FAR. THANK YOU, LITTLE CHILD, FRIEND OF MY OLD FRIEND. MY NAME IS…"

His name sounded more like a song. Listening to the easy rhythm, I started to get sleepy.

Giants' names were made up of the names of generations of their ancestors, so it went on for more than twenty minutes. Tama, Pochi, and Nana started to nod off, and I could hardly blame them.

His name was written in the AR display, so I didn't really need to memorize it, but even in human language it would still take upward of five minutes to say. The legendary Jugemu would be impressed.

"…BUT THAT MAY BE TOO LONG FOR YOU TO SAY EASILY. YOU MAY CALL ME 'STONEHAMMER.'"

"THANK YOU FOR YOUR KIND WELCOME. SINCE I HAVE ALREADY GIVEN MY NAME, PLEASE ALLOW ME TO INTRODUCE MY COMPANIONS."

"…Mia."

I brought Mia forward, and she mumbled her name shortly, covering her ears with a cross look on her face.

Apparently, the loud bass of Stonehammer's voice had hurt her ears.

"OH-HO, AN ELF OF BOLENAN FOREST, ARE YOU? NOT SINCE SIR YUSARATOYA VISITED ONE HUNDRED YEARS AGO HAVE I SEEN YOUR KIND. ALLOW ME TO WELCOME YOU ON BEHALF OF OUR ENTIRE VILLAGE."

The giant was referring to the elfin manager of the general store in Seiryuu City.

So he's been here, too, huh?

I continued to introduce the rest of the group. We had a bit of trouble with the last one, Miss Karina.

"M-my name is Karina Muno. I am the second daughter of Baron Muno—"

"Muno, you say! So a relative of that rotten marquis has strayed into our village to lose her head?!"

The brownie beside the giants turned bright red with rage and interrupted Miss Karina's introduction. This guy blew up at everything.

Miss Karina hid behind me, unaccustomed to being the target of such malice.

As she pressed up against my back, I could have fainted with joy.

As thanks for this blessing, I figured I should probably defend her. I'd have to use my "Making Excuses" skill or my rarely used "Mediation" skill here.

"JUST A MOMENT, PLEASE!"

I spread my arms to defend Miss Karina as she hid behind me.

"Satou...," I heard her whisper. I was pretty sure that was the first time she'd called me by name.

Thus encouraged, I continued to speak in a loud, tense voice.

"MARQUIS MUNO'S FAMILY HAS BEEN DESTROYED. HER FATHER HAS ONLY INHERITED THE NAME AND IS IN NO WAY RELATED TO THE FORMER MARQUIS'S HOUSE."

I tried to defend her, but the indignant brownie clearly refused to listen.

Perhaps under the effect of my skills, Stonehammer stopped the brownie for me.

"THAT IS ENOUGH."

"B-BUT—"

"ENOUGH, I SAID."

At his lord's orders, the brownie sank into a sulky silence.

"LITTLE CHILD, SATOU. I WILL NOT ASK YOU WHY YOU HAVE BROUGHT A YOUNG WOMAN BEARING THE NAME OF MUNO TO THIS LAND."

This time, Stonehammer faced me as he spoke.

Shoot. At this rate, there was no way that Miss Karina would be able to achieve her goal here.

However, the giant wasn't finished speaking.

"THE WITCH'S LETTER STATED THAT YOUR PURPOSE IS TO SEE UNKNOWN LANDS. ALLOW ME TO PREPARE YOU A ROOM IN THE MANSION OF ONE OF OUR VILLAGE'S LITTLE GIANTS. IT IS MY THANKS TO YOU FOR DELIVERING THE LETTER. PLEASE FEEL FREE TO REST IN OUR VILLAGE FOR AS LONG AS YOU DESIRE."

Nice one, Miss Witch!

I recalled the image of the mild old witch in profile as I praised her appreciatively in my mind.

Uh-oh, it'll be bad if he says Miss Karina has to leave alone. I'd better make sure.

"LORD STONEHAMMER, I AM TERRIBLY SORRY TO MAKE SUCH A BRAZEN REQUEST, BUT MIGHT I PLEASE ASK YOUR PERMISSION FOR MY FRIEND—THE DAUGHTER OF BARON MUNO—TO STAY AS WELL?"

"...VERY WELL. THE YOUNG MUNO WOMAN MAY REMAIN WITH YOU."

After a short pause, Stonehammer did give his permission.

Hopefully now Miss Karina would be able to negotiate with Stonehammer and the other giants during our visit.

Even though it had been only a few days, she was a member of our traveling party now. I figured I could at least try to come up with a plan to help her in between sightseeing.

"WE TRULY APPRECIATE YOUR KIND GENEROSITY."

I thanked Stonehammer deeply, then exited the hall.

We were escorted to a room next to the hall, where we waited obediently for someone from the forest giant village to welcome us.

Liza positioned herself next to the door as a gatekeeper.

"Sir Satou, we are grateful for your assistance." Raka thanked me on behalf of Miss Karina.

Miss Karina seemed shaken by what must have been her first experience as a target of ill will; her face was pale as she mumbled her thanks.

Pochi and Tama sat on either side of her, looking up at her anxiously.

"I don't think it'll be easy, but I wish you luck."

"Yes, I had no idea..."

Arisa patted Miss Karina's shoulder encouragingly.

"There is no benefit to being disheartened, I advise. If you have time to feel downcast, you must use it to move forward instead, I recite."

"That's right, Lady Karina! There's hardly anything that can't be solved by a proper meal and a good night's sleep."

Nana and Lulu did their best to cheer up Miss Karina, too. Come to think of it, Arisa had mentioned that Lulu had been treated very poorly in her hometown.

Before long, a group of ten-foot-tall little giants came to greet us with a palanquin to carry us to the village.

"Sorry to have kept you waiting, daho. It took some time to prepare the palanquin, daho."

The apparent leader spoke with an unusual verbal quirk as the little giants brought us out of the Mountain-Tree.

Outside the tree was a trench-like road to the village, which was almost a mile away. The village was about twice as far from the trunk as the edge of the Mountain-Tree's canopy was.

The lowest branches grew about three hundred feet up, but the tips hung down almost to the ground. A few earthen towers were stationed there.

In the distance, I could see little giants doing some kind of work at the top of the tower.

Apparently, they were collecting fruit from the branches of the Mountain-Tree.

The fruits were large enough that the little giants were picking them in pairs, so they must have been six or seven feet around in diameter.

Outside the trench, I could see an earthen wall about ten feet high.

According to the map, there were several of these walls forming concentric circles around the Mountain-Tree, at intervals of about six hundred and fifty feet. They were too low to be defensive barriers, and there were periodic gaps in them.

When we had nearly arrived at the village, we heard the sound of alarm bells.

"What could that be?"

"A fruit must have fallen from the Mountain-Tree, daho," explained the leader of the little giants.

Indeed, if a fruit fell from a higher branch in the nearly mile-high Mountain-Tree, it certainly could cause a disaster.

So the earth walls weren't to keep out enemies but to defend against falling fruit.

Overhead, I saw something shaking the leaves and branches of the tree as it descended. It was about seven hundred feet away from here.

"The defense lid will cover us soon enough, so please do not worry, daho."

Placing our palanquin on the ground, the leader addressed us in a calm voice.

Even as he spoke, an arched, transparent barrier appeared over the walls of the passage. It was probably a Shelter wall made with Foundation Magic.

Then a vermilion fruit appeared from the branches.

Because of its unusual size, it seemed to be falling slowly, but in truth it was probably descending at a considerable speed.

As if to prove this, the earth rumbled and trembled as the fruit hit the ground.

Arisa and Mia (who were sitting on my knees), Tama and Pochi (to my left and right), and even Lulu and Miss Karina (behind me) all latched on to my arms.

I felt a wonderful softness of various sizes press into my back.

However, Miss Karina must have unconsciously invoked her Strength Enhancement or something. Her grip on my arm kinda hurt.

Liza and Nana didn't miss a beat, keenly watching where the fruit had fallen.

A few more tremors followed shortly after.

"Uh-oh, daho. Must be a bouncer, daho."

Since we couldn't see what was going on very well from the trench, he had probably drawn his conclusion from the repeated quakes.

The fruit crashed into the soil wall in front of the village and reached a halt.

But, the next moment, we saw the wall crack apart, and the fruit rolled on into the village.

"Oh dear. That's the spriggan general's house, daho. We'll all have to help with repairs tomorrow, daho."

It sounded less like a major disaster and more like a frequently occurring inconvenience.

The magic defense ceiling above us was canceled out, and our palanquin was lifted up again, giving us a view of the aftermath.

Three had fallen altogether, two of them stopping in the trough they'd dug in the earth.

I could see plenty of other places where holes had been filled in, too.

"Does fruit fall like that very often?"

"Oh, no. Aside from during harvest season, there's usually no more than one a month, daho."

Then I guess a bunch of them must've fallen at once at one point...

"Normally, the elder sparrows eat the fruit at the top of the tree, daho. But in the last month or so, there haven't been as many, so lots of the ripe fruit has been falling, daho."

...or not.

Elder sparrows were giant, round birds like the one the witch of the Forest of Illusions had ridden.

What could've caused their numbers to decrease?

"I seem to recall those birds being quite large. Is there a dangerous predator around or something?"

"Not anymore, so don't worry, daho. But during the most recent new moon, a flock of hydra came through the barrier, daho. Many of the sparrows were eaten, daho," the little giants' leader answered sorrowfully.

Hydra again, huh? Powerful and mobile. Those pests must be hard to manage.

"The great forest giants drove them away by throwing hard-shelled fruit at them, but several were hit by the hydras' poison breath, daho."

"That sounds terrible."

I would be fine as long as I killed the thing instantly from a distance so it couldn't counterattack, but if I did end up on the receiving end of that poison breath, I bet washing my clothes would be a huge pain afterward. It might even damage the fibers and make them unwearable.

"It was, daho. That was the first time in the three hundred years I've been alive that we were attacked by monsters, so I really panicked, daho."

Maybe I was just being paranoid, but I wondered if the hell demon had provoked the hydra flock to attack the village.

"The adult forest giants were healed by a gnomish antidote, at least, but there are still three forest giant children who're bedridden from the poison, daho."

The poison was still in their systems a month later?

I tried searching for forest giants on the map.

Sure enough, three forest giant children had the status condition **Poison/Hydra [Chronic]**. Their HP gauges were down to a third or fourth of their original number, and their magic and stamina gauges were on the verge of depletion, too.

"Does the antidote not work on children?"

"Well... I heard that they only had enough materials for snake venom antidote, so it wasn't very effective, daho. So now one forest giant, Lord Braidbeard, is off hunting the hydra so we can make the real antidote, daho."

Ah! That must be the one forest giant I found when I searched the map of the barony before.

At the moment, he was near the barrier.

A search of his possessions revealed that he had a severed hydra head, so he must have been able to safely secure the antidote materials.

I had a hydra corpse in my Storage, too, but it would be uncouth to render his efforts moot just before his triumphant return, so I decided to keep that to myself.

The palanquin carrying our group stopped in front of the biggest house in the village.

"Welcome home, dear. So these are the great forest giants' guests?"

"Yes, daho. There is an elf among them as well, so please treat them with courtesy, daho."

"Oh my. I think it's been near a hundred years since we last welcomed an elf into our home."

The two were husband and wife, both over three hundred years old.

"I am Whitefinger, wife of the village chief, Lank. It's a pleasure to meet you."

So the leader of our little giant entourage was the village chief.

The names she gave were apparently shortened versions of their lengthy names, like the forest giants'. They were most likely direct translations from giant language into Shigan.

Since Mia was hiding behind me and making no attempt to introduce herself, I greeted them instead.

"I beg your pardon—Mia is quite shy. I am a humanfolk peddler by the name of Satou."

"I see. So her name is Lady Mia? Worry not—we are well aware that elves are often silent. The only words Lord Yusaratoya ever spoke to us in his visit were *Yuya*, *thanks*, and *farewell*."

She said this jokingly, so I doubted she was trying to be sarcastic.

After everyone else had been introduced and we'd been shown to our rooms, Mia finally mumbled her name to Whitefinger.

"Mia."

"My, elves have such wonderful voices! I'll make you a meal with the fruit of the Mountain-Tree tonight. Are there any foods that you don't like?"

The pitch of Whitefinger's voice rose when Mia spoke, and she leaned in toward the elf.

"Meat," Mia replied, forming an X over her mouth with her fingers and pulling back slightly.

"I'll be sure not to make any dishes with meat, then," Whitefinger answered with zeal.

Despair appeared on the beastfolk girls' faces, so I discreetly requested that she include meat in everyone's dishes but Mia's.

On our way to the chief's house, I'd seen a cowherd with a herd of animals that looked like longhaired cattle, so meat wasn't too scarce here.

Shortly thereafter, Lank stated that he was going to get some of the fruit from the Mountain-Tree, so I asked him to take Liza and me along.

I was a little worried about Miss Karina. She'd immediately shut herself away in her room, claiming she was tired, so I went to see how she was doing while the village chief got prepared.

Armed with baked goods and freshly brewed blue-green tea from Storage, I visited Miss Karina's room.

"Please eat a little something. Lulu says an empty stomach only worsens a bad mood."

"I have no appetite at all…"

As if in protest, her stomach immediately let out a growl.

I offered again, and after reluctantly accepting it, she started eating right away.

The way she held the pastry in both hands as she munched on it reminded me of a cute little squirrel.

"Why…?" Miss Karina murmured quietly. "Why must I be hated so by people I've never even met?" The fear and anger in her trembling voice clearly expressed the complexity of her heart.

"Perhaps since Marquis Muno did such terrible things—"

"But why?! I have no ties or blood relation to such a person!"

Miss Karina passionately stood, grabbing my collar and putting her face close to mine. Her eyes were full of anger and sadness at this unreasonable world.

"To them, all they see is that you're a human with the name of 'Muno,' I imagine."

Even in a parallel world, one thing can be all it takes to hate someone.

At my words, Miss Karina simply repeated, "Why…?" and pressed her forehead into my chest.

Faintly, I could hear her starting to weep.

I couldn't take my eyes off her quivering eyelashes and glossy lips.

How can a woman in a moment of weakness be so lovely…?

I hugged her lightly to comfort her, and she leaned into me like a child.

With her soft chest against me, I desperately fought the terrible urge to fall back onto the bed with her.

At that moment, Liza opened the door.

"Master, Lord Lank says he is just about ready to— Oh, pardon me. I shall come back later."

"Wait! That won't be necessary."

Liza took in the situation and made to leave tactfully, but I quickly stopped her.

Thanks to her arrival, the battle between the angel and demon in my soul ended in a narrow victory for the side of good.

That was close. If I were to lay a hand on a noble's daughter, I'd either end up on the wanted list or the fast track to marriage.

I relaxed my arm around Miss Karina and instead patted her lightly on the back to soothe her.

Then I made another attempt to cheer her up after asking Liza to wait a moment.

"Lady Karina, it's too soon to give up. It's just as a famous leader of my kingdom once said: When you give up, it's all over."

I paused for a moment, waiting for her reaction.

She didn't seem thrilled, but at least she was listening to me.

"Lady Karina, even if they don't show you a smidgen of kindness, you can't retreat yet. You'll just have to take action to win their favor."

"...Favor?" Miss Karina looked up at me hopefully, so I nodded.

If I said this to one of my non-nerd friends, they'd probably make fun of me for treating everything like a game.

Miss Karina didn't seem to understand completely, so I tried to explain.

"That's right. There aren't many people who will do something nice for someone they hate. So you just have to start by befriending them."

"Befriending them...? However would I go about such a thing?"

"We'll just have to try to find a way. At least we have permission to stay, for starters."

The life was returning to Miss Karina's eyes, but she still seemed anxious.

"Don't worry. It'll work out somehow."

I took her hand reassuringly, smiling as lightly as possible.

"Thank you...Satou."

My "Keen Hearing" skill ensured Miss Karina's mumbled thanks reached me.

My rash promise seemed to have worked, as the shadows were finally disappearing from her expression. Her cheeks were turning pink, too. Her eyes were still faintly clouded from crying—she looked just like a maiden in love.

She'd be all right now.

"Liza and I are going with Lord Lank to gather information, all right?"

"Let me co—"

"Wait, Lady Karina. If we accompany them, we will only hinder their attempts to collect information. We must be prudent."

"Mr. Raka…"

Miss Karina wanted to come along, but Raka stopped her.

Oh yeah, Raka's here, too, huh?

"Leave the investigating to us. I'll get some good tidbits and come back."

I smiled again to put her worries at ease, then left the room.

Before we set out, I visited Arisa and asked her to go talk with Miss Karina.

Liza and I marched along with Lank on the main street of Mountain-Tree Village.

The little community consisted of about a hundred and eighty houses, but unlike a human village, the buildings here came in vastly different sizes. Not only that, but apparently, each race had its own style of architecture, so it was fascinating to see the variety of roofs, windows, and so on.

"This is a nice village."

"That's kind of you to say, daho. We're all very proud of our village, daho."

Lank considerately matched his pace with ours, and we took in the sights of the street as we proceeded toward the fruit-processing plant.

Along the way, we saw some children racing down the street; the young fairies were smaller than Pochi and Tama, but the little giants were taller than me.

Now, you'd never find a fantastical scene like this on Earth. I wouldn't forget the sight of a spriggan boy riding proudly on a little giant child's back anytime soon.

I decided to explore the village with everyone tomorrow. Arisa in particular would probably be overjoyed.

Soon enough, we arrived at the fruit-processing plant, which looked like a workshop with no outer walls.

Enormous colorful fruits waited in rows for the little giants to cut them open with large axes and saws.

I rapped experimentally on a dark-gray fruit lying nearby, and it felt almost like steel. Next to it was a yellow fruit about as firm as a coconut. Clearly, there were large differences among each of the varieties.

"This one's too hard. Lank, take over for me."

"Duty calls, daho. I'll be right back, daho."

One of the little giants pleaded with Lank for help after failing to cleave the fruit with an ax.

The sturdy rind also gave Lank trouble, as his ax bounced off it harmlessly.

"Could I maybe give it a try, too?"

I generally don't like to draw attention, but I really wanted to experience this for myself.

With abilities like Body Strengthening in this world, it shouldn't be too strange for a human to be able to wield a giant ax.

Besides, this village didn't seem to have a lot of contact with the outside world, so they probably wouldn't spread any strange rumors. If anything, the authority of Mia and the Silent Bell of Bolenan should protect me here.

"Are you sure you can hold it, daho?"

"I'll be all right. I have a Body Strengthening magic tool."

As usual, my "Fabrication" skill was working to great effect here.

I borrowed the giant ax and tested out its weight. Since my own body was so light, I couldn't do much about the inertia of the ax.

Near the wall, there was a large, thin-bladed sword that looked a little lighter, so I borrowed that instead and gave it a swing.

"Ooh, amazing, daho. I've never seen anyone cut one of those on their first swing, daho."

"What an arm! Do you think he might even be able to break an ironshell?"

"It's worth a try, daho. If it works, we'll be able to drink ironshell wine at tonight's banquet, daho."

This "ironshell" was probably the dark-gray fruit I'd seen near the entrance. It was as hard as steel, so only the forest giants' shell-breaking tools could crack it.

Ironshell wine, they explained, tasted sweet and strong, and it had a high alcohol content.

Perhaps this was the key ingredient of the Giant's Tears wine I'd drank in Sedum City back in Kuhanou County?

With an intense glare at the fruit towering over me, I made a swing at it with the sword.

The thin blade broke with a resounding *crack*.

"I'm sorry…"

"Well, an ironshell was probably too much to hope for."

"Yeah, it's only to be expected…"

I apologized, and the plant workers responded with disappointment.

"…H-hey, look there!"

One of the workers shouted and pointed at the ironshell.

A fissure had appeared high on the fruit, and as if encouraged by the cry of surprise, the crack was growing.

"H-he cut it!"

"Whoa!!"

"A-amazing, daho. Satou, you are a master swordsman, daho."

A chorus of surprise and adulation rose from the crowd of workers.

Picking up the remains of the blade from the floor, I finished my apology.

"…I broke the sword."

"It's no problem, daho. Axes and swords break all the time while we're splitting fruit, daho. If we bring some wine to the blacksmith later, he'll be happy to fix it, daho. Just leave that to the guys at the plant, daho."

Lank's casual reply encouraged me.

Just in case, I apologized to the other workers, but far from being angry, they insisted that I could break as many as I liked as long as I cut open more ironshells for them.

As I split three more, the number of onlookers steadily increased.

> Title Acquired: Street Performer

Just as I acquired the title, a woman with the head of a dog appeared in the workshop.

"I heard there was a master swordsman here. Is it really true that he can split the ironshell fruit?"

"Just look around, Miss Kobold! Can't you see the pile of halves right here?"

"…S-so it is true."

Wow, so that's a kobold?

So their race had rather pale skin and a dog head—no, wait. The "head" was actually a helmet.

"Show me with this sword, then. It's a blue-steel sword forged by kobolds."

The girl came up to me and shoved a large curved blade into my hands.

I could see a tooth protruding from her lips that was like a little fang. The headgear covered most of her face, but her mouth was that of a dazzling woman.

I unsheathed the sword she handed me. It was a beautiful weapon. The handle had a guard to protect the wielder's hand, and the single-edge blade was slightly curved. It was a bit too long for me to hold with one hand, but it was definitely a saber of some kind.

In addition, true to the metal's name, the steel blade had a blue sheen to it.

According to my AR, the material was called **kobold alloy blue steel**. But the kobold alloy kitchen knife I had was the same color as ordinary metal…

Well, there was no point in nitpicking about the materials of a parallel world.

I gave a light practice swing to test the balance. It weighed about the same as an ordinary steel sword.

Then, taking a breath, I readied the blue-steel sword in front of an ironshell fruit.

If I used Spellblade, I could ensure that the sword wouldn't break, but the stats in the AR display indicated that it should be fine either way, so I simply took a swing.

"Splendid."

I somehow lopped the fruit open without breaking the sword. The kobold girl seemed impressed.

"This is a good weapon."

I shook off the traces of sap from the sword, returned it to its scabbard, and handed it back to the young woman.

"Having seen your skill, I have a favor to ask of you, sir. If you would, I request that you take me to Bolehart, where the dwarves live, or Bolenan Forest, the home of the elves. As a reward, I will give you this blue-steel sword, Bluefang."

Speaking quickly and resolutely, the girl held it out toward me with one hand.

Considering how heavy that thing was, she had to be strong.

"Do you mind if I ask your reason?"

From her tone, I didn't think she was planning to bring trouble to the elf village or anything, but if it was an urgent errand, she probably wouldn't want to accompany us on our easygoing sightseeing journey.

If that was the case, she'd be better off borrowing an elder sparrow from the forest giants and flying there alone.

After warning me she couldn't speak about it here, the girl brought Liza and me to the back of the factory to explain.

"The reason I asked to travel with you is that it would be too difficult for us to get to Bolenan Forest alone."

Right, there were only three kobolds here. The girl was a low level, too, so she needed a bodyguard.

"Why do you want to see the elves of Bolenan Forest?"

"Because the very existence of the kobolds is at stake."

"Existence?"

"When a kobold child is born, a gemstone called a blue crystal is needed, but our mines have all run dry."

The mines dried up...?

Hmm? Could it be...?

"Is that why the silver mines in Kuhanou County were attacked?"

"That's right. Baron Muno's magistrate told us that there were blue crystals hidden deep in those silver mines."

The magistrate... Isn't that the hell demon?

I wonder if I can search that on the map?

It would be rough to investigate the mountains at random, so even if I could find sources of ore nearby, that would make the search easier.

"So are blue crystals always found near silver veins?"

"No, there's no guarantee of that. However, the elves or dwarves should surely have access to them in their bluesilver mines."

Blue steel, bluesilver, blue crystals... These guys really like blue.

If it were green like my mithril sword, would it be called greensilver?

"The crystals have a beautiful color, like the leaves of the Mountain-Tree," she said, indicating the deep-evergreen foliage.

Maybe their perception of color was different?

I reached into the back of my robe, pulled out the mithril dagger from Storage, and showed it to her.

"Is this made of bluesilver, then?"

"Ooh, what a beautiful dagger. Yes, surely that's the source of its lovely blue color."

In other words, then, they had to find a mithril vein.

Figuring I might as well, I searched the mountains of the Muno Barony for mithril veins.

First, I tried the nearest mountain to the village as the target, but I didn't find anything there.

I knew it wouldn't be easy, but… Oh right! If I remembered correctly, there had been papers about proposed mine sites in the Lesser Garage Bag I found in the haunted fortress.

In the documents, I discovered a description of a possible vein within the large forest.

It was a wide area for a search, so I checked the mountains in the forest one by one until I discovered a mithril vein in the third one.

And in a cave at the bottom of the mithril vein, I found the blue crystals in question.

Now, how would I explain this to her…?

Time for my "Fabrication" skill to go to work.

"I don't know whether there are blue crystals there, but I do happen to know of a mithril vein."

"R-really?!"

"Yeah, a mysterious man calling himself 'the masked hermit' told me about it."

I drew a map in the dirt to the mountain where the vein was located.

"The hermit lives in this mountain. He explained that he was searching for a mithril mine to obtain a powerful sword."

"Then if I give him this one…"

The kobold girl leaped up joyfully, but then she paused.

"No, that won't work. I've already promised to give it to you. And all I have other than that are some tools…"

What a conscientious girl.

"The only thing I did was give you information. If you feel you must pay me, perhaps you could spare a tool made of blue steel?"

"Are you sure that's enough?"

"Yeah, definitely."

The girl left to make preparations to travel to the mountain, so I began to brainstorm how to make my little tale a reality.

I should probably go to the mountain tonight and create a tunnel to the blue crystals there. It would be an easy matter if I used my Pitfall spell.

Then I could make a log cabin at the entrance of the tunnel and leave a carved wooden mask inside with a paper handing over the vein to the next person to find it. Since she might not be able to read Shigan letters, I'd have to place some mithril ore and blue crystals with it, too.

Tonight's going to be a busy night.

As it turned out, things were busy even before night fell.

After we'd drawn out the liquor from the ironshells and carved out samples of the fruit with small knives, the plant workers and I heard a *thud* and felt the ground shake.

Braidbeard, the giant who'd been on an expedition outside the barrier, had returned.

"I HAVE BROUGHT THE HEAD OF A HYDRA, GNOME. USE IT TO MAKE MEDICINE."

The thirty-foot-tall giant loomed outside the workshop. As his name suggested, he had an impressively woven beard.

A little gnome came tumbling out of the alchemy store next to the workshop.

Then, as he examined the hydra head the giant had placed on the ground, he shook his own head sorrowfully.

"Lord Braidbeard, I cannot use this head. Since the poison glands have been destroyed, the venom I need to create the material has drained away..."

"WHAT?!"

The gnome quivered before the irrational anger of the giant. The other people of the village, too, shuddered at the giant's incensed roar.

Even Liza looked ready to faint, so I supported her with an arm.

Quickly, I checked the hydra corpse I had in Storage.

It was no good. Since the heads had been smashed to bits, there were no venom glands remaining.

...No, it was too soon to give up. The poison itself was the key here.

"Sir Gnome, would you happen to have any Black Warped Stone?"

"Why would I have such an impractical ingredient? I don't know who you are, but I'm busy right now."

Just as I thought...

"Sir Swordsman, I do."

A spriggan man came forward and said he would go and get it from his house. An onlooker told me that he was a prospector who searched for ore and gemstones.

"Sir Gnome. I am Satou, a peddler currently imposing upon the home of Sir Lank. I have in my possession Dragon Stone and Serpent's Blood Stone. If that spriggan gentleman is kind enough to bring back some Black Warped Stone, you should be able to create a universal antidote, correct?"

I grinned broadly as I spoke, but the gnome's face was still pale.

"I'm sorry. I have not the skills to make such an advanced medicine. My master would likely be able to, but..."

This was unexpected. It hadn't occurred to me that he wouldn't be able to make it.

I had no choice, then. I couldn't bear to make the suffering children wait until someone could get another hydra head.

"...Let me make it, then. I may not look the part, but I have studied under the witch of the Forest of Illusions. I have no doubt that I can succeed."

After that, I received a large bag full of Black Warped Stone from the spriggan man, and I gave him three intermediate health potions as compensation. Despite his being a prospector, he didn't seem to be a very greedy man.

Borrowing the alchemy shop's equipment, I was able to make three small casks' worth of **antidote: universal**. The reason I made it by the cask was to account for the forest giants' large build.

Liza and I rode on Braidbeard's shoulder to the Mountain-Tree.

Even though he was walking slowly, the size of his strides meant that he was moving as fast as a car.

Since Liza was afraid of heights, she clung onto me during the entire trip. It was adorable. I would never have expected it from her.

On our way to the Mountain-Tree, a fruit came falling from above, but the giant Braidbeard simply caught it deftly in his hand.

Returning to the living quarters of the forest giants, Braidbeard told Stonehammer and the others that he had the antidote, and we went to the children's room.

Stonehammer and the other forest giants followed behind us.

The tremors on the ground were something else. The brownies working in the forest giants' neighborhood were rolling and tumbling all around below us.

"MEDICINE. FOR THE CHILDREN."

"WHO IS THE HUMANFOLK BOY?"

"HE MADE THE MEDICINE."

"HUMANFOLK MEDICINE? I'M NOT SURE…"

It was only natural that a mother would be reluctant to give her child medicine made by a random stranger.

"SIR SATOU IS AN ATTENDANT OF THE ELF LADY MIA. YOU CAN TRUST HIM."

Although Stonehammer vouched for me, the mothers still seemed unconvinced.

"THEN I WILL TASTE IT FIRST."

I spoke up in the giants' language, scooped out a dose of the medicine with a vial, and drank it down.

This convinced them at last, and the giant mothers gave the medicine to their children. The children were upward of sixteen feet tall, so it was a remarkable sight.

Having drunk the medicine, the children lay down limply on their beds.

This should have healed them, but their **Poisoned** status didn't go away.

A dejected silence fell on the forest giants as they watched over the children.

…That's strange. I'm sure I made the medicine properly. Didn't I?

As if in answer to my question, the children's breathing stabilized, and their faces cleared.

Perhaps because the children were so large and the poison so severe, the antidote took some time to go into effect.

At last, their status in the AR display changed from **Poison/Hydra [Chronic]** to **Asleep**.

Having been poisoned for so long, their bodies were probably weakened and exhausted.

Shortly afterward, the gnome who seemed to be the attending physician confirmed with his "Analyze Person" skill that the children were no longer poisoned.

I received hugs and kisses of thanks from each of the mothers in turn, which only reminded me how much bigger they were than me.

My body got all sticky, and their busts were many sizes larger than Miss Karina's and threatened to suffocate me. The only thing I felt was that I could really use a nap.

> Title Acquired: Friend of the Giants

When the forest giants calmed down, their chief, Stonehammer, gave me his thanks.

"WE ARE TRULY GRATEFUL FOR YOUR HELP. IF THERE IS ANYTHING YOU WISH FOR, YOU NEED ONLY ASK. IF IT IS WITHIN OUR POWER, WE WILL GLADLY GRANT IT."

For a moment, Miss Karina's face came to mind, but I didn't mention her request.

It seemed inexcusable to ask the forest giants to go to a humanfolk city and drive out a hell demon when there were only ten of them. If it came down to it, it'd be easier if I put on my silver mask and took care of it myself.

"YOU SEE, A HELL DEMON IS RUNNING RAMPANT IN MY FRIEND'S HOMETOWN—"

"VERY WELL. FOR YOUR SAKE, WE SHALL GLADLY SET OUT AND FIGHT THIS DEMON."

Braidbeard cut into the middle of my sentence to volunteer. His bearded face looked truly impressive.

"NO, THAT WOULD BE FAR TOO MUCH TO ASK, I BELIEVE. I WISH ONLY TO INQUIRE IF YOU MIGHT LEND ME SOME WEAPON OR TOOL THAT MIGHT WEAKEN A HELL DEMON, IF YOU HAPPEN TO HAVE SUCH A THING?"

"IN THAT CASE, WE DO INDEED HAVE SOMETHING THAT WILL BE OF USE. IT IS KNOWN AS THE DEMON-SEALING BELL, CRAFTED LONG AGO IN THE FLUE KINGDOM. IT IS SAID A SINGLE SWING WILL REVEAL THE DEMON'S IDENTITY AND TEMPORARILY LESSEN ITS POWER."

That sounded like a good deal to me. It might be the perfect item for Miss Karina.

I felt like I'd heard the name "Flue Kingdom" before, so I checked in Storage and found the currency of that area in my spoils from the

Valley of Dragons. It wasn't the Orc Empire the old folks' leader had mentioned before.

A group of gnomes came forward with two wagons full of handbells and magic weapons.

The weapons included swords, spears, axes, and bows. My AR display informed me that they were all well made.

Along with the handbell, there was a large sword, a battle-ax, and a longbow that were leagues above my weapons in performance, except for my Holy Swords.

"CHOOSE ANY WEAPON YOU LIKE. WHILE WE CANNOT GIVE ALL OF THEM TO YOU, ANY ONE SHOULD SERVE YOU WELL."

Hmm… The sword wasn't as strong as my Holy Swords, and I wasn't really into battle-axes. But you couldn't go wrong with a long-distance physical attack, so I decided to go with the bow.

"THEN, IF I MAY, THIS SCARLET LONGBOW—"

"SO THAT IS YOUR CHOICE…," Stonehammer murmured in a voice steeped with emotion. "THE MAGIC SWORDSMAN WHO PRESENTED US WITH THAT MAGIC BOW WAS A SPRIGGAN WHO ACQUIRED IT AS PROOF HE HAD DEFEATED A POWERFUL MONSTER CALLED A FLOORMASTER."

As he spoke of the Magic Bow's history, the giant took it from the wagon and skillfully drew its string with the tip of his fingernail.

So it was a drop from a mini-boss in a labyrinth? No wonder it seemed so powerful, then.

"THIS BOW CAN PIERCE ROCK FROM A GREAT DISTANCE AWAY, EVEN HARM A DRAGON'S SCALES…"

Stonehammer released the string, and the vibration created a mysterious sound.

"AND THUS, IT CHOOSES ITS OWN MASTER."

Staring down at me with expectation in his eyes, Stonehammer handed me the bow.

"LITTLE CHILD, SATOU. LET US SEE YOU DRAW ITS BOW-STRING."

I accepted the highly decorated Magic Bow. It was made of an enchanted red metal called scarletite, with an orichalcum string that glowed gold.

When I tried giving it a light tug, the resistance surprised me.

This time, I took correct posture and drew it in earnest. I was worried that the string might break, but that turned out to be a needless concern.

When I fully drew the string and let it loose toward the sky, a buzz arose among the giants and attendants.

> **Title Acquired: Powerful Bowman**
> **Title Acquired: Magic Archer**
> **Title Acquired: Magic-Bow Master**

"ADMIRABLY DONE! THIS MAGIC BOW NOW BELONGS TO YOU."

"I WILL BE SURE TO TAKE GOOD CARE OF IT."

Stonehammer nodded with satisfaction and pointed at the bow.

"IT APPEARS THAT THE BOW HAS ACCEPTED YOU AS ITS NEW MASTER, AS WELL."

I didn't necessarily believe the giant's dramatic claim, but for whatever reason, I did notice a slight glow from the patterns on the weapon.

"IT SEEMS YOU ARE QUITE SKILLED, SATOU. I IMAGINE YOU MAY HAVE USED SOME FORM OF STRENGTH-ENHANCING SKILL, BUT NEVERTHELESS, THIS IS THE FIRST TIME IN SEVEN HUNDRED YEARS THAT ANYONE BUT A GIANT HAS BEEN ABLE TO DRAW THAT BOWSTRING."

"I NEVER IMAGINED THAT ANYONE BUT US WOULD BE ABLE TO DO IT."

The other giants praised me, too, grinning heartily.

Around then, the little giants came in with casks of wine to celebrate the children's recovery, and the conversation turned toward holding a banquet.

"WE SHALL HAVE A GREAT FEAST THIS NIGHT. LET US INVITE EVERYONE IN THE VILLAGE FOR A GRAND CELEBRATION!"

"YES!"

The giants seemed uncharacteristically excited, probably due to the children's recovery.

Though the banquet was decided suddenly, there was no shortage of participants or food from the village.

Miss Karina didn't participate, but Whitefinger brought my kids along. We sat as guests of honor at the head table next to the giants.

Amusingly, given the enormous meat, fruit, and other dishes surrounding us, we felt as if we'd been shrunk.

Tama and Pochi grinned widely as they made an impressive attack on a piece of meat that was bigger than both of them.

Apparently envious, the other kids started taking bites out of it, and soon they were smiling, too.

Of course, I joined in on the fun, laughing as we tore off big bites of the enormous hunk. It was good to cut loose once in a while.

There were a few minor accidents, too. Once, Arisa and Mia clambered around on a giant fruit, scooping out pieces, and plunged into the center. They nearly drowned in the juice.

When I mentioned between joking with the forest giants that I'd like a piece of the Mountain-Tree fruit as a souvenir, they were happy to oblige.

They were getting pretty drunk, so they cheerfully informed me that I could take half of the fruits from the top of the tree where the elder sparrows lived.

I think they were mostly joking, but they might've been serious, too.

With a small cask of high-quality liquor from Sedum City under one arm, I mingled with all kinds of people.

I learned the birdfolk language and pantherfolk language, and they told me all about their home on the eastern continent.

A small weaselfolk hunter even offered us a spare boat, so we'd be able to enjoy a trip across the lake and downriver on our way back.

In exchange for the boat, we agreed to take care of a sixty-foot-long monster called a lake snake that lived outside the barrier. My map told me it was only around level 20, which meant defeating it wouldn't reveal my power. I had no problem accepting his request.

It would take them about three days to outfit the boat, so it was decided that we'd continue sightseeing throughout the village in the meantime.

After the banquet ended, I got the dryad to transport me to the top of the Mountain-Tree, where I harvested about half the fruits, mostly the ones liable to break off and fall.

When I'd traveled about two-thirds of the way around the top of the giant tree, I remembered the kobold's mining expedition.

"Are you there, dryad?"

I knocked on the trunk of the Mountain-Tree, and the nude, green little girl appeared on top.

"What's up?"

"Sorry, but can you transport me to that nearby mountain over there?"

"Sure! As long as I can get some seconds, of course."

I pointed at the mountain where the mithril vein was, and the dryad cheerfully agreed.

Of course, she had to leech my magic supply with her lips again, but I was drunk enough that I didn't really pay it any mind.

Excavating a mining tunnel with magic alone, as I'd planned, proved unexpectedly difficult.

As I worked, I came across stones and bedrock that prevented me from using the Pitfall spell to create holes.

I put the stones away in Storage and hewed my way through the bedrock with the help of Magic Arrows and Holy Swords.

> **Skill Acquired: "Mining"**
> **Title Acquired: Prospector**
> **Title Acquired: Miner**
> **Title Acquired: Mining Engineer**

With the support of my new skills, I was able to come up with optimal methods using the tools and magic I had on hand.

In order to prevent cave-ins, I dug the tunnel in a spiral and carefully avoided accidentally digging into the wall of the tunnel. I used a warhammer to create footholds along the sides.

Then I just had to keep repeating the process.

Along the way, I found mithril, silver, and even cobalt ore. The cobalt ore was toxic, so it would be dangerous for anyone who didn't have poison resistance like me.

After an hour or so, I'd reached the cavern with the blue crystals.

And when I emerged into that hollow...

"So these are blue crystals? ...They're beautiful."

...I saw a sight so fantastic that I couldn't help murmuring to myself.

I had seen crystalline caverns in TV specials before, but rather than reflecting the light around them, these blue minerals were glowing from within.

...No, wait. It wasn't the crystals that were glowing.

I took one clump of the blue crystals and collected the glowing white light stones underneath. If I crushed these, I could create light powder, an LED-like material used in creating illumination-type magic tools.

It was a mystery why there would be light stones so deep underground.

According to my documents, they were found only in places deep in the mountains with a strong light source...

Well, I'd leave that kind of investigation to scholars.

I'd found my goal and gained an extra prize while I was at it, so I left the cavern and covered the entrance with a clearly marked rock. I'd just realized that exposing the blue crystals to air could degrade their quality.

Once I got back to the surface, I decided to build a small log cabin at the entrance to the tunnel.

With the help of my high strength stat, my "Logging" skill, and the outlandishly sharp Holy Sword Excalibur, gathering the lumber took only about five minutes. Of course, that was because Storage was excellent for transporting it.

Then, with the additional help of my "Woodworking" skill and new "Construction" skill, I completed the log cabin in no time at all. *Honestly, there should be a limit to how much cheating I can do.*

I furnished it with a desk I'd bought in Sedum City and left a paper on it with the same mark I'd drawn on the entrance to the cave. I weighted it with a blue crystal and a chunk of mithril ore.

Nobody seemed to live around this mountain, so in order to make it easier for the kobolds to find the place, I cut down a few trees and set them aflame. I took care to ensure that it wouldn't start a forest fire, of course.

"Good morning. You look unusually tired, master."

"Good morning, Lulu. I ended up working through most of the night, that's all."

It was our twentieth morning in the Muno Barony. When I returned to the Mountain-Tree banquet hall, wearing an innocent expression, Lulu's cheerful smile greeted me. She must have enjoyed herself at the banquet yesterday; that grin was enough to overcome my exhaustion from the all-nighter.

We were at the site of yesterday's feast with the people of the village. The goal was to have the leftovers as breakfast.

"You must've worked hard, master. Would you like some yellow peach juice?"

"Thank you, Lulu."

I sipped the drink Lulu handed to me, made from one of the Mountain-Tree's fruits. It was delicious and refreshing.

Just then, the younger kids returned with their plates full of food.

"Burning the midnight oil…? Don't tell me you were cavorting with giant ladies all night!"

"Mrrr, lewd."

I told them the same thing I'd told Lulu, yet somehow they managed to misunderstand.

"I didn't do anything shady; it was just normal manual labor."

I parried their baseless accusations.

That's what I get for working my ass off to protect the town from falling fruit and save the kobold race from possible extinction.

"S-Satou…"

I turned toward the voice that had called my name and saw Miss Karina. Her color was much better than yesterday. Whitefinger must have brought her here.

She stood with her hands folded in front of her, speaking quietly. A good night's sleep must have calmed her.

"After our talk, I consulted with Mr. Raka for a while, but we still have no idea what they might want us to do. Which is why…"

Then she met my gaze directly and firmly for the first time.

"I think I shall speak to Sir Stonehammer myself. If the forest giants wish for anything from the outside world, perhaps I can ask them to help me get rid of the hell demon in return. Surely there must be something they desire."

Miss Karina's bearing was determined.

"It is just as you say, Lady Karina. As long as you do not give up, a path will surely open for you."

Raka warmly encouraged her decision.

…Right, I guess she must not have heard about the poisoned children, since she wasn't here yesterday.

The other kids, who already knew, shifted uncomfortably in their seats.

I made eye contact with Arisa to silently ask, *You haven't talked to her yet?* and just as I'd expected, she shook her head.

"So I would like you to help me collect information as well, if you might."

Ah, she's back to calling me "you." What was up with the first-name treatment earlier?

"As a peddler, you are undoubtedly skilled at entering social circles, Sir Satou."

I hated to discourage Miss Karina when she was trying to be proactive, but I had to tell her, especially if I wanted to eat a tasty breakfast anytime soon.

"About that, actually… Yesterday—"

At that moment, the forest giant children came tottering over to me.

"SATOU!"

"SATOU THE HUMAN."

"THANK YOU."

Having recovered in just one night, the children showered me with thanks, picking me up gently and rubbing against me with their cheeks.

Anyone else would probably have some broken ribs after this treatment, but for me it meant only mild discomfort, so I let them do as they liked.

This continued until the forest giant mothers hurried over and instructed their children to release me.

"…W-well, it seems you've already become quite friendly."

Miss Karina raised her eyebrows at the display of affection.

At this point, I explained the events of the previous day. Once I was finished, Miss Karina pressed her hands to her cheeks and shrieked like that one Munch painting.

Now that I had revealed everything, my conscience was no longer burdened, and we all enjoyed breakfast. We paid little attention to Miss Karina's confusing mixture of joy and complaining.

Then, after breakfast, she struck up another conversation.

"Say, you, why are you able to do everything so easily?"

"I just got lucky. I happened to have the medicine they needed, and they asked what I would want in exchange, so I asked for an item that might help you achieve your goal."

I held the demon-sealing bell out to Miss Karina as I explained.

With tears welling up in her eyes, she clasped my hands, magic bell and all.

"What can the Muno Barony possibly do to thank you? Knighthood? Or perhaps…"

Miss Karina's face was approaching.

"Arisa uses Impenetrable Barrier!"

"Mm, barrier."

At that moment, Arisa and Mia dove in between us, pulling the two of us apart.

"Master, you mustn't get so close."

"Master, what is our next mission? I inquire."

Lulu and Nana tugged on my arms.

Nana was expressionless as usual, but Lulu was puffing up her cheeks in a rare bout of adorable jealousy. It was enough to make me want to whip my cell phone out of Storage and take a picture, but obviously I restrained myself.

The others were oddly quiet, so I turned to see Liza on standby with Pochi and Tama held under each arm.

Now I had to respond to Miss Karina, but I wasn't sure how...

Knighthood and aristocracy seemed like a hassle, so perhaps requesting permission to buy Magic Scrolls, like I'd done in Kuhanou County, would be best.

If I were still the same age as I'd been in my own world, maybe I'd choose the more stable route of wedding a magic-breasted beauty like Miss Karina and becoming a noble.

But, since I'd regained my youth, I would rather choose to explore and see the sights of this parallel world.

"As far as my reward, I think I'll have to ask the baron directly."

"Directly...," Miss Karina repeated, then cleared her throat with a gulp and continued in a voice as quiet as a mosquito's whine. "V-very well. I shall prepare myself, then."

She seemed to have misunderstood, but I could probably just resolve that once I met with the baron.

Looking back at everyone else, I decided it was time to focus on our main goal again.

"Now, shall we head out to tour the sights of the village?"

Miss Karina wanted to bring the bell home and defeat the demon right away, but I explained that we would have a boat. It would be faster to wait for the vessel and take it down the river, which would justify our current sightseeing trip.

If we left now, all our efforts in getting here would be in vain.

We set off triumphantly, totally forgetting that there would be nobody in the village.

Thus, we reluctantly changed our destination and took the horses near a herd of unicorns. We even spotted gjallarhorns from a distance.

According to legends, unicorns would allow only virgins to approach them, but they didn't seem to mind when I touched them for some reason.

However, they were just as moody as the legends said, so Mia and I were the only ones who managed to ride on one.

The gjallarhorns were pure white, mountain goat–looking creatures with horns that bore a strong resemblance to the Holy Sword derived from them.

They were much more vigilant than the unicorns, and they would flee even when we were so far away that only the sharp-eyed Tama and Pochi could catch a glimpse of them.

They had the race-specific inherent skills of "Short-Range Teleportation" and "Flight," so it was unlikely that we'd be able to get anywhere near them.

After that, we devoted the next two days until the boat was ready to touring the village.

We stopped by a workshop that processed fruit skins and tried our hands at textile manufacturing. There, we acquired some elastic thread made from the skin of the rubbery bouncer fruit, which Arisa and I used to make socks and underwear that were more like the modern styles we were used to.

I also tried out armor crafted from the rind of the ironshell fruit and hydra leather. Both made for light armor with excellent resistance to shock and blades, so I made some for everybody, not just the vanguard group.

For the rearguard, I designed an inner bodysuit for emergencies, which should be more than enough protection in combination with their leather armor.

As for the advance guard, their armor now had better defense than full-plate mail.

During our two days of tourism, the situation around Muno City began to change a little.

On our twenty-second day in the Muno Barony, as I did my usual morning check, I noticed an army of fifteen hundred had deployed from Muno City.

That might not sound like much, but given the low population of the territory, the number was suspiciously high.

One of the possessed knights led the group. The doppelgänger responsible for this could use Psychic Magic, which might explain why all the soldiers were under the **Frenzied** status.

Judging by the direction of their march, their goal was most likely to subdue a large band of almost seven hundred bandits who had set up a base in the large forest.

However, since the soldiers all had more bounties than the bandits they were going after, it was hard to tell who the real villains were.

The next morning was our twenty-third day in the Muno Barony.

After our daily spell-chanting practice, I took another look at what the demon was up to and noticed something strange.

There was a hell-demon doppelgänger in the goblin settlement inside the large forest, but what was really strange was the number of goblins.

Ten days ago, there had been about seven hundred and fifty of them, but now there were over twenty times more. That seemed impossible, but—maybe it was the gabo fruit? There had been a town that was mass-producing them.

And if I remembered correctly, the gabo fruit was discovered during investigations into an exploding goblin population.

If the demon had been working behind the scenes to breed them, then this number might make sense.

These goblins were starting to move toward Muno City, separating into three large armies as they did so.

And the army that would normally be protecting the city was currently in the forest, doing battle with the bandits.

The kid bandits and the old folks should be far enough out of the way to be safe, but the villages closer to Muno City could be in serious danger.

And since the demon was probably responsible for this proliferation, there was no telling whether Muno City itself would be safe behind its walls.

There were just under a hundred soldiers left in the city. Miss Karina's family was there, too, so it would probably be best to go to alert the citizens of the danger right away.

The Defense of Muno City

Satou here. When I was a kid and everyone was into ESP, what I wanted most of all was teleportation. It'd be convenient if I could use it myself, but there's nothing more annoying than an enemy who can use it.

"Go ahead, please, dryad."

That morning, after I noticed the strange occurrences around Muno City, I had everyone change into new equipment and prepare for departure, bidding a hasty farewell to the forest giants and villagers. Now, we stood inside the dryad's fairy ring.

I didn't want everyone to have to keep seeing me kiss a little girl, so I had taken care of the magic transfer beforehand.

"All righty, here we gooo."

With a lazy reply, the dryad transported us from the fairy ring inside the Mountain-Tree to one in a forest not far from Muno City.

A journey of ten days took a mere instant. This magic supposedly had its own constraints, but dryad teleportation was still way too convenient.

Like a dangerous drug, it would be all too easy to become addicted to convenience. All it cost was the taboo act of kissing a little girl.

The sudden transportation startled the horses, so I soothed them while reviewing the map.

The walls of Muno City were only three miles from here in a straight line, with harvested fields in the middle.

Muno City was almost twice the size of Seiryuu City, the first place I'd visited in this parallel world, yet its population was only half of the latter.

There was a small hill on the southeast side of the city, and Muno

Castle stood at its peak. Three layers of walls protected the castle, encircling nearly a third of the city.

As I confirmed the city's layout, I decided to check the position of the demon as well.

The demon's real body had gone all the way down to level 26. Since the new doppelgängers weren't automatically marked or anything, I had to keep an eye on the demon's level.

There were eleven new doppelgängers in total, not including the magistrate or the ones possessing the knights.

One of them was moving toward the southwest end of the territory.

He appeared to be heading for the hydra herd, perhaps gunning for an MPK-style mass slaughter.

Well, I'm always up for getting some more cooking ingredients. Hydra meat is delicious, after all.

I wasn't sure what the other ten doppelgängers were planning, but they were in position, surrounding the army from the outside.

The battle between the army and the large band of thieves had started, too; their numbers were lower than they'd been this morning.

I finished all this in a matter of seconds and closed the map.

"Wh-where are we?"

"In a forest near Muno City. Look, you can see the outer wall of the city on the other side of the bushes."

At my words, Miss Karina and the other kids turned on their horses to look where I was pointing.

"I-it's true… What exactly are you?"

"I'm just a peddler. The kindly dryad simply brought us here."

I shrugged off Miss Karina's surprise.

"More importantly, since the dryad was nice enough to give us a shortcut, let's head straight for Muno City."

"V-very well. It is just as you say. Come along, then, everyone."

Holding on to her horse's neck, Miss Karina trotted enthusiastically out of the forest.

"Karina, waaait?"

"You mustn't act on your own, ma'am!"

Apparently tempted, Pochi and Tama looked back at me inquisitively.

"Yes, let's go, too."

On my signal, everyone galloped along after her.

To be honest, I didn't want to take my kids into an area where a hell demon was wreaking havoc, but since Mountain-Tree Village could easily be invaded by hydras or fallen upon by huge fruits, I didn't feel safe leaving them there, either. And since the demon could be involved in the hydra invasions, I'd be particularly worried about letting them stay in the village.

If they'd be in danger no matter where they were, I'd prefer to have them close by so that I could keep them safe.

The Muno City guard must have noticed the goblin outbreak, or perhaps they were on the defensive because of the absence of their army, because Muno City's gates were closed.

"Open the gate! Baron Muno's daughter, Lady Karina Muno, has arrived! Open the gate at once!"

Instead of Miss Karina herself, Raka called for the soldiers on the ramparts to open the gates.

Miss Karina could be quite shy, especially toward men, so she probably had a hard time calling out to the well-built soldiers.

After about ten minutes, there was finally some movement.

The steel side gate next to the main gate swung open, and a few soldiers emerged. I could see armed soldiers on the other side. They were on high alert.

"The baron's daughter, you say? Let's see something to prove it, then."

The bearded, middle-aged soldier stared at Miss Karina with undisguised suspicion.

"Proof, you say?"

"That's right. We underling soldiers don't know the faces of the baron's family. Show me a ring or dagger or something with the family crest on it."

"How rude," Miss Karina huffed, retreating behind me to hide from the older soldier.

"Lady Karina, do you have anything of the sort?"

"Well, perhaps the clasp of my overcoat will do, then."

Miss Karina removed the fastener and handed it to me. Without it, her overcoat fell open, revealing a glimpse of her dress and the enchanting breasts underneath it.

This caused a commotion among the soldiers. Naturally, their eyes were all focused on the same area.

She truly had a magical pair of breasts. They carried incredible clout, it seemed.

"Mr. Guard, will this do?"

"…Th-this is…"

The middle-aged soldier fell speechless as he saw the coat of arms on the clasp, then kneeled to beg for forgiveness.

"P-please pardon my terrible rudeness…"

"You are forgiven," Miss Karina mumbled, taking the clasp back from me.

The enthralling breasts were once again hidden in the shadows of the cloak, raising a sigh of disappointment from the soldiers.

Following the middle-aged soldier, we led our horses through the side entrance.

Muno City's main gate plaza was very large. It was about as big as the yard of a normal school. In the center of the square was a dried-up fountain with a statue of an armored knight holding a staff and sword and riding a dragon.

There was a group of impoverished-looking people gathered on the western edge of the square, listening to a speech.

"…The revival of the demon lord is nigh! If you wish to survive the destruction and rejoice in the new world, join us in knocking on the door of freedom. This is the only way to survive the Season of the Demon Lord…"

My "Keen Hearing" skill caught some disturbing claims.

If this were my old world, I would've assumed it was a street performer or an actor practicing lines, but here it was undoubtedly a real speech that could easily be perceived as encouraging treason.

When I noticed one of the soldiers glowering hatefully at the crowd, I asked about it.

"That gathering there…"

"Yeah, it's that group of demon lord worshippers calling themselves the Wings of Freedom."

Yikes, people actually worship the demon lord? I did hear that belief in the impending apocalypse had been popular around the turn of the century back home, so I guess some things never changed no matter what world you were in.

"Are they troublemakers, then?"

"They don't really do anything bad, so they're harmless enough, but…" She hesitantly trailed off.

Another soldier behind her explained tersely, "The magistrate has instructed us not to interfere if we see them."

"…The magistrate?"

Well, if the magistrate was a demon, it would make sense that he'd be all right with demon worshipping.

"Yeah, well, the ancestral king did establish freedom of religion when this kingdom was founded."

My suspicions that the ancestral king Yamato had been Japanese were only deepening.

"Well, that's the official stance, but the real reason's probably that the guy giving these speeches is the good-for-nothing son of a leading merchant from the duchy."

This made sense, too. There were probably few merchants willing to travel to Muno City when the barony was in such a sorry state.

I checked just to be sure, but the merchant's son and his comrades didn't have any abnormal status conditions.

I felt like I should put a marker on him just in case but decided against it, since that might hinder my monitoring the demon. I added **Wings of Freedom** to my list of search keywords so that I'd be able to keep an eye on them at any time.

We proceeded to the castle with a group of six soldiers guarding our front and rear.

The city's main street was an impressive thirty feet wide, but since many of the shop fronts on either side were closed or vacant, it felt more like a ghost town than a thriving metropolis.

"Is everything on top of that hill part of the castle?"

"That's right, Arisa. In terms of size, our Muno Castle is second only to the royal palace and the castle of the old capital."

As Miss Karina and Arisa chatted, the great bastion loomed large atop the hill. I already knew all this from my map, but looking up at it from the bottom of the slope only emphasized its enormity.

When we passed through the castle gates, we proceeded up a winding ramp. There were low walls around it with narrow openings, probably for archers to ward off invaders in case of emergency.

When we came out past the second castle wall, we entered an area that was divided into several hundred-foot halls by ten-foot-tall walls.

We couldn't see where we were going, so the identically shaped halls felt like a maze. That would help rob invaders of their sense of direction.

The castle itself wasn't even visible, so soldiers working in the castle would probably feel lost, too, until they got used to it.

When we made it out of the series of connected halls, we reached a wide area that could accommodate maybe even thousands of soldiers. There were several buildings nearby, probably soldiers' barracks.

Then, after crossing a dry moat and passing through the third wall, we were able to get a full view of the castle.

The real thing was far more intimidating than numbers on a map and imparted a true sense of its enormity.

However…it was also a little run-down.

I think it must have been a beautiful white castle when it was first built, but the ivy-covered walls were crumbling in one place, and cracks ran all over it. On top of that, there were several places with what looked like scorch marks.

This was probably the result of the battle with the Undead King Zen's troops.

"Master, take a look at this, if you would."

Liza was pointing at a Magic Cannon installed in one of the towers at the corners of the castle.

The old folks at the river had said that Zen had destroyed the cannon, but the demon magistrate must have repaired it or something—as far as I could tell from below, it was in perfect working condition.

It was identical to the Magic Cannon Liza and I had found in the underground treasury of the wraith's fortress.

"Ah, you're familiar with Magic Cannons, Liza? My father had it removed when he became the lord of this territory, but the magistrate had a dummy reinstalled to maintain public order."

"A dummy…? Is it broken, then?"

"Indeed. We did take a look at it to see if it could be used to defeat the demon, but the control device had been completely gouged out. It was probably destroyed by Dark Magic or Space Magic."

Raka answered my question in Miss Karina's stead.

If the Undead King Zen was the one who destroyed it, he'd probably used Shadow Magic.

In that case, he must have actually been going easy on us when we fought in Seiryuu City. Although it had sure seemed like he was going all out with that shadow whip.

"Perhaps you could fix it, though?"

"I'm afraid that's impossible."

Miss Karina glanced at me hopefully, but I was quick to say no.

I did have the skills and materials to do so but not the machinery or equipment. Besides, if I chose to repair a weapon of mass destruction that could easily be turned on the people, and then it was actually used in battle, I wouldn't be able to sleep at night.

Arriving at the main gate of the building, we were greeted by a number of maids in simple navy-blue dresses. The soldier who'd gone ahead of us had probably let them know we were coming.

"Lady Karina! Thank goodness you're safe!"

"Yes, I'm home, Pina."

One slender maid embraced Miss Karina, celebrating their reunion.

Normally, I'd think it would be a problem for a servant to hug her master in front of guests, but nobody here seemed to mind.

As I watched the scene unfold, Tama tugged on my coat, peering up at me with mild distress.

"What is it?"

"Mmm, the ground is weeeird," Tama muttered at the floor beneath us. "Let's leeeave?"

"Tama, you mustn't bother master so much." Liza rebuked Tama, who responded by clinging to her leg and rubbing her face against it.

My "Sense Danger" and "Trap Detection" skills weren't pinging anything, so what could be scaring her?

Checking the map, I saw that there was a prison underneath us, where the demon magistrate was currently located.

Tama was probably upset because she was sensing his presence. I didn't know if that was her "Enemy Detection" skill or just her wild instincts, but I was impressed.

After a while, one of the lower-ranking maids prodded Pina to remind her of our presence. Pina apologized for her rudeness, then led us upstairs to the private room where Baron Muno was waiting.

We were invited into a hall with such a high ceiling that it was practically a ballroom.

However, it was quiet, and a partitioning screen and some furniture in one corner created a room within a room. Maybe this place was too large for someone to relax in.

As we approached the screen in the corner, we could see the baron and his companions beyond it. There was a plump middle-aged man with black hair and a mustache, a beautiful raven-haired woman with blue eyes who resembled Miss Karina, and an unnecessarily handsome young man in his twenties, all sitting on a sofa.

These were the baron, his eldest daughter, and the fake hero. I didn't even need to confirm it with my AR display.

"Father, sister, I've come home."

"K-Karina?!"

The baron exclaimed with surprise and leaped up from the sofa. Apparently word that Miss Karina was back hadn't reached them.

He must have been greatly worried, as dark bags shadowed his kindly eyes.

"Karinaaaa!!"

The baron practically tripped over himself as he rushed up to Miss Karina.

On the other hand, the eldest daughter simply remarked, "Oh my!" with bland surprise. She had the handsome fake hero help her up and walked toward us.

As she was Karina's sister, it was no surprise that her chest jiggled with each step.

This woman, who had round, soft-looking eyes, was twenty-four years old and single. Since early marriage was the norm in this world, this struck me as unusual for a noble's daughter.

The men around here must have knotholes for eyes if they'd ignore a beauty with breasts comparable to Miss Karina's.

Heedless of my amoral, wandering eyes, Miss Karina and the baron rejoiced at their reunion.

"Y-you're all right… I'm so glad you're all right…!"

The baron wailed as he hugged Miss Karina.

"Welcome back, Karina."

"Soluna, my dear sister."

Miss Soluna hugged the pair lightly, patted Miss Karina's hair, and gently admonished her with affection. "Father hasn't slept a wink with worry since you left, you know."

"…I'm sorry, Father."

Miss Karina looked to the baron apologetically.

Behind them, the false hero crossed his arms lightly and nodded along. Noticing my gaze, he shot me a dashing wink. I guess that gesture was a thing here, too.

Arisa shrieked something about her "Satou x Fake Hero OTP" behind me, so I had Lulu rebuke her. It was more effective than my telling her off myself.

Watching us with a bemused smile, the handsome fake hero amicably addressed me.

"Nice to meet you. I'm Hauto, a hero."

His name was just a slight misspelling of the actual hero's name, Masaki Hayato. Of course, he didn't have the Hero title, and while he did have skills like "Shield" and "One-Handed Sword," he was only level 7.

He didn't have any status conditions or bounties, though.

"Ah, so you're a hero, sir? I am Satou, a peddler."

"No need for the 'sir.' Just call me Hauto. An apostle gave me this Holy Sword Gjallarhorn and appointed me a hero, but I was originally just a humble farmer."

Listening to Hauto's self-introduction, Arisa muttered something quietly.

"…Gjallarhorn? The lost Holy Sword of Shiga Kingdom? The real thing?"

It was a fake, of course. I knew because I had the real thing.

The AR display called the fake **Demon Blade Gjallarhorn**, so the demon probably gave it to him, disguised as an apostle of a god.

As I chatted with the false hero until the baron settled down, I learned that he'd lived in a poor village inhabited only by the elderly until a man bathed in light appeared before him, told him that he was a hero, and bestowed upon him the Holy Sword.

Then the magistrate came to get him the next day, and he'd been training with the soldiers at the castle ever since.

In any case, it seemed like he was a good, ordinary man. Why would the demon go to the trouble of making him into a fake hero?

If you wanted to sully the name of heroes, wouldn't it be easier to use someone more corrupt as your imposter?

Wait, the demon has the "Transformation" skill, too.

Maybe it was planning to build trust in the fake hero and then disguise itself as him.

Well, whatever. No matter what the demon was planning, it wouldn't matter if I defeated him first.

Okay, well, that was a worthless conjecture. Time to think of something else.

My radar showed that the demon magistrate and one of the possessed knights would be arriving in this room any moment now.

"Something's comiiing?"

"What is, sir?"

Tama and Pochi, who were currently under Liza's arms to prevent any funny business, looked at each other.

Apparently, Tama had sensed the approach of the hell demon.

"Lulu, take Mia and Arisa and move to the side of that wall. Nana, guard them, please. Liza, Pochi, Tama, you'll be in front of Nana. Wait for my signal before you draw your weapons."

"What's going on, Satou?"

As I suddenly started giving instructions, the fake hero looked at me curiously.

Without answering him, I shucked the bag containing everyone's weapons off my shoulder and handed it to Liza.

Just then, the demonic magistrate appeared from behind the door with the possessed knight in tow.

"Lady Karina! That's him."

"Father, please stay back. Mr. Raka, Strengthening, please."

"Karina? What was that voice just now...?"

Not understanding the situation, the baron continued clinging to Miss Karina as she pulled out the demon-sealing bell from a cloth bag at her waist.

"Lady Karina, it is good to see you safe. Who might these commoners be, incidentally?"

The magistrate, a lean man with pale skin and black hair, twirled his handlebar mustache as he glanced over at us and questioned the fake hero.

Behind me, a blue light shone from Miss Karina's direction, and the baron and Miss Soluna shrieked. Most likely, she'd used her Strength Enhancement to forcibly peel the baron off her.

"Magistrate—no, demon! Your evil scheme ends here."

"Lady Karina, whatever do you—?"

"There's no use in trying to deceive me!"

Without allowing the magistrate to finish, Miss Karina raised the demon-sealing bell above her head.

The foul knight escorting the magistrate quickly cut in front of him, perhaps expecting her to throw it.

The demon-sealing bell rang out with a clear, cool sound.

"MYUWEEEEEN!" His true form revealed, the demon magistrate let out a shrill screech.

The knight, too, dropped to one knee as a semitransparent demon half rose out of his body. It quickly retreated back inside the knight, but the half that had shown itself was identical to the demon. Clearly, a doppelgänger was possessing the knight.

"Lady Karina, now!"

"Yes, I'm ready!"

Raka gave the signal, and Miss Karina charged toward the demon.

I had hoped the doppelgänger would be chased out of the knight's body first, but he was only level 1. Miss Karina should be able to handle him without a problem.

I slipped a bronze nail out of Storage into my hand.

If anything unexpected happened, I planned to use Spellblade on the nail and throw it. If I stealthily recovered it and lied that the giants had given it to me as a one-time-use trump card, it shouldn't be a problem.

With Raka's strength aiding her, Miss Karina shot toward the hellish magistrate like an arrow.

"Miss Karina, have you gone mad?!"

Alarmed by her speed and unaware that the magistrate had morphed into a demon behind him, the knight raised his kite shield to block her way.

The demon was completely hidden by the large knight's shadow.

"You are in my way, good sir!"

Miss Karina launched a flying kick at the knight's shield.

However, even if he was rotten, he was still a level-20 knight. He moved the kite shield skillfully to parry Miss Karina and launch her backward.

She rolled across the floor. Then the hell demon howled again.

I sidestepped the intrusive guard to take care of the demon magistrate in Miss Karina's stead, but he wasn't there. Instead, I saw his tail for just a moment, disappearing into the body of the knight.

Don't tell me.

"Miss Karina, the bell!"

"It's no use, Sir Satou. Lady Karina has fainted."

Since Raka was protecting her, a tumble like that shouldn't have affected her so much. The hell demon's howl must have been Psychic Magic.

Without hesitation, I ran over to Miss Karina.

The bell was probably the only thing that could drive the demon out of the knight's body.

I picked it up and waved it at the same instant as he gained control over the knight.

However, I was too late. The demon started flickering back out of the knight's body like a double, but only for a moment, and the knight's head transformed into a cluster of tentacles like a sea anemone. The knight's race had changed from **Human** to **Demon**, too. Perhaps because there were two copies of the demon, he had two tentacle heads.

Now that he had taken over the knight's body, the demon's level had changed to level 20 to match his host.

"How dare you, a little girl, ruining our plans!"

I had no idea what he was talking out of, but his anger was certainly clear.

"Demon! I will be your opponent. Satou, you must take the baron and his family and flee from this place!"

The fake hero drew his fake Holy Sword and strode toward the very real demon. His fear was obvious from his strange gait and trembling hands, though.

Still, the fake hero—Hauto did his best to smile reassuringly at us.

The demon had chosen the right man for the job. If he could just level up and get stronger, this guy had the makings of a real hero on the inside.

Well, I had no desire to let Hauto die in vain. We'd just have to be his reinforcements.

Since this thing could use only Psychic Magic, Arisa should be able to jam it.

"Liza, Pochi, Tama, take this demon down. Nana, you and I will handle his attacks."

After finishing her Body Strengthening, Nana stood before the beastfolk girls.

Even suited up in her new equipment, it wouldn't be safe to let Nana serve as the only defense against a level-20 opponent, so I joined her on the front lines.

The demon slashed with his sword, and Nana brought up her round shield to block it.

To make it easier for her, I aimed for the moment the two collided and delivered a firm kick to the demon's shield to throw off his balance.

As soon as he was still, Liza moved to strike with her spear, but the tentacles on his head blocked her.

Just then, Tama and Pochi came up behind the demon and stabbed at his feet with their short swords.

The demon could feel pain, and he swept the sword behind him to drive the beastfolk girls away.

The two of them avoided the attack, but unfortunately, it struck Hauto instead.

He rolled across the floor a way and didn't move for a moment. The wound didn't seem to be serious, though, and he stood up unsteadily and returned to the front lines with his not–Holy Sword in hand.

"Arisa, I'm counting on you to jam his magic."

"Okeydoke!"

The instant the demon started howling the beginnings of a spell, Arisa interrupted him with a chantless Mind Blow.

Nana used that opening to make a Shield with Foundation Magic, making it even easier for her to block the demon's magic attacks safely.

"Mia, please try to heal everyone. Lulu, you'll be Mia's guard. Don't use the gun."

"Mm."

"R-right! I-I'll do my best."

Mia held up a staff from the Garage Bag, and Lulu raised a frying pan in front of her chest with trembling hands.

Part of the reason I warned her not to use the gun was that I didn't want to show off a rare magic tool, but I also wanted to avoid friendly fire.

Arisa interrupted the demon's magic, Liza and Nana held him down at the front, and Tama and Pochi whittled away at the demon's health. It was our usual pattern of cooperation.

Hauto recklessly rushed in front of the demon and got his arm fractured by a tentacle attack, but Tama and Pochi rescued him before the demon could follow up, so his life wasn't in serious danger. Mia immediately started giving him first-aid treatment with healing magic.

I also made sure to ring the demon-sealing bell regularly to keep the demon weakened.

As Tama and Pochi were using mithril alloy short swords this time, the enemy's HP was disappearing more quickly than usual.

I didn't want to drag things out too long, so I occasionally helped with a few kicks on the front lines.

"Take this, sir!"

Pochi landed one last satisfying critical hit, and the demon became a cloud of black dust that sifted through the gaps in the full-plate mail.

When the powder was gone, the armor and helmet dropped to the floor and scattered.

"Gooone?"

"There's no more meat inside, sir."

"You mustn't let your guards down, you two."

A fragment of the demon had transformed into a rat scuttling out of the armor.

But Liza was still on high alert, and she immediately impaled the rodent with her Magic Cricket Spear and turned it to black dust.

"Liza's amaziiing!"

"Indeed, sir!"

Tama and Pochi praised Liza as they warily scanned their surroundings.

Just in case, I checked the log to make sure we'd defeated the demon and did another search on the map to reassure myself there weren't any more demons or doppelgängers in Muno City.

"Good work, everyone. You can stop being in battle mode now."

At my words, the beastfolk girls relaxed and put away their weapons.

"Cooore?"

"There's a core here, too, sir."

Tama had found a small stone inside the armor. Pochi picked up a tiny one near where Liza had defeated the demon rat.

So were demons considered a kind of monster?

The greater hell demon I'd defeated in Seiryuu City hadn't left a core behind, as far as I knew. I didn't remember any from the lesser one, either.

What was the difference here? Was it because I'd used a Holy Sword?

I put a lid on this unanswerable question, collected the dazed Miss Karina from the side of the wall, and brought her to the baron.

Arisa had dispelled the effects of the demon's Psychic Magic, but Miss Karina still showed no signs of opening her eyes.

"So the magistrate and Sir Eral the knight became demons? Y-you... Do you know what's going on here?"

"Nice to meet you, Lord Baron. I am Satou, a traveling merchant."

I introduced myself to the alarmed, suspicious baron, then laid Miss Karina down on the sofa.

The fact that I got to hold her princess-style certainly had its perks, but I wasn't about to revel in those in front of her family.

"All I know is what I heard from Raka and Lady Karina. Is that all right?"

"...That will be fine. Who is this Raka anyway? Is it one of these young ladies...?"

As soon as the exhausted baron shifted his attention to my kids, his gaze became a stare.

He's not a lolicon, right? What's going on?

"...Animal-eared folk? S-Sir Satou, don't tell me you're a hero, too?!"

Startled by the baron's passion, Pochi and Tama flattened their ears fearfully.

Come to think of it, Miss Karina was surprised when we first met, too.

"Just as I said, I am only a humble peddler. My comrades are not heroes, either."

I wasn't lying. I was just a peddler who happened to have the Hero title.

Not that anyone had a lie-detecting skill. Still, there could be trouble if a careless fib triggered Raka's Perceive Malice function.

"Lord Baron, I am the one known as Raka."

The baron blinked in surprise when Raka's voice issued forth from Miss Karina's pendant.

So her father didn't know about Raka. It wasn't a family heirloom?

Raka explained to the bewildered noble how he and Miss Karina had met.

The short version was Miss Karina had been walking through the ruins of Marquis Muno's villa and happened upon a hidden chamber under a floor where Raka was enshrined, thus becoming his new master.

I waited for an appropriate lull in the conversation, then redirected the topic.

"Lord Baron, may I continue?"

"Yes, pardon me. Please go on."

"Very well. If I may…"

I told the baron what I'd heard from Miss Karina.

I explained how she discovered through Raka that the magistrate was a demon, visited the Mountain-Tree Village to request help in defeating him, met us on the way, and borrowed the artifact from the forest giants.

While we were talking, some maids arrived and said a room had been prepared for us, so the baron and I sent the others ahead while we went to his office to finish our conversation.

Considering the size of the castle, the number of servants struck me as very small. Maybe he had budgetary constraints. There wasn't even a maid in the office, never mind a civil official.

When I'd finished the tale, I took a deep drink of the weak herbal tea that a maid had brought earlier.

"So that's what happened…"

"The story doesn't end there, Lord Baron. A spirit in the giants' village warned me that a great crisis is approaching Muno City."

Since I couldn't just blurt out that I'd seen it on my map, I claimed to have heard it from a "spirit"—the dryad. Raka wasn't around, so I could get away with taking a few creative liberties.

"A crisis?!"

"Yes. There has been an immense outbreak of goblins near the city. I was told that the number might well exceed ten thousand."

"Ten thousand…?!"

The blood drained from the baron's face.

Far from coming up with a plan or calling on a subordinate to do so, the baron simply stared at his feet in shock. He didn't appear terribly competent as a statesman.

Taking this into account, I tried to give an innocuous proposal.

"Forgive my arrogance, but perhaps it might be best to have the people in the nearby villages take refuge inside the city walls or evacuate them far away?"

"Y-yes, of course! That's perfect. I'll call the magistrate right—"

For a moment, the light returned to the baron's eyes with my encouragement, but he faltered again when he remembered that the magistrate had been a demon.

"Perhaps a civil official would be preferable?" I offered, and then he was able to dispatch soldiers to help evacuate the villagers safely.

I also suggested that he send out a messenger to call back the army fighting the bandits.

We would have only about half our troops to protect the city in the meantime, but there was no helping that.

"Lord Baron, there is actually a bit more to the story."

"Th-there's still more?!"

Well, I had to let him know about the demon. We'd have trouble if he thought the copies we'd taken care of were the end of the matter.

"Yes. The same spirit also told me that there are more demons than the ones we defeated earlier…"

While I spoke, I checked the demon's current position on the map. The doppelgänger heading toward the hydras' habitat had reached his destination, but other than that, there were no further changes.

However, the number of dots that indicated the soldiers and thieves was decreasing at an alarming rate. There were only four or five hundred people left—only a fifth of the initial number.

Even soldiers with no opponents nearby were getting injured.

There must be some kind of infighting.

I understood why when I checked their status conditions.

The soldiers had the **Confusion** condition. Those doppelgängers did have Psychic Magic, after all, and now they were surrounding the army.

There was no reason for me to go rescue a bunch of bad guys, but it was still upsetting to witness all those casualties.

I wanted to charge into battle and get rid of the demon once and for all, but even with my speed, it'd take at least an hour. Unfortunately, I probably wouldn't make it there in time.

I hid my frustration with the "Poker Face" skill and continued my discussion with the baron.

"The spirit told me there were sightings of multiple demons in the hydra den and the thieves' fortress in the forest."

"M-multiple demons?! …C-couldn't this be an omen of a demon lord's revival?!"

A demon lord? I certainly hoped not.

I checked the map just to be safe, but I didn't see anyone in the territory with the title Demon Lord, "Unknown" skills like Arisa, or anything like that. But the blank area where the demons had been hanging about was right below the baron's castle—

$$* \qquad * \qquad *$$

"The ground is weeeird?"

I remembered what Tama had said when we'd entered the castle.

At the time, I'd assumed she meant the demon magistrate that was in the prison beneath us, but...he didn't have a demon lord egg or something rolling around down there, right?

"Lord Baron, I was also warned to 'beware the basement.' Would you happen to have any idea what that might mean?"

I casually left out the part about who'd given me this advice.

"When this was the marquis's castle, the Undead King Zen laid a curse on the City Core in the basement... Perhaps it's referring to that."

...Listen, old man. Don't go blabbing about the City Core in front of a random outsider! That's supposed to be a big secret known only to lords!

I bit back an outburst with the help of my "Poker Face" skill and took a deep breath to calm myself.

The baron seemed unaware of the faux pas, so I pretended not to have heard it and carried on.

"So there is a curse?"

"That's right. If any nobles or other ambitious folks set foot in the basement, they'll be afflicted by a curse that will gradually sap their strength and energy until they eventually die."

"Wouldn't it be best to have a priest without ambitions remove the curse, then?"

I assumed they'd tried that already, but I was pursuing the subject out of curiosity.

"When I became the lord of this land, I asked the holy woman and head priestess of the Tenion Temple to do so, but even they could only make it halfway down the staircase before it became too much to bear."

I assumed the curse had dissipated once I set Zen's soul to rest, and even if not, I would probably immediately get a "Curse Resistance" skill as soon as I set foot on the stairs and would make it down to the basement easily enough.

I bet this "holy woman" was a pure and beautiful lady, though. Once I reached the old capital, I would have to get a look at her, even if it was from far away.

"In that case, how about letting a civilian soldier or civil official go investigate?"

"Impossible. I once had the bravest of all the commoners in the territory, Sir Zotol the knight, investigate, but…he only made it halfway down before he was overcome with panic and fled. An ordinary civil official couldn't even approach the stairs."

I see. So nobles and priests were met with a Drain curse, while commoners would experience Fear.

Hmm? Wait, so commoners can become knights? …Well, that doesn't matter right now.

"I set out toward the basement myself at the time of my inauguration, but I was overwhelmed with terror and fled back upstairs."

…What? So the baron didn't have control of the City Core?

I opened the map to look at his status, and I found that unlike Count Kuhanou, he didn't have the Lord title.

Maybe the reason the territory was suffering from a drought was that they couldn't use the Ritual Magic provided by the City Core.

I checked the path to the City Core on the map. It was unguarded.

I still had Miss Karina's demon-sealing bell, too. It wouldn't hurt to check it out. I could even take a stab at lifting the curse while I was at it.

Anyway, all that aside, there was still nobody here who could keep the people of the city from panicking when the demon led the goblins here to attack.

Arisa could probably use her Psychic Magic and generally charismatic nature to calm the public, but that would be a last resort.

Right, what happened to the original magistrate before the demon took his place?

Did the demon possess and kill him, like that Sir Eral guy?

I searched for **magistrate** on the map but didn't find anything in the territory, so I asked the baron about it.

"Lord Baron, do you have any idea of where the real magistrate might be?"

"The magistrate… Right, that was that old fellow, I believe. No, wait, he passed away during the epidemic three years ago. So I asked the duke to dispatch a suitable replacement, I think…"

The baron searched his memories. Apparently, he couldn't remember the magistrate's name, as if the information had been erased.

I couldn't say for sure, since the AR display didn't show any abnormal status conditions, but my hypothesis was that the demon tampered with his memories using Psychic Magic. I'd have to ask Arisa about this later.

They probably wouldn't appoint a commoner as magistrate, so I searched for nobles on the map.

Other than the baron's family, there was only one noble in Muno City.

"Are you familiar with someone by the name and title of Viscount Nina Lottel?"

"Nina... Nina the Iron-Blooded? Yes, I know of her. Duke Ougoch sent her to our territory three years ago as a prospective replacement magistrate..."

The baron answered my question smoothly. Then he blinked, and his expression stiffened.

A viscount to be the baron's magistrate?

I thought viscount was a higher rank than baron... Well, whatever.

"...That's right. Where is Miss Nina? I do remember holding her hand and asking her to take the old man's place... When was that...?"

"Most likely, the demon has erased your memories. If Lady Nina is alive, perhaps she is imprisoned?"

On my words, the baron leaped out of the room, hurrying downstairs to rescue Miss Nina.

There were also priests and people with the "Analyze" skill among the prisoners, so if he freed them as well, that should improve our chances in battle.

I took another glance at the battleground as the baron rushed out of the room, only to find that the army and the band of thieves had been annihilated completely, much earlier than I'd predicted.

I was tempted to take off and eliminate the demons myself, but if one of the flying pests got past me and put my kids in danger, it'd be a serious problem.

It was probably better to let the opponent get closer so I could easily return to the city if needed.

It was a little frustrating to wait for the enemy to take the initiative, but I couldn't fly through the sky or teleport around like some omnipotent hero of legends. I had to keep my priorities in order.

◆

I wasn't sure whether to follow the baron, but it was possible I could help him take control of the City Core. I sallied forth to the basement stairs that would lead me underneath the castle.

The ornate gate in front of the stairs wasn't locked, so I opened the door normally and ventured inside.

And as soon as I set foot on the first step…

> **Skill Acquired: "Curse Resistance"**
> **Skill Acquired: "Drain Resistance"**
> **Title Acquired: Saint**

The Saint title must be because I withstood the curse?

Well, whatever. I maxed out the two resistance skills and descended.

Each step sent a cold chill down my spine. If this was what it was like with my skills, no wonder ordinary people couldn't handle it.

My radar display changed when I was about halfway there, so I used "Search Entire Map" to investigate, but there was only one room at the bottom of the spiral staircase, not a single human or demon to be found.

The solitary room was a dome with a radius of about one hundred and fifty feet, and over a short platform in the center hovered a twenty-sided, luminous blue crystal.

The AR display designated it as **City Core: Muno**.

The passage to the core was a wide, short set of stairs; except for this pathway, the rest of the area was threaded with waterways where clear water smoothly flowed over glowing blue stones.

The gentle burble of cool water and the soft, steady beat of the City Core had a soothing effect as I traveled along the passage.

When I'd gotten about halfway across, a semitransparent black shadow rose from the floor in the middle of the hallway.

"Intruder. I am a shadow of he who is known as the Undead King Zen. If you be truly pure and noble of heart, show me that you are worthy of being a lord."

Uh, I'm not a lord, though.

The AR display gave its name as **cursed soul**. This was probably the essence of the curse, then.

I changed my title to Hero and took out the Holy Sword Gjallarhorn from Storage. This was the Holy Sword I'd inherited from the Undead King Zen and used to send him on to the afterlife.

"Zen has passed on to the next world. That means your role here is done, too."

I raised the Holy Sword above my head as I spoke to the cursed remnant of its creator.

The Holy Sword Gjallarhorn sliced through the shadow in a trail of blue. As soon as the sword touched it, the soul began to fade away.

I never really found out whether I'd proven myself as a lord or not, but the soul's expression during the exorcism was peaceful, just like Zen's.

With that, my work was done. Still, I was already here, so why not take a closer look at the City Core?

"Welcome, O king, ruler over a superior territory. Do you wish to register this land as a satellite city?"

As soon as I walked up to the floating core, a voice issued forth from it. The heavy echoes made it difficult to tell which gender it belonged to.

> **> Title Acquired: King**
> **> Title Acquired: Nameless King**
> **> Title Acquired: Hero King**
> **> Title Acquired: Lord**

Who are you calling a "king"?

I mentally snapped at whoever was responsible for the system messages appearing in my log.

The titles Nameless King and Hero King probably came from my blank name and currently equipped Hero title respectively.

This "superior territory" thing must have been about the Valley of Dragons mana source. The strongest dragon god once ruled it, after all.

"No, I'm not registering anything. The lord of this city is Baron Muno."

"Search completed. There are three individuals in this land by the name of Muno. Please clarify."

With the help of the map, I found the baron's name.

"Mr. Leon Muno."

"Registration completed. Henceforth, I shall serve Lord Leon Muno."

"Great, thank you."

"Acknowledged, O unnamed king."

It was getting stuffy down there, so I waved good-bye to the core and returned to the surface.

Of course, I changed my name and title back to normal when I returned to the Muno Barony territory.

Once I was back upstairs, I continued monitoring the doppelgängers on the map.

The demon had fused back with his doppelgängers to reach level 36 and was now at the battlefield of the soldiers and thieves with one possessed knight and fifteen wraiths.

As I watched, zombies began appearing around the wraiths.

This must be the effect of "Create Servant," a race-specific ability of the wraiths.

A bunch of monsters had entered the vast stretch of cultivated land in front of Muno City, so I decided I would cremate the lot of them with a barrage of Fire Shots. As long as I did it under cover of nightfall, nobody should find out my identity.

The farthest doppelgänger was still prowling around the hydra den.

Most likely, his goal was to possess a hydra. Well, a bigger target would just be that much easier for me to take down.

The goblins had regrouped and were advancing toward Muno City in three large squadrons.

Demi-goblin lords and demi-goblin tamers had started to appear among them; the goblins might have been raising their levels with cannibalism.

Their names sounded impressive, but they were only level 10 at best, so I should be able to take them all out at once. If they kept this pace, they would arrive before sundown.

◆

"Are you Satou?"

A maid had guided me to a room where a woman in her early thirties sitting up in bed greeted me. Her rugged appearance would be more accurately described as "cool" rather than "beautiful."

The baron was perched in a chair next to the bed.

I was the only one who'd been summoned there, by the way. Since the goblins would be showing up soon, my kids were busy checking their weapons and armor.

"Sorry you have to see me like this. I'm Nina, the magistrate."

"Nice to meet you. I'm Satou, a traveling merchant."

The baron had told me that she'd been imprisoned for almost two years, but her eyes were bright with resolve despite her sunken cheeks, and her husky voice sounded strong. Considering her nickname was "the Iron-Blooded," she was obviously stout of heart.

I wasn't sure why the demon hadn't killed her, but he probably had some evil purpose for it.

"I heard you and your vassals defeated the demon that was nesting in our castle. Thank you." Miss Nina ducked her head. "So, is it true there are still more demons about?"

"Yes, that is what I was told."

"I see… Man, if we could use that thing, we could beat 'em without a problem, but…"

At first, I thought she meant the City Core, but apparently, she was referring to the Magic Cannon on the turret.

Just then, a messenger came rushing into the room.

"I have a report, sir! A huge horde of goblins has just been sighted on the edge of the forest!"

"Is it only goblins?"

"They appear to be riding praying mantis monsters, and there was an unidentified quadruped with a cylindrical body among their number, sir."

I already knew that thanks to my map, of course, but I couldn't reveal that here.

The goblins were accompanied by a level-27 monster called a rock shooter, which had four legs and the girth of a four-ton truck, as well as some soldier mantises with levels in the upper teens.

The rock shooter had merely been possessed earlier, but now it had been taken over entirely, as its race had changed to **Demon**. Its only skill was Psychic Magic, so it was probably merely hosting one of the doppelgängers.

Just to be sure, I checked for any other monsters or creatures under the demon's control in the area.

The remaining possessed knight had lost his body completely and become a demon knight. He was leading a horde of zombies this way. They moved surprisingly quickly, but it would probably still take an hour or two for them to reach the edge of the forest.

The farthest doppelgänger had finally succeeded in possessing a hydra and was flying toward Muno City with two more hydras in tow. They still had a long way to go, but at this rate they would arrive around the same time as the demon knight and the zombies.

It would be wise to start with the rock shooter and the demon knight, then dispose of the hydra hosting the main demon.

I had to be careful of the order of attack, or else the demon might switch out with a doppelgänger just as I was about to defeat him.

Miss Nina sent a messenger to the garrison soldiers and asked the civil official, a young woman waiting anxiously in the next room, to speak to the bureaucracy of the territory.

"I'm going to the observation room. You there, help me out."

I carried Miss Nina up to the top of the castle.

The baron's daughters, Hauto, and the kids had all finished checking their arms and assembled there. They were talking and pointing at something past the city gate.

As if to reflect everyone's anxiety, clouds had gathered to obscure the sun.

"Satou."

"Masterrr?"

Mia and Tama were the first to notice my arrival and turned toward me.

"Black things are swarming out of the forest, sir!"

Pochi, who'd climbed onto the fence around the observation room, pointed toward the forest as she made her report.

"I'm impressed you could see them from so far away."

"Soluna let me borrow her longpoke, sir."

Apparently even Pochi couldn't make out figures more than four miles away, so they'd used a telescope-like magic tool called a "longscope."

Miss Nina snatched the longscope from Miss Karina, observing for herself the horde of goblins emerging from the forest.

"There's so many..."

Miss Nina passed the longscope to the baron, who looked through it and gulped.

Coming to a decision, the baron handed me the longscope as he spoke.

"Lady Nina. I am putting you in charge of this situation."

That sounded like passing the buck to me, but the baron's expression was serious, so everyone waited in silence for him to continue.

"I—I am going to claim control of the room in the basement. That is my duty as a l-lord."

The baron's voice trembled as he finished speaking.

Miss Nina seemed to be the only one who understood the situation, as his daughters just responded with confusion.

"...If it isn't possible, turn back right away," said Miss Nina.

Encouraged, the baron headed toward the basement, accompanied by a maid.

Miss Soluna tried to follow him, but Miss Nina stopped her.

As I saw the baron off, I noticed something strange on the map.

Miss Nina asked a different maid on standby in the room to arrange a lifeline and bell to facilitate the baron's safe return. If the sound of the bell stopped, a manservant would be waiting at the entrance to the basement to pull the lifeline.

Once she'd finished giving these instructions, I approached her.

"Lady Nina, pardon me, but I have a question..."

"What is it?"

"Did you order an evacuation out of the city?"

"...What are you talking about?"

Miss Nina accepted the longscope from me to survey the entrance to the city.

"The main gate of the outer wall is open?"

A few high-ranking government officials and military officers were gathered near the gate, along with their families.

They were escaping from Muno City with an escort of soldiers along the main road toward the Ougoch Duchy.

There were no soldiers at the open gate, leaving Muno City completely defenseless against the goblin horde rushing toward it.

"This simply won't do. We must go and close the gate!" Miss Karina cried.

"Karinaaa?"

"It's dangerous to go alone, sir!"

Miss Karina rushed out of the room, and Tama and Pochi looked to me pleadingly.

"Let me go! I shall protect your sister, Lady Soluna."

"You mustn't, Hauto. You're injured, aren't you?"

Hauto brandished the fake Holy Sword in one hand.

True, his injured arm would probably be a hindrance. I handed him a good-quality lesser recovery potion to fix the bone fracture and went to protect Miss Karina myself.

"Sir Hauto, please protect Lady Soluna and Lady Nina. We'll take care of the rest."

"...All right. Make sure Lady Karina is safe."

Hauto gripped my hands fervently. I nodded at him and the others, then left the room with my kids.

Lulu came along, too, of course. She was bad at combat, but it'd probably be more dangerous to leave her at the castle.

While we galloped on horseback down the main street, a stampede of townspeople came rushing toward us, meaning the goblins had invaded.

If Mia used the Balloon spell to push them aside, someone would probably get hurt.

"Arisa, I'm counting on you."

"Okeydoke! ...*Repellent Field Kihi Kuukan!*"

Once Arisa's Psychic Magic had done its work, the fleeing citizens gave us a wide berth as if we were repugnant to them.

With a clear line of sight, we could see Miss Karina fighting alone and a handful of citizens who'd been caught and pushed down by goblins.

Countless monsters surrounded Miss Karina, but Raka's powerful protection and Strength Enhancement kept her from being overwhelmed, so her tremendous bust was as peerless as ever.

Up close, the goblins looked like the devils you might see in a painting of hell, with hairless black skin and green blood that made for a truly monstrous presence.

Despite being humanoid, they didn't seem to have language, since hearing their gurgling shrieks didn't net me a new linguistic skill.

Since they were monsters not demi-humans, there was no point in holding back.

"Mia, Tama, take aim. These guys are monsters, not people. It's okay to kill them."

"Mm."

"'kaaay."

I left the reins to Lulu, who was riding the horse with me, and started firing my short bow at the goblins.

Since it was a very wide street and Arisa's magic was funneling the civilians into certain escape routes, it was easy to take aim.

"Everyone! Flee to the castle!" Arisa shouted as loudly as she could with her little lungs to direct the citizens. "The great hero is there! He'll protect you!"

The citizens seemed perplexed at first, but as soon as they heard about the hero, they started sprinting in small groups toward the hilltop.

"Karinaaa!"

"We're here to help, ma'am!"

"You came…"

Miss Karina grew emotional at the sight of her reinforcements, but now wasn't really the time for that.

"Liza! Let's trample these goblins and push them back toward the gate," I called.

"Understood! Pochi, Tama, Nana, let's go."

"Aye-aye, siiir!"

"Roger, sir!"

"Orders registered, I report."

The vanguard team joined forces with Miss Karina and started to run the goblins down.

I advanced with the rearguard team, shooting down any escapees from the first group.

We did see a bloodied citizen or two, but they had family members lending a shoulder to help them escape.

At the castle, there were priests who had been freed from the prison, plus the maids. Everyone should be able to get treatment there.

We joined up with the soldiers in front of the main gate, working together to take down the rest of the invaders.

The goblins were pretty weak, so we were able to claim the gate within about a half hour without any major incidents.

"Mia, now!"

"…■ ■ ■ ■ ■ *Balloon Kyuubouchou!*"

A new squadron tried to charge the gate, but Mia's magic created green steam that pushed them back.

The vapor was the blood of the previous goblin invaders.

"Close the gates!" I called.

"Understood!"

"Aye-ayeee!"

"Raah, sir!"

I joined Miss Karina and the vanguard team in helping to lock the main gate.

It creaked shut with a heavy *thud*, and the nearby soldiers operated the crank to lock the gate.

These troops had seen the goblins invading and rushed over from other lookout towers.

"All right, the crank is turned. No need to push anymore, lads!"

We caught our breath, surveying the corpses of a hundred or more goblins in front of the main gate.

Some of my kids had light injuries, so I put Lulu and Mia in charge of treating them, then ascended the main gate tower with Miss Karina and Arisa.

The five soldiers at the top were shooting arrows at their enemies with a look of desperation.

"There are quite a lot of them, aren't there?"

"I'd say so."

"Geh, I feel like I'll be seeing this in my nightmares."

Beyond the great gate was a clamoring black throng so thick that the ground couldn't be seen under them. It was like something out of a horror movie.

"Given how crowded together they are, couldn't that catapult take out tons of them at once?"

"Afraid not."

I pointed at the catapult and spoke to a soldier, but he answered brusquely.

"We don't have any stones for it."

"You didn't replenish the stores?" Miss Karina asked. "Whyever not?"

"The magistrate said there wasn't a budget for it… We ran out of heavy quarrels for the ballista during that swarm of spiderbears not long ago, too."

The soldier responded to Miss Karina's interrogation with barely suppressed anger.

Apparently, the demon magistrate had been busy preparing for the attack on Muno City.

Well, no point in shaking a fist at it now. I used my item search on the map to find large quarrels and stones in Muno City.

All right, this should work.

My kids had finished their medical treatment and were coming up the stairs, so I gave them their next instructions.

"Nana, I need you to run an errand for me, please. Behind that building with the red roof is a company that deals in weapons. They should have a lot of ammo for the ballista. Make sure they have normal arrows, too."

I took out a bag stuffed with gold coins from under my coat and handed it to Nana as I spoke.

"Master, I do not have a telescopic sight unit equipped, so I cannot acquire a visual lock on the red roof, I report."

"I can see it, sir!"

"All right, then please go with Nana, Pochi."

"Yes, sir."

Pochi and Nana ran off to buy the arrows.

"Liza and Tama, head to the stone wholesaler near the outer wall. You should be able to get plenty of good rocks for the catapult there."

"Understood. Let's go, Tama."

"Aye-aye, siiir!"

I gave Liza and Tama another bag of money, and they rushed down the stairs.

"Lulu and Arisa, can you find out if we can use the nearest inn as a hospital in case anyone is seriously injured?"

"Okeydoke!"

"Certainly, sir."

Arisa and Lulu pattered off after the other kids.

"Mia, I'll have you stay here and help me make sure the goblins don't get any closer."

"Mm."

Mia and I set out to shoot down the goblins attempting to climb the outer wall.

"Whoa, you guys are good. You never miss the mark…"

One of the soldiers whistled in admiration.

Whoops, did I go overboard? I should try and miss once every five shots or so.

"E-excuse me. What, erm… What might I do to be of use?"

Miss Karina looked at me a bit timidly. It was hard to believe that the brave heroine who'd charged in to rescue the townspeople was the same girl gazing at me like a lost child now.

"Oh right. Lady Karina, you should go back to the castle—"

"N-no, I shan't! I shall fight here as well!" Miss Karina immediately cut me off.

"…Please let me finish. I'd like you to go back to the castle and gather Sir Hauto and any others who might be able to fight and bring them here."

"…Me?"

"That's right. This is something only you can do, Lady Karina."

"I—I know that. I'll be off, then!"

With that, Miss Karina jumped down from the building and broke into a run with a blue glow in her wake.

This girl is way too reckless. I get that she can run quickly with Raka's Strength Enhancement, but wouldn't it be faster to go by horse?

An hour had passed since we closed the gates, and our defensive capabilities had considerably improved.

The kids brought back plenty of heavy quarrels, and Hauto arrived with a recruited civilian militia of about two hundred. Maids equipped with the possessions of former soldiers accompanied Miss Karina.

In addition, Arisa used her Psychic Magic to buff everyone with Brave Heart Field, so morale would stay high even in the face of overwhelming odds.

Of course, Hauto, who was at the forefront encouraging the troops despite his own trembling, played a big part in this as well.

Outside, the goblins tried again and again to climb over the wall by using one another, but each time we successfully repelled them, often by using boiling oil.

On top of that, we snuck in Arisa's Fear spell whenever possible to scare them back and caused them to attack one another with Confusion.

Nobody else could tell, but Arisa was a remarkable help in this defensive battle. I'd have to cook her favorite food or something later as thanks.

As for me, I wanted to slip away and disguise myself as the

silver-masked hero to go defeat the demons as soon as possible, but I couldn't seem to find a good opportunity.

The demons and their reinforcements would arrive within a half hour, so I would have to make a chance for myself soon…

"What's thaaat?"

"A tube, sir?"

Tama and Pochi were pointing to a cylindrical four-legged monster that had appeared about half a mile away—the rock shooter that the demon had taken over.

My "Sense Danger" skill started tingling faintly.

…A white light shone on the horizon.

Just as the howling wind reached my ear, an intense vibration shook the castle.

"Satou."

"Geh!"

I supported Mia and Arisa as they lost their balance, then tried to figure out what had happened.

Looking down from the observation room, I saw a rock about the size of a basketball sticking out of the wall. The projectile must have come from the rock shooter.

It wasn't strong enough to bring down the ramparts in a single blow.

In the distance, I could see goblins reloading the rock shooter.

You think I'm gonna let you do that?

I loaded a heavy quarrel into the ballista and aimed it upward.

"It's no use. That's never going to reach that far!"

As the soldier shouted at me, my "Shooting" skill also informed me that it would never reach its target at this rate.

My longbow was a normal weapon, so it would shoot only up to about a thousand feet away, maybe fifteen hundred feet if precision didn't matter.

So there's no way it will hit an enemy almost half a mile away…

Another attack from the rock shooter hit the main gate, shaking the building above it where we stood.

"Satou?"

Mia looked up at me nervously, so I smiled back.

…but that's only if I'm shooting normally.

I invoked the spell Blow from my magic menu, creating a strong tailwind around the building above the gate.

Then, I fired seven arrows into the wind in rapid succession.

With help from the strong air currents and my "Shooting," "Sniping," and "Aim" skills, the arrows hit their marks on the rock shooter's three eyes and front legs, one after another.

Since the sudden gale had knocked the soldiers on top of our tower off balance, they probably hadn't seen anything.

Angered by the pain, the rock shooter readied to fire its next shot, but with its front legs buckling, it couldn't get a high-enough angle.

Instead, the missile just scattered a bunch of goblin archers and rolled to a stop on the ground.

Perfect. We shouldn't have to worry about the rock shooter for a while now.

Meanwhile, the goblins on my radar had started crossing beyond the gate. The second shot had blown a hole big enough for goblins to come through.

Nana and the beastfolk girls had already run down from the tower to easily defeat the goblins pouring in through the gap.

Since the defense tower's stockpile of magic recovery potions had run out, I sent Arisa to Lulu, who was on standby at the inn, to replenish our stores.

"Mia, go down there, too, and cover them, please."

"Mm."

Mia nodded and headed down the stairs.

On the other side of the catapult, Miss Karina was using Raka's Strength Enhancement to hurl boulders at the goblins, but when she saw us, she paused to give orders to the maids guarding her.

"You all ought to go and help Liza and the others, too."

"But Lady Karina!"

"That is an order."

The armed maids left Miss Karina's side to help get rid of the goblins.

"I shan't let you set one foot inside this tower!"

More goblins clambered over one another in an attempt to enter our base, but Miss Karina warded them off using more stones.

With all the goblins she was defeating, Miss Karina's level had risen from 5 to 7, and judging by her EXP bar in the AR display, she'd be hitting 8 before long.

"Miss Karina, please stop and take a break soon."

"I assure you, I am perfectly fine. If anything, you're the one who ought to take a—"

Miss Karina suddenly dropped to one knee. As I'd expected, this was a symptom of level-up sickness. It wasn't a disease or anything, and she would be back to normal after a few hours of rest.

As I looked after Miss Karina, who seemed distressed by the sudden drop in her physical capabilities, a group of militiamen arrived with more ammunition.

"We've brought stones for the catapult, sir."

"Pile them up over there, please."

I sat Miss Karina against the wall to take a breather, then turned toward the militia.

The guy in the very back of the group of three men looked familiar...

The corner of his mouth curled up in a sneer under the shadow of his helmet as he withdrew a dagger from beneath his clothes.

The demon lord worshipper who was giving a speech in the plaza!

I could've easily knocked the man out before he drew his dagger, but for now, I pretended not to see anything.

"Death to all who bear the blood of Muno!"

The demon lord devotee readied his poisoned dagger before his chest, then charged toward Miss Karina.

I quickly stepped in front of him and took the blow from the assassin's dagger in her stead—or made it look like I had, anyway—then tossed the man to the ground and relieved him of his weapon.

The bright-red liquid that sprayed into the air was animal blood that I'd had in Storage for use in magic potions.

The other two militiamen who'd come up with the would-be assassin quickly pinned him down.

"Satou! Hold still, I shall suck the poison out at once."

Miss Karina dragged her weakened body toward me. I pretended to stagger away, leaning against the wall on the city side.

"Bwa-ha-ha, you'd do well to suck it up! That dagger was coated in deadly hydra poison. It's toxic enough to kill people on contact! Suck the poison out and you can die along with him!"

...Is hydra poison the latest fad right now or what?

Oblivious to my bemused reaction, the man cackled maniacally to accompany his unnecessary exposition.

Well, the other two militiamen could probably take it from here.

I fell over the wall from the tower, busting through the ceiling of the barn below and landing in a pile of hay, scattering it everywhere.

"Master!"

Liza burst through the wall of the stable at tremendous speed.

Startled by her unexpected behavior, I nonetheless gave her an order.

"Liza, carry me to the inn where Lulu's on standby, please."

"Of course, sir."

Carrying me bridal-style, Liza brought me to a room at the inn at the speed of a gale-force wind.

"M-master, are you all right?!"

"Oh... Oh no..."

There were other people in the room besides Lulu and Arisa, so I whispered in Liza's ear and had her clear the room.

Once everyone else was gone, I confessed to the three girls that it was only an act.

"Sorry if I alarmed you. I'm perfectly fine."

"D-don't ever scare us like that again!"

"Th-thank goodness..."

I assumed Liza's silence was because she was angry, so I turned toward her, only to find that huge tears were pouring down her cheeks.

Hugging her gently, I murmured an apology in her ear.

"I'm sorry, Liza. I didn't mean to worry you."

I explained the reason behind my act to the three of them and asked them to back up my alibi.

"Lulu, take this."

"Is this...a monster-repellent Holy Stone?"

"Yeah, I want you to activate it here. That way, even if the worst happens and the enemy breaks through, the effect will make the goblins reluctant to come into the city."

I handed the Holy Stone and the Garage Bag to Lulu as I explained. It wasn't glamorous, but it was still important work.

"I'm counting on you, Lulu."

"Right! I'll do my best!"

Lulu nodded intently, so I patted her black hair and stood up from the bed.

"B-but fighting a demon on your own? That's insanity!" cried Arisa.

"Not for our master," Liza said. "I may have become distraught earlier, but I trust that he can handle it."

"Wh-what makes you so sure?"

Liza looked to me uncertainly, so I nodded my permission.

"Because I saw him defeat a giant hydra, which had destroyed a fortress, in a single attack. Truly, the only enemy that might pose a threat to master might be a dragon or a demon lord."

"...A-are you really that strong?"

"Yeah. So don't worry. Just wait here for the good news."

"A-all right, then. But don't get hurt, okay? I don't want to see a single scratch on that pure young skin of y—"

A little too reassured, Arisa started to say something stupid, so I bonked her on the head.

"Good luck, sir."

"Please be safe, master."

I nodded to the other two, put on the silver mask, and headed into a back alley.

As I left the room behind, I heard Tama and Pochi enter. Nana and Mia had come along behind them, too.

Mentally apologizing to everyone for worrying them, I set about changing my title, name, and equipment.

Now, time to be a hero.

I sprang over the outer wall on the southwest side, cutting through the left flank of the five-thousand-goblin army.

Running up a hill, I jumped into the air.

Using the Blow spell, I created a gust that sent me several thousand feet higher.

> Title Acquired: Free Floater

"Time to burn."

I created a barrage of Fire Shots from the magic menu, surrounding the goblins and torching them with each blast.

After six rounds, I'd burned up about 20 percent of the left flank and created a wall of fire that prevented the rest of them from escaping.

The demon wasn't anywhere in this group.

I didn't need to annihilate them, but it would be good to reduce their numbers as much as possible.

As I dashed between the outer wall of Muno City and the left section of the troops, I tossed more Fire Shots into the ring of flames.

A demi-goblin mounted on a soldier mantis came leaping toward me over the wall of flame.

I used Short Stun to smash through the mantis's wings, knocking the pair into the fire.

Sorry, but I don't have time to mess around with small-fry.

I crossed two miles of the battlefield at a speed of two hundred miles per hour, setting my sights on the demon that was fused with the rock shooter.

The creature was still about half a mile away, but my Magic Arrow spell should still reach at this distance.

A full-powered salvo of one hundred twenty enchanted bolts pummeled into the demon rock shooter.

The monster filled with holes even faster than the hydra I'd killed at the fortress had.

But though it was now falling apart, the thing still wasn't dead.

This must be the effect of its "Lesser Magic Resistance" skill.

Well, in that case...

I took a steel short spear out of Storage and flung it.

The spear bored a huge hole right through the thing's flank, but it still wouldn't die.

Right... Zena had said in Seiryuu City that only magic or magic weapons could hurt demons.

Thinking back, when we beat the demon magistrate before, we hadn't been using ordinary weapons.

Rushing up to the demon rock shooter, I cut it down with the Holy Sword Excalibur.

Despite how stubborn it'd been before, a single touch from Excalibur was enough for it to crumble to black dust in no time flat. Leave it to a Holy Sword.

Seeing that I'd defeated the demon, the nearby goblins began to flee into the woods.

All the unharmed goblins from the left flank saw this and started running away, too.

At the same time, the undead monsters under the demon knight's command emerged from the forest right where the fleeing goblins had been.

The demon knight swung his sword, and immediately the horde of undead began rushing this way.

Personally, I refused to accept zombies that can run, but it wasn't surprising given how quickly they'd marched here.

Before they got any closer, I decided to reduce with magic the number of the bolting monsters.

Just as I opened my magic menu, I felt a series of vibrations from inside the large forest.

I could see the foliage shaking. Closing the magic menu for a moment, I opened my map, and…

…knocking the trees about like twigs, an enormous human figure emerged onto the battlefield.

"TALLY-HO!"

…*Huh?*

The ground shook as the forest giant jumped into the fray, cutting swathes in the horde of goblins with his giant battle-ax.

A group of demi-goblin knights mounted on soldier mantises boldly rushed toward him, but a single swing of his battle-ax lopped off the head of one of the mounts and sliced its rider in two.

The one charging into battle with an enormous, Spellblade-lit ax was none other than Braidbeard the forest giant.

He must have run here all the way from the Mountain-Tree Village to back us up.

"THANK YOU FOR COMING, LORD BRAIDBEARD."

"IF ONE IS TO BE THANKED, IT IS SATOU THE HUMAN."

Three more forest giants lined up next to Braidbeard and began exterminating the imps.

"I'LL LEAVE THE GOBLINS TO YOU, THEN. I'M GOING TO TAKE ON THE UNDEAD MONSTERS."

Without waiting for Braidbeard's reply, I began roasting the undead with Fire Shots.

Armed with a lance, the demon knight charged straight at me. He had somehow taken over the horse as well as the knight he was possessing.

I attacked the demon with Magic Arrow. I'd expected the assault to tear him apart, but that didn't happen.

The demon knight had blocked my attack with his shield. According to the AR display, the buckler was called a **Screaming Shield**; a relief of a human face was embossed into the surface.

I tried coming at it with Fire Shot instead, but the shield deflected that, too.

Well, if magic wouldn't work, I'd have to get physical.

I triggered Spellblade on a bronze nail from Storage and hurled it at the demon knight as he charged toward me.

The demon knight raised his shield to block my attack.

With a sharp *clang*, the Spellblade nail penetrated the shield and knocked both knight and horse to the ground, but the demon still wasn't defeated. This shield could hold its own even against physical attacks.

I charged at the demon knight with the Holy Sword Excalibur in hand.

I tried activating Spellblade on Excalibur, but I stopped when I felt a strange resistance.

Maybe it doesn't work well with Holy Swords?

Taking advantage of my momentary pause, the demon knight let loose a triple attack with his lance, which pulsed as though alive.

I intercepted the attack at once with the Holy Sword. Each time it touched my blade, the lance sparked red and took another dent.

As I'd hoped, Holy Swords were effective against both demons and their weapons.

I kicked the Screaming Shield out of the demon knight's hands, and he stumbled.

Then, while the demon was vulnerable, I lopped off the tentacle-like head with the Holy Sword to defeat him.

From afar, the roar of a giant monster echoed across the battlefield.

Clearly, the real demon host was coming this way.

Three hydras appeared on the battlefield, tangled together as if they were fighting one another.

...No, wait, they really *were* feuding.

The tentacle-headed demon hydra was battling the two normal hydras in midair. The monsters snapped at one another's heads, and the tangled mass looked ready to crash at any moment.

Well, that works for me. Might as well finish them off now.

I took a Holy Arrow out of Storage.

This unique bolt was made of wood from the Mountain-Tree, with an obsidian arrowhead that would easily facilitate magic, and I'd carved the blue magic circuit for a Holy Sword into both parts.

It wasn't very durable, but since I needed it to hit only once, that shouldn't be a problem.

I took out the Magic Bow I'd gotten from the giants, nocking the Holy Arrow. I'd made only three prototypes, so I'd have to aim carefully.

I poured as much magical power into the projectile as it would hold and it glowed blue.

Noticing the light, the demon hydra chewed off his own captured head to get away from the others.

After they were shaken off, the two hydras crashed into the ground near me.

The demon hydra was frantically racing away, but no matter how quickly he moved, he wouldn't reach a speed of two hundred miles per hour.

During my test fire, this bow and arrow had a range of two miles. When I let go, the arrow would be faster than the speed of sound.

Eat this!

I fired the arrow with all my might.

Flying from the Magic Bow, the Holy Arrow soared through the sky in a streak of blue.

It broke through the sound barrier and caught up to the demon hydra from behind in the blink of an eye, turning him into an explosion of black dust.

The black dust formed several black rings in the air, perhaps due to the blue glow, then scattered on the wind.

After instantaneously destroying the demon, the arrow zipped onward through the clouds and vanished into the blue sky.

Surprised by the unexpected power of my Holy Arrow, I checked the log.

The line **hydra demon defeated** had appeared there.

Great, looks like I finished it— Wait, no, not quite. The red dot that indicated the demon was still on my radar.

The double-headed hydra that had crashed near me now had tentacles for heads.

He had used his own devoured head to take over another body.

The other hydra, a three-headed one, had been killed in the crash.

"I never expect a real hero to appear..."

Whoa, it's talking.

While the thing spoke, I scanned the map for any remaining doppelgängers or possessed creatures.

"But it seem you be too late."

No, this guy was the only demon left. He didn't have any other hosts, either.

"I have plunge this land into despair, and the malice and resentment of the people be collected in my chaos jar and transformed to miasma."

Oh, so that's what he's doing?

I examined the hydra corpse, but there were no signs the demon had invaded its body.

"What now, hero? Do you not wish to know where the chaos jar be?"

Now that he mentioned it, I tried searching for this **chaos jar** on the map.

It was in the luggage of one of the high-ranking government officials who'd fled earlier.

"You never catch up with it now! The chaos jar on its way to sacred shrine in the very hands of you humans."

"Oh, I don't know about that. Actually, though, would you mind explaining the shrine you mentioned?"

The demon hydra seemed pleased that I had responded and cackled uproariously from both heads.

"I tell you no more. Go ahead and struggle, hero. The golden sovereign will resurrected, and then you will regret your foolishness."

Okay, so the chaos jar is necessary for the resurrection of some "golden sovereign" guy or whatever, then?

It was probably used for a kind of ritual to revive a demon lord, then.

But, as they say, too much scheming will be the schemer's downfall.

"Nah, I don't think I'll be regretting anything. The chaos jar isn't going to reach its destination."

I blandly shrugged at the demon hydra.

After all, the officials carrying the chaos jar were currently under attack from a group of thieves near the territory border.

His plan was going to be ruined by robbers who were around only because of the unrest he himself had spread throughout the barony; it seemed like excellent karmic retribution to me.

"How you be so sure?"

"…I will tell you no more."

I repeated the demon's words back at him, ending the conversation.

One of the heads howled with anger, firing the Psychic Magic spell Mind Blow at me from point-blank range.

My "Psychic Resistance" skill let me withstand the spell with only slight discomfort, and I poured some magic into the Holy Sword Excalibur to strengthen it.

Unlike the Holy Arrow, the sword didn't have a limit on how much magic it could hold.

Since its capacity was apparently endless, I stopped at about one thousand points of magic and swung the blade toward the demon hydra as he started to leap into the air.

Just then, the supposedly dead three-headed hydra got in the way.

Behind it was a wraith the demon had created. The specter had probably used one of its race-specific abilities to make the three-headed creature into an undead monster.

I cut through the zombie hydra standing before me to turn it back into a corpse, then popped the body into Storage so that it couldn't be used again.

After that, I selected Fire Shot from my magic menu and reduced the wraith to ashes.

Finally, I took aim at the demon hydra as he spread his wings to take off into the sky and fired a hundred and twenty Magic Arrows.

Just like the four-headed hydra I'd encountered at the border, the demon's heads were quickly pulverized into chunks of meat by the magic.

The demon began breaking away from the corpse as it crashed to the earth, so I cut through him with the Holy Sword, turning him to black dust.

…*It's not over yet.*

"Come out. It's no use playing dead against me."

"I impressed that you notice."

Tearing through the belly of the grounded carcass, the demon appeared before me.

The AR display said his level was 36—in other words, this time really would be the last.

Ready to defeat him in one blow, I leaped into the air and swung the Holy Sword Excalibur in one motion.

Blue light arced through the sky.

Where did it go?

"Very scary. What a hero you be."

The demon was now standing where I'd defeated the demon knight before.

His upper body was sprouting from the lower half of a gjallarhorn. Most likely, it had only seemed dead in the stomach of the demon hydra.

His disappearance a moment ago must have been the gjallarhorn's inherent skill "Short-Range Teleportation."

First, I'd better take down that annoying gjallarhorn body. I opened the magic column of the menu and fired Magic Arrow.

However, the Screaming Shield from before got in the way.

He must have teleported in order to recover the shield.

The demon used two more "Short-Range Teleportations" to put some distance between us, then took to the sky toward Muno Castle.

Quickly, I grabbed a Holy Arrow and nocked it on my Magic Bow.

However, just as I infused it with magic, the demon used another "Short-Range Teleportation" and escaped into Muno City.

I put the fully charged arrow into Storage for now and raced back to Muno City at top speed.

My enemy was out of the range of my radar now, so I gave chase with the map open.

I couldn't be sure that he wouldn't make more doppelgängers while he was out of sight, too, so I made sure to search the map repeatedly as I ran.

When I had Muno Castle in sight again, the demon was at the top of the tower housing the defunct Magic Cannon.

But the supposedly broken weapon was moving on its own.

According to my AR display, it was now a **poltergeist**.

He can even turn objects into undead monsters? Seriously?!

"Now watch as I burning Muno City to the ground."

My "Keen Hearing" skill picked up on the faraway demon's voice.

The demon had flung off the body of the gjallarhorn and merged with the Magic Cannon poltergeist.

Shit. I'm not in a good position.

The Screaming Shield could ward off my precise Magic Arrows, and the Holy Arrow I'd used earlier would be way too powerful.

If I used it from here, it might blow away the nearby castle.

"Recall the power of Magic Cannon, which once douse the cities of Muno in flame."

As the demon cackled loudly, the Magic Cannon began transforming into a futuristic long barrel.

The fear that my kids might be harmed clouded my mind with panic, making it difficult to devise another solution.

What do I do?

Would I have to risk the people in the castle to destroy it, for the safety of my kids…?

Running through an alley, I tried to calm my frantic mind as it jumped from conclusion to conclusion.

Nine more seconds until he's in range of my Holy Sword.

"With the magic power of the source, there be no limit to Magic Cannon's ammunition."

The glowing particles in the barrel of his weapon began whirling about.

So on top of being crazy powerful, it has unlimited ammo?

I jumped over the first of the walls.

"Now, let me hearing your screams as the beauty of flames arise! They shall be the beacon that herald the resurrection of our king!"

Looking down at me, the demon aimed the cannon toward the main gate, right where my kids were engaged in battle.

I can't stop him.

I landed on the tower of the second wall, whipping out the Magic Bow.

"You too late!"

But then, suddenly, the light in the barrel of the cannon disappeared.

"What? My connection to the source be broken?"

On my open map, I saw the baron's dot of light at the location of the City Core.

Deep in my heart, I applauded the brave baron for overcoming his fear of the curse.

Then, in that moment of reflection, I realized something.

If I only need to destroy the Magic Cannon, can't I just use an ordinary weapon?

I took out a short spear from Storage and hurled it.

In the blink of an eye, the poltergeist floated out of the wreckage of the fearsome weapon.

At that moment, a loud noise shook the air, and a barrier of white light surrounded the main building of the castle.

"I-impossible!"

The barrier repelled the demon and launched him into the air, and the poltergeist, unable to withstand the force, was destroyed.

"They say the barrier made by a City Core can even defend against attacks from intermediate and greater hell demons."

I recalled what Arisa had said to me some time ago.

The demon tried to escape, and I drew the string of the Magic Bow without an arrow.

Quickly, the demon raised the Screaming Shield toward me.

Well, no need to worry about damaging the castle, then.

I took the Holy Arrow brimming with power out of Storage and once again nocked it to the Magic Bow.

Checkmate.

A streak of blue light soared through the sky over Muno City, and the demon that had staged his evil schemes in this city was annihilated once and for all.

A New Family Name

Satou here. In modern Japan, it's standard for normal families to have a family name, but ordinary people often don't have one in games and such, thanks to game planners like Mr. Tubs who think it's annoying to come up with them.

With the demon disposed of, I lowered the hood of my red coat, exposing my long blond wig and silver mask to the public as I soared through the central street toward the main gate.

The wig and mask were designed to stay in place even when I was running, so it wasn't a problem.

There were still hundreds of goblins at the main gate fighting to invade the city.

However, now they were trying to escape the rampaging forest giants outside the town.

"...■ ■ ■ ■ ■ *Balloon Kyuubouchou!*"

Mia's Water Magic hurled the goblins back over the gate.

Arisa and Nana were at Mia's side, and the beastfolk girls and Miss Karina were near the gate. Hauto was in the tower on top of the gate with many of the civilian soldiers, while Lulu was assigning duties in the inn.

The goblins were throwing stones over the gate, but Nana blocked them with her shield, and Arisa's Psychic Magic spell Mind Blow knocked out the little imps.

The beastfolk girls and Miss Karina beat down any enemies that tumbled into the city from Mia's spell.

The other soldiers were providing cover for these four from the rear.

I passed behind Mia as she chugged a magic recovery potion, stopping in front of the castle gate.

"Lady Karina!!"

"Who is that?!"

"A hero."

I answered loudly, courtesy of my "Ventriloquism" skill. That was my best imitation of the voice actor Nakaji Jouta.

I moved past the surprised Miss Karina and used Short Stun to knock back the goblins encroaching on the gate, placing my hand on the warped steel.

With a little force, I bent the steel like putty.

In less than a second, the opening in the gate was gone. It wasn't the most professional repair job, but a craftsman could probably fine-tune it later.

I went back to stand before Miss Karina and the others and asked her to deliver a message to the baron and Miss Nina.

"Young lady. Let it be known to the baron that all the demons in the territory have been destroyed."

I was careful to speak differently from Satou.

Then, I leaped to the top of the tower. It would've looked cool to get there in a single bound, but I ended up doing three little jumps off a few footholds on the outer wall and the adjacent tower.

"You protected the city well. Leave the rest to me."

I landed next to Hauto, thanking him for his service.

Raising an open hand toward the goblins, I laid waste to them with a rain of Short Stuns.

Since goblins were so fragile, this spell was the most efficient method to deal with them.

A rumble of surprise rose from the militia, but I ignored them and mopped up the rest of the goblins outside the city with Short Stun and Magic Arrow.

With the map, I identified remaining enemies besides the ones near the forest giants, sniping them with Magic Arrows.

In the process, I learned that the range of this spell was over a mile and a half.

Once I'd disposed of the fourteen hundred goblins and two hundred zombies outside the main gate, I left the tower. There was no trace of the wraiths that the demon had made.

I told Hauto the same thing I'd said to Miss Karina, to take the report to the castle. The information was redundant, but my main goal was to get Miss Karina and Hauto to go back to the castle without stopping to check on Satou first.

Then I bounded out of the city, disappearing from the people's sight.

After that, just as I'd intended, Miss Karina and Hauto returned to the castle without stopping by to see me.

After I left the city, I visited the thieves' hideout hidden in the mountains four miles away from Muno City to collect the chaos jar the demon had described.

The attacking thieves had not only murdered the bureaucrats and their guards but stolen all their valuables.

The thieves responsible for the crime had given in to curiosity and opened the lid of the chaos jar. They all lay dead with expressions of fear frozen on their faces.

I had a feeling they'd turn into undead if I left them like that, so I made a deep hole with Pitfall and cremated them in it with Fire Shot.

Finally, I stowed away the chaos jar and left the place behind.

I'd recovered the treasures that the bandits stole, too, of course. I thought they could come in handy for rebuilding Muno City.

I returned to the battlefield in the light of the setting sun.

Illuminated by the sunset, the corpses of monsters and the now-motionless bodies that were once zombies made for a sobering reminder of the impermanence of life.

I paused to give a moment of silence for them and started to leave, then had a sudden realization.

If I left them here like this, they might poison the earth or water supply.

If I remembered correctly, there was a part in a Warring States time-travel novel I'd read where some villagers died of disease while clearing away bodies.

I guess I can cheat a bit with my map and Storage here.

I marked the corpses on my map and set them to appear on my radar as yellow dots.

Then, I ran around the battlefield with the yellow dots on my radar as my guide, collecting each body as soon as it was in range of Storage.

I lost track of how many rounds I made. Finally, as dusk was settling over the battleground, I finished recovering all of them.

…That was pretty tiring.

The monster corpses were fine in Storage, but the human bodies would have to be returned to the bereaved families in the city.

I sorted the corpses in Storage according to their former station in life, laying them down in four-foot-deep pits dug with magic.

Their relatives could decide whether to cremate or bury them. After another moment of silent prayer, I left the graveyard.

My work finally done, I sneaked into the city under cover of darkness, returning to the room in the inn where everyone was waiting. This was after I removed my Hero disguise and title, of course.

"I've returned."

"Welcome back, master," said Liza, and everyone else followed suit.

"Welcome baaack!"

"We were worried, sir!"

Pochi and Tama had been worried about me this whole time; they climbed all over me, nuzzling their faces against my head.

Their relief soon gave way to fatigue, and they started nodding off as they clung to me. I stroked their heads and laid them down on the bed.

"Master, here."

Lulu handed the Garage Bag and Holy Stone back to me. She'd been in this room activating it again and again so that the invading monsters wouldn't spread into the city.

"Great work, Lulu."

I patted her head gently in thanks for her hard work behind the scenes.

Lulu smiled a little proudly.

"Hero?" Mia mumbled something and tilted her head.

Maybe she meant to ask if I was really a hero and not a peddler?

"Mia figured out that it was you before we even said anything! She said a spirit told her," Arisa explained quietly in my ear. That was all well and good, but I'd have appreciated it more if she hadn't tried to lick my ear in the process.

Was the dryad the "spirit" she was talking about?

Since I'd still had the Hero title when the dryad helped me escape from the Cradle, she'd probably figured it out then. I'd have to ask her not to spread that information around too much next time we met.

"Master acquired the title of Hero and a Holy Sword when he fought my former master to save Mia, I report." Nana explained the situation to Mia for me.

That wasn't quite accurate, but the elf seemed satisfied with this account, so I left it at that.

I was a bit too tired to go to the trouble of clarifying things anyway.

"Master, I need more magic supply, I request."

"Sorry, but can you use a magic potion for now? I'll do it in the morning."

Normally, I'd be more than happy to help, but I wasn't really up for it right now.

Somehow, despite her expressionless face, Nana adopted the dejected air of an abandoned puppy.

I told everyone to keep the fact that I was a hero a secret, and we decided to spend the night right there in the inn.

Pochi and Tama still didn't know that I was the hero.

I wasn't sure whether to tell them myself or not, but Liza and Arisa suggested that I keep it from them until they were older, so I decided not to say anything unless it was necessary.

We shouldn't get caught up in any major strife in the future, so I doubted it would be a problem.

The forest giants had returned to the forest while I was dealing with the thieves, so I wasn't able to see them off.

The next morning, Miss Karina came and brought us to the audience room of Muno Castle.

"Satou, as a father, I am deeply appreciative to you for saving Karina's life. And as a lord, I thank you for your tremendous contributions toward defeating the demon."

These were the baron's very first words to me as we entered the castle.

Still, shouldn't those things have been in the reverse order? *Goodness, what a doting baron.*

After that, Miss Nina joined the nobleman in thanking us repeatedly for rescuing the barony from its grave crisis. Finally, she took over to discuss my reward for saving the territory.

"Now, we will certainly confer a medal of honor upon you later, but our debt to you is quite large. A medal alone isn't nearly enough. As far as prizes that the baron has the authority to give..."

As Miss Nina spoke, Miss Karina's face blushed red. Miss Nina glanced at her, then at the girls behind me.

"...A beautiful woman or a title. Which would you desire?"

The reason money wasn't presented among the options was probably because the city's finances were in such dire straits.

At this rate, I had a sneaking suspicion I was about to end up on the road to marriage with Miss Karina.

She was certainly gorgeous, but if she became my wife, I'd doubtless end up having to spend my life in the service of the Muno Barony and probably wind up being buried here, too.

Personally, I'd like to continue to be free to travel the world.

"My apologies, but I have no need for either. A medal is more than enough."

"How noble, to be so free of desire." Miss Nina raised her eyebrows at me doubtfully.

Miss Karina's expression clouded, but I had to harden my heart and ignore her. I couldn't make everyone happy all the time.

"It's not as though I have no desires at all. My greatest wish is to travel and see as much of the world as possible with my own eyes, you see. A noble who cannot stay and serve his territory is hardly worth having, right? Besides, I'm far too young to take a bride."

"There's nothing unusual about marrying an adult, is there? Those girls behind you aren't your wives?"

The moment Miss Nina asked that question, I felt an incredible sense of pressure from the kids behind me.

Okay, time to follow the example of harem protagonists throughout history and act totally oblivious.

"Well, they're all like family to me, but none of them is my wife."

I felt a chorus of disappointed sighs behind me, along with a relieved one from Miss Karina.

"How about Lady Karina, then? She may be slightly past her prime, but she's beautiful and has childbearing hips. Surely you wish to have strong, healthy children?"

Miss Karina pouted unhappily at Miss Nina's rude comments, though the compliment toward her beauty made her blush. It was kind of cute, but if I let that show, Miss Nina would take that as encouragement, so I rode it out with the help of my "Poker Face" skill.

Miss Soluna stood calmly next to Hauto.

"But for a mere commoner to aspire to marry a baron's daughter—," I began, but then Miss Soluna turned toward me with a smile, and I quickly corrected myself.

That was close. I'd forgotten that Hauto, who was clearly her sweetheart, was a commoner, too.

"—would be wonderful, of course. But as long as I am traveling the world, I have no intention of taking a bride."

"I see..."

Miss Nina put a hand to her chin thoughtfully.

Then she whispered something in the baron's ear, and he gave his consent.

"Very well, Satou. We shall make you an honorary hereditary knight."

"Lady Nina—"

I started to protest, but she raised a hand to silence me.

"We will not ask you to do any work for the barony. Your duty would be to travel the lands as a vassal of the territory."

Say what? Do they want me to gather intelligence about other territories?

"We would not ask you to play at being a spy, of course."

Wait, they wouldn't? What does she want me to do, then?

Miss Nina cut me off as I opened my mouth again. "However, it is important that you visit many different lands as our vassal."

"I'm afraid I don't understand. What is it you wish to ask of me, Miss Nina?" I still didn't get it, so I decided to just cut to the chase.

"Are you aware that the Muno Barony is rumored to be a 'cursed territory'?"

"Yes, though I do not know the reason." I nodded slowly.

"They say any noble who visits this place will be doomed to misfortune. There were many other nobles who claimed to be the lords of this area before our baron Muno, but almost all of them met with accidental or mysterious deaths. To make matters worse, most of the nobles who've visited after Baron Muno's inauguration have since suffered illnesses or become bedridden. Because of all that, an absurd rumor spread that our territory is cursed."

The former was probably thanks to Zen or his subordinates, and the latter had most likely been the result of trying to enter the City Core room and falling victim to Zen's curse.

"My role would be to spread the word to other territories that the Muno Barony is safe, then?"

"That's right. We haven't been able to dispose of the rumors ourselves because we've been unable to solicit the help of any capable nobles." Miss Nina nodded and continued, "Besides, it really is necessary for you to receive a rank. On top of everything else, we can't have people thinking that we are so stingy that we'd reward such great services with a mere medal. It's not that we think you would spread any such rumor, of course. But there is always gossip wherever one goes."

Miss Nina shrugged and sighed.

"At any rate, there's no need to be so cautious about it. An honorary hereditary knight's title is hardly a huge affair. It's the lowest class of nobility. Older noble families might even treat you as a fake. Still, it should prove useful to you!"

I couldn't think of any reason why it would, but Miss Nina grinned.

"Our barony and our neighbors in the Ougoch Duchy aside, discrimination against demi-humans is quite strong in northern territories, is it not? If you become an honorary hereditary knight, commoners will treat you as a nobleman. In other words, your slaves will be treated with respect as the property of an aristocrat. That should make for better service than you'd get as a lowly commoner."

I had to admit, that sounded appealing. It'd be worth it just to not be refused accommodation at inns anymore.

In the end, Miss Nina's trump card won out, and Baron Muno granted me the position of honorary hereditary knight.

After that, we were given rooms in Muno Castle where we would stay until the knighting ceremony, but these days ended up being very busy.

For instance, I consulted Miss Nina about the fortress where the escaped and abandoned serfs were staying, and for some reason, she decided they should be my servants with the fortress as my villa.

I helped apprehend soldiers who'd committed felonies and find the hidden assets of embezzling officials.

I secretly gifted the gold I'd found in Marquis Muno's hidden treasury to the barony in the name of the "Silver-Masked Hero."

I wrote a letter to Zena about the wraith we battled in the ruined fortress and sent it to Seiryuu City.

I paid in full to have the maids create Victorian-era outfits and adopt them as their uniform.

Lulu and I got the head chef of the castle to teach us some cooking basics in exchange for slipping him recipes for things like fried chicken and mayonnaise.

I watched Liza and the others taking on some bandits as training. One chivalrous thief disavowed his group and joined the army, just like a protagonist from historical fiction.

I helped make a real gabo-fruit field inside Muno City by hiring people from the slums to work in exchange for monster meat and residence in the barracks.

I had the opportunity to listen to Baron Muno excitedly discuss his research on heroes at a tea party with Miss Soluna, Pochi, Tama, and others.

I wasn't able to get any new scrolls at the magic shop, but it turned out that the baron had a viscount cousin who ran the only scrollmaking studio in the kingdom, so he wrote a letter of introduction for me.

I also borrowed a studio that no one was using to work on various projects, like making a new carriage.

I used hydra materials to make a hang glider and rode it to the giants' village, where I thanked them with a whole roast of rocket wolf and a barrel of Shigan sake from Muno City.

I disposed of the monster the weaselfolk fisherman had mentioned previously and received the boat in return.

On the way back, I stopped by the mountain hut I'd made to find a letter of thanks and the bluesilver sword from the kobold girl, so I knew she'd been able to mine the blue crystals successfully.

Finally, I exterminated the monsters that had dammed the river near Muno City, restoring the flow to normal.

Now the farmland in front of Muno City should be easier to cultivate, too.

There was a ton of gabo fruits left from the demon magistrate's goblin-breeding efforts in the nearby towns, so Miss Nina said they should have enough food for a while.

*   *   *

In addition, Miss Nina taught me various things about my new rank.

Just as I'd thought before, a viscount really was higher than a baron.

The honorary nobility of one generation was technically treated along the same lines as permanent nobility, so I could think of the order as viscount, honorary viscount, then baron.

When I asked why the honorary viscount Nina would be the magistrate of Baron Muno, then, she said it was because he was the lord of a territory.

She went on to explain that in the Shiga Kingdom, the custom was to treat any lord with just as much respect as a count, regardless of the lord's original position. This was probably due to the City Cores.

On top of that, since Baron Muno had taken control of the City Core—or "become the true lord," as Miss Nina put it—he would be officially promoted to the position of count at the next kingdom meeting.

In that case, this confusing rank-reversal situation would be solved as well.

◆

"Do you have any preferences about your family name?"

"My family name?"

Ten days after the decision to grant me the title of honorary hereditary knight, I was called into Miss Nina's office and instructed to decide on my name as a noble.

According to her, she'd finally gotten her case for urgency approved and was making preparations for my knighting ceremony.

"An honorary noble title is limited to one generation, isn't it? Is a family name really necessary?"

"It is indeed only one generation, but a surprising number of houses continue to receive honorary titles for many generations."

I nodded thoughtfully at her explanation.

"Right! Even if a single-generation noble is viewed as an upstart, they still have more money than a poor or fallen noble. There are some territories where you can buy a title with money, and you can get an excellent education for your children, after all."

Arisa, who was helping Miss Nina with paperwork, piped up from behind a stack of documents.

Because Miss Nina had eliminated so many corrupt officials when she came back into power, the government was short on manpower.

At first, Arisa had only been delivering lost items to officials, but she sympathized when she saw how busy they were and offered to help by sorting office documents.

Then, she naturally moved from sorting to assisting with processing the paperwork, and eventually wound up with the position of being Miss Nina's assistant. Apparently, Arisa had a knack for accounting.

"Is Arisa being helpful?"

"Yeah, enough that I wish you'd leave her here to work as my aide."

"Oh my, that wouldn't do. I'm fully dedicated to my master in mind and body alike!" Arisa shot me an exaggerated wink, so I rolled my eyes and patted her on the head.

"Well, I'm sure you can't come up with one on the spot, right? I'll give you a couple of days to decide."

"How about, say, Tachibana?"

As I recall, that was Arisa's last name in her previous life.

"I'll pass, thanks."

"Yes, I believe there's already a hereditary knight named Tachibana. You can check with the civil official Yuyurina about whether a certain family name's available or not. She studied heraldry at the royal academy, so she'd know better than I would."

"All right. I'll try and come up with a few possibilities to ask about."

Her business with me finished, Miss Nina returned to her paperwork.

If I remembered right, Yuyurina was the quiet civil official with brown hair in a refined braid.

After a few words with Arisa, I left the office.

I racked my brain for a good family name as I strode through the corridor, but nothing came to mind.

Of course there was my real surname, Suzuki, but then my name in this world would sound so Japanese that I might forget my real one, so I decided against it.

As you might've guessed from my character name, I'd always been pretty arbitrary in naming things, so I decided to poll everyone else for ideas.

"Familyyy?"

"Family's great, sir!"

The nearest members of my group were Tama and Pochi in one of the Muno family's private rooms, but they didn't know what a "family name" was.

The two of them were sitting next to Miss Soluna and munching on something that looked like fried fish with bones sticking out. Kinda dull for a teatime snack, if you ask me.

These three were the only people in the room. The baron was in the office next door and would be battling paperwork until the next day. Hauto was patrolling the city with Liza and Nana.

"A family name? Well, if you marry our darling Karina, I'm sure you could take over the Donano family name."

Miss Soluna smiled mischievously. Donano had been the baron's family's surname until they took over the Muno name.

Baron Muno also had the title of Baronet Donano, so whoever married Miss Soluna or Miss Karina in the future would take that family name and rank.

"That seems quite intimidating, so I'm afraid I'll have to decline."

"Oh well. Karina has a tough road ahead of her."

Miss Soluna giggled after me as I left the room.

"Sorry, but could you let me through?"

"Ah, Sir Knight!"

"Please, go right ahead!"

The cluster of maids in front of the kitchen entrance moved aside to let me in.

"Oh-ho, good to see you, Sir Knight."

"Welcome back, master."

Lulu, who was deep-frying something with the head chef, Miss Gert, turned toward me.

"That's a nice color," I said. "I think the fire's a little too strong, though. You should probably tone it down some before the outside gets burned to a crisp."

"Ah, I'm sorry!"

I took over for Lulu to adjust the fire.

Before Miss Nina had sent for me, the three of us had been frying wild-boar cutlets.

"It's remarkable that you can tell the temperature just by looking."

I smiled at the astonished Miss Gert, then moved the boar cutlets to the net that served as a draining rack.

Cutting one in half with a kitchen knife, I made sure that it had cooked all the way through. The coating had turned black, but it should still be edible, at least.

"What should we do? Pawn them off on the maids who didn't get lunch?"

"Yes, please do! It's all right if it's not perfect!"

"We'll eat anything you cook, Sir Knight!"

I presented to one of the maids a plate complete with sauce and mayonnaise.

Personally, I didn't think mayonnaise and pork cutlets went together very well, but I held my tongue. The maids loved mayo.

"Hooray! Two per person, all right?"

"Delicious!"

"No fair, Erina! Don't put so much mayo on one piece!"

"Girls, if you're going to be this noisy, I won't give you any more samples!"

"We're sorry, Miss Gert!"

After roaring at the bickering maids, Miss Gert went back to preparing the next pork cutlets with Lulu.

As I helped them out, I decided to get Lulu's opinion on a family name.

"A family name? How about Kuvork, then?"

Kuvork was the kingdom that Arisa and Lulu had come from. It had also been Arisa's family name when she was a princess.

"I don't think that would be wise. It'd be like picking a fight with the regions that invaded the Kuvork Kingdom."

"I suppose so… Ah, then maybe…? Oh, never mind."

Lulu seemed to have an idea, but she wouldn't spit it out. When I pressed the subject, she offered the surname "Watari."

Lulu's great-grandfather had been Japanese, so this must have been his last name.

"It's the family name of my great-grandfather, from his faraway country. But in the Kuvork Kingdom where I was born, only nobles were permitted to have a family name, so nobody used it."

Satou Watari.

It sounded a bit old-fashioned, but it wasn't bad.

"I'm not sure whether I'll use it, but I'll certainly write it down as one of the candidates, if that's all right."

"Yes!" Lulu smiled brightly at my response.

Yes, she was beautiful as ever today.

After I'd shown Lulu and Miss Gert a few tricks for frying delicious pork cutlets, I visited the garden where Mia was playing music.

I passed through the rear lawn, where countless sheets were billowing in the wind, and toward the shade of Mia's favorite tree in the baron's private space.

Maybe it was because the baron could use the City Core now, but this place always seemed to be pleasantly warm.

"Satou."

"Hi, Mia."

Small animals had gathered around Mia as she played the lute in the sunshine.

When she noticed me and turned, her movement startled the little birds and squirrels, and they darted away in a panic.

"Mm."

Mia didn't seem to mind this particularly and simply patted the ground next to her for me to sit.

I asked Mia for her opinion on the family name.

"Bolenan."

...That would be Mia's family name—or more precisely, the name of her clan.

"I don't think I can take a different clan's name as my own, Mia. The leaders of the elf village would get mad at me."

"Mrrr..."

Mia puffed out her cheeks, but I restored her good spirits by handing her a prototype crepe.

I'd discovered how to make whipped cream in the process of churning butter, so I'd immediately tried frying up some crepes.

I'd acquired baking powder, too, so I'd attempted to make various pastries while I had access to Muno Castle's oven.

As I munched on the dessert with Mia, I got her to teach me the names of various plants and animals as potential surnames. None of them seemed quite right, so I promised to add a few to the list of candidates and headed out.

*   *   *

"Master, I have returned, I report."

"We've received the processed feathers, master."

Nana and Liza dismounted from their horses as they debriefed me.

I'd commissioned a craftsman in the city to prepare some feathers for making a down quilt.

We didn't have enough, so the advance-guard team and I had gone bird hunting near the main road while taking out thieves along the way.

"Great, thanks."

"They are remarkably soft and fluffy, I report."

Nana was enjoying the texture of the feather-filled bag.

I asked them if they had any family name ideas.

"Nagasaki, I recommend. It was my former master's surname."

"How about Kishreshigarza? It is the name of my clan, but nobody should be claiming it as a family name."

Nana and Liza gave their respective suggestions.

Satou Nagasaki.

Satou Kishreshigarza.

Neither of them really jumped out at me.

Just then, a few soldiers arrived.

"Miss Liza, Miss Nana, we're about to start practice. Would you like to—? Oh, Sir Knight. Why not join us as well?"

The one who'd called out to us was named Zotol. We'd met him when Liza and I went out patrolling for bandits and defeated him after a close fight.

He was a skilled opponent who could beat Liza one-on-one and could hold his own against all four members of the vanguard team.

Unable to stand the cruel orders of the demon magistrate and the corruption of their fellow soldiers, he and his band of followers had left the military. They had traveled around working as guards for merchants passing through the territory or getting rid of monsters at the request of villages.

They were more like mercenaries than thieves, but corrupt bureaucrats who viewed them as a threat had tricked them and put them on the wanted list as thieves.

Now he and his group had been reemployed as soldiers of the barony.

Unfortunately, he couldn't return to being a knight right away, so he was ranked as a soldier for now.

"Sorry, I have business to take care of, so I'll pass on training for today."

"You'd better join us next time, then! Oh, and if you see Hauto, please tell him to come to the practice field."

I agreed to pass on the message and left Liza and Nana to train with the flexing soldier.

"Family name? There were no nobles in my village, so I don't know the first thing about that."

That was Hauto's answer when I found him in the dining hall and asked him about it.

Hauto was currently working as a junior knight-in-training for the baron. He had learned that he wasn't really a hero after touching a Yamato stone a few days prior.

An analysis had proven that his "Holy Sword" Gjallarhorn was actually a cursed demon blade, so it had been sealed away in a chamber in the basement of Muno Castle. The sword at his waist was just an ordinary iron blade.

Though no longer a hero, Hauto still had a relationship with Miss Soluna, so he was undergoing intensive training to become a proper knight and marry her.

Miss Soluna was teaching him culture and language, while he was training in fencing and strategy with Zotol every day.

"I've found you at last! Today is the day you shall finally train with me!"

"What good fortune that Sir Hauto is here, too."

Miss Karina appeared in the dining hall, clad in the same shirt and pants as the soldiers.

"Are you trying to run away from your etiquette teacher to train again?"

"B-but of course not. Today is devoted solely to combat training."

There was no such day in the schedule that Miss Nina had made for Miss Karina's education.

Incidentally, her etiquette teacher was Miss Soluna.

"Why not ask Lady Karina for advice about it?"

"Advice? Whatever about?"

At Hauto's prompting, I took a shot in the dark and asked Miss Karina for family name suggestions.

"You're having difficulty in choosing a family name, are you? I know just the one."

"What is it?"

"How about Pendragon? It's a hero's name. Lord Orion Pendragon."

"Ahem…" A youthful civil official with a braid, who was eating nearby, timidly entered the conversation. This was Yuyurina, the one Miss Nina had mentioned before. She was usually very quiet, so this was unexpected. "Isn't that the name of a fictional character?"

"That's right! It's the hero of my very favorite story. He journeys around on a dragon, overcomes the seven trials given him by the gods, and in the end defeats the great demon lord in a brilliant epic saga."

This was like a weird mix of King Arthur's legend and Greek mythology.

"He rides a dragon?"

"Yes, and no mere wyvern, either! He rides none other than a red dragon, named Welsh."

I did seem to remember King Arthur's father's name being Pendragon. Wasn't he a dragon-slaying hero?

That might actually work. I do have Excalibur, after all, so I could even change my first name to Arthur and go around as Arthur Pendragon.

And so, after two full days of brainstorming, I finally decided on a family name.

◆

"…■ ■ *Confer Peerage Jojaku!*"

In a room of Muno Castle designated for peerage ceremonies, I received my noble rank from Baron Muno.

The rank field in my status changed to **Noble [Hereditary Knight]**, and my affiliation changed to **Shiga Kingdom, Muno Barony**.

The three medals I'd received yesterday were listed in my **Awards** and **Bounties** column, too. Of course, I'd also received physical medals to convey my honors to others whenever I was formally dressed.

The reason I hadn't gained the "Confer Peerage" skill in the process was probably that it was a Ritual Magic spell that was a function of the City Core.

"Satou, please touch the Yamato stone to confirm that the ritual was successful."

"All right."

This time, I changed a few values in my networking tab before touching the Yamato stone.

Since I now had a powerful supporter, even if he wasn't the most reliable, I disclosed a little more about my skills and level so that I could operate a bit more easily. I'd consulted with Arisa about this decision the day before.

Once the ceremony was over, Miss Nina led the baron's daughters and my kids into the room.

The last to enter was the civil official Yuyurina.

"All right, let us begin. ■ ■ *Name Order Meimei!* 'Satou Pendragon.'"

The young woman with the braids nervously invoked her "Name Order" skill.

> Skill Acquired: "Name Order"

The new name was granted to me as everyone looked on. It didn't change automatically in my menu's networking tab, so I changed it myself.

Then, we used a Yamato stone to confirm the change and create new identification. Unlike the papers of ordinary commoners, my information was now engraved on a silver plate.

"Heh-heh… Karina Pendragon, eh? Not bad, if I do say so myself."

I caught wind of some disturbing remarks but pretended not to hear. She'd murmured so quietly that aside from me with my "Keen Hearing" skill, most likely only Raka had heard it.

"Arisa Pendragon… Sounds a bit too much like Arthur, but at least it's got oomph." Arisa grinned to herself, tapping her chin as she schemed away.

"Hee-hee, it would be nice to be called Lulu Pendragon someday…"

Et tu, Lulu?

Of course, Lulu had whispered softly like Miss Karina. Nobody else could hear it but me.

"Pochi Pendragon, sir!"

"Tama Pendragooon?"

Pochi and Tama ran circles around me as their way of saying congratulations.

If they had wings, they probably would've rocketed off into the sky right there.

"Very elegant, master."

Liza wiped tears from the corners of her eyes, overcome with emotion.

"Mrrr. Bolenan…" Mia hadn't given up yet.

"Master. Master Pendragon. Which shall I call you, I inquire?"

"Just 'master' is fine," I told Nana.

"Now then, Sir Satou Pendragon, hereditary knight. I look forward to working with you in the future."

"The pleasure is all mine, Viscount Nina Lottel."

Miss Nina extended her hand for a handshake. I didn't know until now that was a practice in this world, too.

One didn't add the word *honorary* when stating someone else's peerage aloud. However, I would have to introduce myself as "honorary hereditary knight Satou."

Still grasping my hand, Miss Nina gave me yet another assignment.

"Be sure to decide on a coat of arms before you leave, as well."

I need to have a coat of arms, too…?

We ended up deciding that I would receive lessons in high society and heraldry from the baron and Yuyurina respectively, starting the next day.

It should go without saying that I gained the skills "Sociability" and "Heraldry" in the process.

As for my crest, I ended up going with a design of a dragon holding a pen like a spear.

I was a little concerned about the plot to resurrect the "golden sovereign" or whatever, but the chaos jar that was key for that ritual was safely in Storage, so I was hoping we'd be able to at least explore the old capital in peace.

Of course, I couldn't rule out the possibility of him getting revived another way, so I'd have to make some preparations just in case.

Looks like my life in this parallel world is going to keep being as hectic as ever.

*   *   *

■   Networking Profile Status   ■────────────

Name: Satou Pendragon
Race: Human
Level: 30
Affiliation: Shiga Kingdom, Muno Barony
Occupation: None
Class: Noble [Hereditary Knight]
Title: None
Skills:
Swordsmanship   Archery   Hand-to-Hand Combat
Throwing
Evasion   Cooking   Calculation   Transmutation
Magic-Tool Crafting   Estimation   Haggling
Sociability
Heraldry
Awards and Bounties:
Muno Barony Radiant Cobalt Medal
Muno Barony Army First-Class Medal
Muno City Civic Honor Medal

─────────────────────────────■

Afterword

Hello, this is Hiro Ainana.

Thank you very much for picking up the fourth volume of *Death March to the Parallel World Rhapsody*!

Thanks to all the readers' support, the book version of *Death March* has just celebrated its first anniversary!

I'll devise more schemes to keep you all from getting bored, so I hope you'll continue reading *Death March* in the future.

Before we start discussing the highlights of this volume, there's something I have to advertise.

If all has gone according to plan, the first volume of the Dragon Comics Age manga adaptation of *Death March to the Parallel World Rhapsody* by Ayamegumu should be on sale at the same time as this volume, so please pick it up if you're interested.

With detailed depictions of characters that aren't illustrated in the books, settings like the street stalls, and all kinds of items and accessories, it's a wonderful expansion of the world of *Death March*.

While reading it, I often found myself admiring the way certain scenes were depicted, thinking, *So that's what that looked like!*

You won't regret buying it! As the original author, I guarantee it.

That little plug went on longer than planned, so let's talk about the highlights of this volume now.

As with the previous volume, this one features new episodes and a better-organized story, and most of it is newly written for the book version.

The story this time is about the Muno Barony, which we heard some nasty rumors about in the previous volume.

In the name of the suffering populace, Satou uses his superhuman powers to defeat an army of evil and banish corrupt aristocrats— Well, it's not exactly as righteous as all that, but you get the idea.

Satou is more the type of person who prefers not to get much more involved than donating food supplies where he can and doing a bit of volunteer work.

However, he ends up being more heroic than his comfort zone

normally entails, including saving a race from the brink of extinction on the side or defeating disastrously strong monsters in passing and using them for cooking ingredients…

But what's changed most from the original version might be the treatment of Miss Karina, who appears in the book's frontispiece.

In the web version, she finally showed herself to Satou at the climax of the story, but this time she shows up much earlier. And since Satou now has a reason to visit the giants' village, the flow of the world in the book is a bit different from the web version.

Plus, I also added some backstory on why the demon was trying to take over the Muno territory.

In addition, the subplots of each chapter now tie into one another, like a long campaign in a tabletop RPG.

Perhaps you might say that the smaller incidents are like gears that eventually turn the wheel of the larger plot…?

Even the incident with the kobolds and the silver mines from the previous book ends up being tied in like that.

To find out what sort of scenario unfolds from all this, please refer to the main story.

If any of you are asking, "What's a tabletop RPG?" I would suggest that you look into a site like Fujimi Shobo's TRPG Online for beginners.

Of course, the main attraction of this volume has to be the illustration of the most magic-breasted character in *Death March*, Karina!

At the time of writing this postscript, I've seen only the initial character designs, but the depiction of her b— That is, her appearance was even better than my own mental image.

Being able to see an ideal vision of Miss Karina like this makes me feel truly lucky as an author.

Well, I'm reaching the upper limit of my page count, so I'll stop going on about volume four's contents now.

Now then, it's time for the usual list of acknowledgments.

My editor Mr. H's comments and revision advice helped me to vastly improve the charm and realism of various scenes. Please continue to guide and encourage me in the future.

I can never thank shri enough for always enlivening the world of *Death March* with such wonderful illustrations. Please keep crafting the visuals of *Death March* from here on out.

I also want to thank everyone involved in the publication and sale of this book, especially everyone at Fujimi Shobo.

Finally, the biggest thank-you of all to you, the readers!!

Thank you very much for reading to the end of the book!

Well, let's meet again at the river in the next volume!

Hiro Ainana